LEE BROOK

The Middleton Woods Stalker

For you, Dad—
Thank you for everything you do.

Contents

Chapter One

When I was eight, I watched as a cat stalked its prey. I couldn't keep my eyes away from the action, and my heart hammered in my chest. It was atop the conservatory, watching a tiny blackbird waiting to strike.

It could have killed the bird whenever it wanted, yet it waited, poised. I thought I knew when the cat would pounce, but I was wrong. Every. Single. Time.

That cat taught me a lesson in patience. It taught me how to stalk. It waited exactly where a predator would wait, but it didn't strike when I thought it would. That cat taught me a great lesson.

I waited for over five minutes for the carnage to happen, but the cat did nothing but watch. Why? Was it afraid? That's what I thought at the time. Killing was scary despite it being hardwired into the brain. It was all Darwin. Survival of the fittest.

And then, a bigger blackbird arrived, chasing the tiny blackbird away. It began to peck at the soft ground for worms, And that's when it happened. The cat pounced.

And it was fucking glorious.

The cat ripped the blackbird to shreds, and the garden was soon covered in blood, guts, and feathers. I still dream about the sinewy ribbons the cat feasted on.

It must have known the bigger animal was going to arrive. I was convinced that was the reason for the cat's patience. The early bird may catch the worm, but a predator stalking in the shadows is most likely to get what they want.

Bigger prey.

When I was nine, my dad told me a joke. "Why did the Christmas turkey join a band?" I remember shaking my head, confused. "Because he had a pair of drumsticks!"

I didn't get the joke—and I still don't—jokes have never been my strong suit. But I do remember that the cracker was red, which made a bang as we pulled it. I liked the way the cardboard gave as I yanked. It was so delicate, as most things are. It made me want to wrench some other stuff.

When I was ten, my dad bought me a Swiss Army Knife. Fucking idiot. I don't know why he did it or what possessed him. He told me his dad had bought him one when he was ten and that it was 'tradition'. So I started using it on myself, carving Roman numerals into my skin. I know every single Roman numeral. Trust me.

When I was thirteen, I took Poppy's kitten into the woods and cut its throat. I'd bought a larger knife by then and desperately wanted to feel something similar to the day I saw the cat kill the blackbird. And I did. I felt the warmth of the kitten's blood as I squeezed its neck after slitting it with my Swiss Army Knife. I still hear the meows in my dreams. The kitten probably had a name, not that I cared.

After that, I killed more animals in the woods, and I remember every single one.

Killing made me feel something, and so I decided I would kill something bigger. Much bigger.

* * *

I recognised Poppy Lavell the minute she walked into the shop. I was sat at my checkout at the Sainsbury's Local in Middleton, watching her as she flitted up and down the claustrophobic aisles. Would she recognise me? Probably not, especially after all these years. She never was the type to take in the details; it was one of the few things that irritated me about her. That was six weeks ago.

Today was Friday, her usual shopping day, and she walked past my checkout, a familiar perfume with notes of almond and jasmine wafting in my direction. I knew what perfume Poppy wore because I spent an hour annoying the sales assistant at the White Rose Shopping Centre, asking for sample after sample until the bint got it right.

As she finally placed her basket on the ledge, I adjusted my name badge, an unconscious habit. It said 'Billy', but that wasn't my real name.

We made eye contact, and she smiled. I thought she had finally recognised me, but I was wrong. It was one of those smiles that hid a sneer. It seemed I was still below her station. Of course, I was. She was a legal assistant for the solicitor around the corner, and I worked on a till in a Sainsbury's Local.

My dad worked for Yorkshire Water and regularly asked me if I wanted to work with him. But his job was fucking boring. He tended to the water pipes in Middleton, getting abuse from the folk whose water didn't quite taste right, smell right, or look right.

That, and I wasn't too fond of the company. The summer had been hot, and Yorkshire Water lost 300 megalitres of water a day from its pipes at a time when water levels in its reservoirs were dropping. That was billions of litres of water wasted yearly, yet they had the cheek to ban hosepipes. Fucking hypocrites.

Yet, in some way, I was jealous of Dad, to be honest with you, because he got to enter a place I'd always wanted to go inside: the water tower at the top of Town Street.

I always knew Poppy Lavell would one day be breathtakingly beautiful. We were the same age, mid-twenties, but she left Middleton in year nine of high school, just as she was blooming. I'd never expected to see her shiny, blonde ringlets again cascading down her back. Yet here she was, staring at me.

People called me 'Jim' at school and took the piss out of me because they thought I looked like Krasinski from The Office. I was OK with it because Krasinski married the beautiful Emily Blunt, which meant there was hope that I could seduce Poppy Lavell.

I met her piercing green eyes and grinned back, hoping she would remember me. But, if she did, she said nothing.

That afternoon six weeks ago was a constant on my mind, but at first, I wasn't sure it was Poppy Lavell. I used the bottle of wine in her basket as an excuse to ask her for her ID. Poppy had laughed charismatically and thanked me for the compliment. The blush against her porcelain skin as I memorised every detail on her driving licence—a blessing of my eidetic memory—was what I dreamed about every night.

"A big Friday night in tonight?" I asked, scanning the Taste the Difference Vintage Cheddar Mac & Cheese and Potato Dauphinoise.

"Yes, that's right," she said, running a manicured hand through her blonde waves, her eyes down on her mobile phone as though she'd rather not chat. She hadn't recognised me at all. Of course, the fake name badge helped.

"Veggie?" I said, grinning.

"Sorry?" I pointed to the food. I'd noticed she never once bought any meat products. "Oh, er, yeah."

"Me too," I lied, beaming, my tone holding more warmth for her than it ever had for anybody else.

"Well, thanks, Billy," she said, eyeing my badge before turning and leaving, taking that alluring waft of perfume with her.

I watched her leave and turn right towards the circus, most likely heading for home. I knew from her licence that she lived on Moor Flatts Avenue, around the corner from the primary school. It wasn't time for my break, but I desperately wanted to follow Poppy, to take in that sweet, nutty scent. I'd bought her a bottle as a gift, which had set me back over £80. I hadn't given it to her yet.

"Oi! Mate! You can stare at that bird at your own leisure." A fat, middle-aged, balding man with a white stain on his blue polo shirt was clicking his fingers. "I could watch that arse wiggle all day too, mate, but you're paid to serve, not to gawk. I want some fags. Twenty Richmond Superkings, a number three, and two fives."

The fat man was referring to the scratch cards I sold hundreds of daily. The number of times I'd been abused because a customer had gambled their last fiver on a card and lost was innumerable. I wanted to kill them all. Every. Last. One.

I handed the items over and blandly provided the total. I was used to not receiving manners from most of my customers, and this guy was no different as he tapped his phone against the contactless hub.

"Bye, fella," the bald man said. "Think I'll be using that

bird as inspiration for a quick wank tonight." He winked and laughed. "They shouldn't dress like that if they don't want to be added to the wank bank, right?"

I thought about the way Poppy arched forward, eyeing my badge, giving me a glorious view of her ample cleavage. I dreamed of those tits every night.

"Women. They're all fucking whores. The lot of 'em. Only interested in fucking if you're providing something."

My lip curled in disdain as I said nothing and watched the man go, my hands clenched tightly, my nails drawing blood from my palms.

I needed to calm down.

And as I closed my eyes, I pictured his polo shirt. Over the man's heart was an image of a tap, with 'Frank Hinchcliffe Plumbing and Heating' below.

Chapter Two

The way Poppy Lavell had said, 'Well, thanks, Billy,' as she arched forward, eyeing my badge, giving me a glorious view of her ample cleavage, was her being flirty. I was sure of it. As was the way she played with her hair before turning and leaving, taking that alluring waft of perfume with her.

It was all I had thought about over the weekend, replaying the moment dozens of times. It was all I thought about as I followed her, as I watched her get the bus into the city centre to meet her friends.

Poppy didn't work weekends, which wasn't ideal as I usually did. It meant I couldn't follow her and watch her as much as I would have liked, but I had learnt enough, especially as I followed her in the mornings and nights.

I usually didn't start work until ten in the morning, and she began at half-eight, so I had plenty of time to watch her make her way to work. There, she often went to the local café for a coffee or the butchers for a sarnie. Sometimes, she'd go to Greggs, but not very often, preferring the independent shops when I tallied it up.

My early morning observations meant I knew Poppy was a keen jogger. It also meant I knew where she went for a jog each morning, for how long, and with who. It was always through Middleton Woods. And Poppy was always out of her door at 6 am. Sometimes, she went with the solicitor from her firm, an older lady with a ghastly tan and bleached-blonde extensions that only made her look older, and other times she went jogging with him. But on Thursdays and Fridays, Poppy always ran alone. Always.

The six weeks since Poppy had re-entered my life had been difficult. I found more and more that I hated Poppy leaving me, especially after discovering Kai Bielby. I was devastated—and furious—when I realised Poppy had a boyfriend. I found out the second time I saw her because she was arranging a date on the phone with him. When I followed her that night into Leeds, I overheard her talking to her friends about him. Kai had matched her on YorkshireFlirt.com, a dating app, and they'd got talking.

Kai was a gym bunny slash sted head who spent most of his time in the gym at the leisure centre. He was, in every way, my opposite. And clearly, to have had Poppy, to have been inside her, to have touched her, kissed her, in every way better than me. Life was so unfair. He had muscles, but I had brains. So why did he get to fuck her when I...

Poppy was like a drug, and I was hooked, awaiting my next fix, yet knowing no matter how many fixes I had, I would never be satisfied.

As the weeks passed, Poppy and Kai spent more and more time together. I watched as they had meals out, went drinking on nights out, and, because of a shared love of exercise, went on frequent jogs together.

And then, a week ago, Kai had disappeared. Thank fuck! She'd come into Sainsbury's, her emerald eyes red-rimmed, her face devoid of her usual smile. I tried to console her to make sure she was OK. That, and I wanted to know why she was so sad. I thought maybe I could fill the void.

Poppy hadn't given in to my gentle prodding, so I watched her through her living room window that weekend. I was also surprised Kai hadn't shown up for their regular Saturday night date.

I was elated that they'd broken up, and my heart soared at the prospect. It was finally time for me to take the next step in my plan.

Her jogging route on Thursdays and Fridays was always the same: down Moor Flatts Road and into the park by the side of the church. Then she'd take a right past the Visitor Centre before turning left and jogging through the woods, always following the road until she reached the Rose Garden, where she would have a drink and a stretch.

That's where I liked to stand and wait, with a bottle in my hand and my black hood up to keep me warm. I enjoyed watching how Poppy's porcelain cheeks had a hint of blush from the exertion of the climb, the way her chest thrust out and then back in. She had her earphones in, and I desperately wanted to know who she was listening to.

Then Poppy would leave me, oblivious to my shadow dawning over her, south, towards the park entrance and down Town Street. I wasn't much of a jogger, but I'd started so that I could see her every morning. The recent October chill made my lungs burn, but it was worth it, as was the money I'd paid for some black running shoes and the other gear to keep me warm.

I found her on YorkshireFlirt.com, the dating app I knew she found Kai on, but she'd never answered my thumbs up with a matching thumbs up of her own to agree to chat. At first, I assumed it was because of the sted head and that she had deleted the app, but I kept checking her profile hourly, hoping she would be active now that prick was out of the picture. I was desperate for any reason that meant she hadn't rejected me.

I sat and watched a film with Poppy on Saturday night. She had left the curtains open, and as we watched The Devil Wears Prada, I wondered what it would feel like to sit next to her on the crimson-coloured sofa, my arm tangled around her warm body as if we were glued together.

So when Poppy entered Sainsbury's today, Wednesday, for her usual, I hyped myself up and decided I would ask her out. She was in later than expected but not late enough for the security guard to arrive, so the shop was empty, except for Afzal and me, who were sorting out stock in the back.

When she walked in, it was just her and me. She looked happier than she had in a while, which was good—good for me, anyway. Perhaps she was ready to move on after all?

"Hello, how are you?" I asked, approaching her casually. I'd noticed on my investigations that she didn't like her personal space being invaded, and so I stopped a reasonable distance away, my best smile on my face. I breathed in her scent, but it only made me want more.

"Good." She pulled a cute face. "Thanks for asking. You?"

This was my chance. I chuckled and said, "Yeah, I'm good." I chanced a step closer, and she didn't retreat, so I said, "Look, this might sound a bit forward, but I've noticed you in here quite a lot recently, and well, do you fancy going out for a drink one night?"

Poppy looked up from the food in the fridge she'd been choosing between and furrowed her brow, a coy smile teasing her lips. "You want to go out with me?" She squinted, looking at my badge. "Billy…" She stepped back from the fridge. "Is that right?"

"That's right," I said, trying to sound confident. Inside, I was shitting myself. "My treat. Dinner, drinks, and dancing." I stepped closer still. "We could go to that wine bar in Morley to start us off. I'm sure I saw you there last week." I saw her raise a perfectly threaded brow. "You like it there? Right?"

I knew she liked it because I'd been there nearly every weekend, watching, waiting.

Then she laughed.

"Sorry?" I said. "Did I say something funny?" I didn't understand humour. Never have, and probably never will.

As I said those words, I felt eyes on the back of my neck. I turned to see the enemy—my high school nemesis, Chanelle Cummings. She was also one of Poppy's best friends.

"Did this loser really just ask you out, Pop?" Chanelle said.

"That's right, Ellie," Poppy said as a smile creased her lips. "Ha! You want me to date you?" She rolled her eyes. "I don't think so, Billy."

Poppy shook her head and walked away whilst my heart sank and my smile faded.

Everything was Chanelle's fault—it always was. It was the same ten years ago, and it was the same now. A raven-haired, satin-black beauty fancied by most people at my high school in Lofthouse, the constant smirk from Chanelle's glossy lips haunted me daily.

Chanelle was always showing off. She turned Poppy into a different person, into a Poppy that had rejected me again. It was Chanelle's fault she'd rejected me when we were teens, and I should have recognised the concealed smile.

Anger rose from within my depths, rising fast, and I had to

clench my fists to stop myself from lashing out. I could feel the warmth from the blood as it reopened old scars. Poppy was a different person when Chanelle wasn't around.

And so, because Chanelle was the reason why Poppy Lavell didn't buy anything for the first time in six weeks and why she didn't leave with a flirty smile on her face, I decided that Poppy would be better off without Chanelle Cummings.

I'd decided I needed to get rid of her.

And then, just when you think things couldn't get any worse, they did.

In came fat plumber Frank wearing the same stained blue polo shirt as last week. I watched as he slowed down at the automatic doors so he could push past Poppy, his chest glancing hers.

My blood boiled.

"Oi! Fags. Twenty Richmond Superkings, a number three, and two fives. Give me fucking winners this time, lad, yeah?"

"OK," I said tightly through gritted teeth. Fury at the embarrassment of her rejection and the rudeness of the plumber, Frank, spiked through my veins.

"Oh, and that bottle of vodka."

I wanted to embarrass him as Chanelle had embarrassed me. "You got any ID on you, mate?" I asked.

"You fucking what?"

"ID?"

"I'm thirty-three. Do I fucking look like I need ID?"

I took a deep breath. "We operate a challenge 25 policy, sir. So yes, ID, please."

"Where's your manager, you little prick?"

Afzal was in the back, and although he was not a manager, he was higher up on the hierarchy, so I lied. "She's not in today, so I'm in charge. How can I help?" I smiled.

The fat, bald man pulled his thick wallet from his too-tight cargo pants. "Here, you little prick!"

I looked at it. Frank Hinchcliffe. Thirty-three? I thought he looked nearer to fifty. Jesus. I looked at the address. I found the same one online for his Plumbing and Heating business.

Perfect.

"Thank you, sir, and please accept my apologies. You're older than you look. That's a good thing, right?"

"Whatever, dickhead," Frank said as he tapped his phone against the contactless hub. "I only come here to bump into that fine piece of ass. You know who I mean, right? The one I just managed to cop a feel of. And her friend. My God! What a tasty morsel. I'd love to be the meat in that sandwich, if you get my drift. Fucking hell."

"Can I help you with anything else, sir?" I asked, wanting to stop talking about Poppy and Chanelle. I felt as if my blood couldn't boil any more.

"You're a fucking joke; you know that? You ruined my mood. Be prepared, loser. I'm going to write a letter to your head office... Billy."

I desperately tried to hide my grin, but it mustn't have worked because the plumber's face turned beetroot. "Yeah, I know your name. It's right there." Frank pressed a chubby finger against the Perspex, indicating my name badge, before shaking his head and leaving.

I'd had enough. I stormed into the stock room, and Afzal jumped as I opened the door with a crash.

"Christ, Bill. Are you OK, mate?" Afzal gave a nervous laugh. He'd always been the jumpy type. I reckoned he was stealing stock when the manager wasn't in. Cigarettes and small bottles of neat alcohol regularly went missing.

"I feel sick. I need to go home. Can you cope until we shut?"

Afzal looked at me, and his smile faded. "Yeah, OK. Security should be here in ten. Can you wait until they show?"

"No," I said, my jaw clenched. "I need to go now." I grabbed my coat from the hook and strode through the fire door without another word. As it banged shut behind me, I took a look around. We had CCTV at the back of the parade of shops, but there were a lot of blind spots. The boss wouldn't know I left early unless Afzal grassed me in.

I wiped the blood from my palms and headed off home.

Frank, the plumber, was going to pay.

And so was Poppy Lavell.

But first, I needed to get rid of Chanelle Cummings.

Chapter Three

There was something outside the house, in the garden.

Chanelle was sure of it. Just as she'd been sure something had been outside every evening during the past week.

She'd shut the living room curtains, keeping out the night sky, and whoever, or whatever, was lurking out there on the small patio beyond the glass of the patio door. Chanelle hadn't heard it at first, but the dog on her lap certainly had. Rosa had been asleep, and then her ears had pricked up before she'd raised her head. She was now staring at the curtain and growling; her pupils widened to black orbs.

Rosa's behaviour unsettled her.

Chanelle knew Rosa's heightened sense of smell and hearing gave her an advantage. That meant there was something out there, and the dog knew it: something alive, menacing, and threatening.

It had begun six nights ago whilst Chanelle was sitting on the sofa in front of the television with Rosa on her lap. Kieron, her boyfriend, worked until late, so she and the dog got into the habit of snuggling together. Chanelle stroked Rosa's soft, brown fur, and the dog slept peacefully. Then suddenly, the dog was awake and on guard, waking Chanelle from the light slumber she had given into. She had been afraid then. And now it was happening again. There was just her and Rosa in the house on Avocet Garth, not far from the pharmacy where she worked.

Her senses were heightened, and Chanelle picked up the remote control and muted the television, not taking her eyes from Rosa. She strained her ears against the silence, but there was nothing: no noise in or outside the house. Outside, the air was still, a chilly but calm autumn night. But Rosa was still on guard, staring menacingly at the curtains, ready to defend if required.

"It's OK, my sweet," Chanelle whispered, stroking her back. "There's nothing out there that can get you." She felt ridiculous talking to Rosa that way and realised she'd said it more for her benefit than the dog's, although she didn't reassure herself any more than Rosa.

Chanelle continued stroking her velvety fur, hoping she would return to sleep, which would mean that whatever was out there had gone and the danger had passed.

She hated that Kieron worked late at the gym, often leaving before she did and returning just before she went to bed. Chanelle had considered dumping him and had come close a month ago before he promised to change. But that change hadn't been what she'd expected. Instead, he'd become detached and angry. Yet he wouldn't tell her why.

Chanelle had confided in both Poppy and Ruby, her two best friends, who had both told her to dump him. But the sex was too good for that. Way too good. In the summer, she was OK being home alone and used for sex at night. But during the colder months, with it being dark by five, she was desperate for some companionship, which was why she'd rescued Rosa.

Chanelle jumped as she thought she heard muttering from

outside. The house she rented regularly creaked with its own sounds, and sometimes, the wind whistled through the trees in her back garden as though the trees were whispering between themselves.

She glanced at her phone and realised it had just gone 9 pm, which was the same time Rosa had been spooked the previous nights. So whatever was outside must have gone, as Rosa had lost interest. Chanelle was glad, and she stroked her protector, watching as her eyes gradually closed and her head relaxed until it rested on her leg again.

It dawned on Chanelle that Rosa's ears remained alert, twitching every so often as if part of her was listening while the rest of her body slept. It occurred to her that Rosa's actions were protective, and she remained alert even when sleeping. A defence mechanism. It did nothing to make Chanelle feel better.

"Rosa," she whispered, twisting her fingers through the fur on Rosa's neck.

A brief moment passed, and then she bolted upright, awake, a low rumble coming from her throat. Something, or someone, was outside again, and a chill ran up Chanelle's spine. It was back again, and Rosa's hackles were rising. Chanelle's heart began to hammer in her chest while Rosa stared at the curtain, ready to attack. Without warning, she jumped from Chanelle's lap onto the arm of the sofa, lying flat and barking furiously.

"Stop, Rosa!" Chanelle said, stroking the dog to calm her down. Her claws would damage the sofa.

Then suddenly, she raced to the patio door, where frenzied, Rosa began scratching at the carpet to be let out. She'd done the same as she had the nights before when she'd heard something.

"No. Naughty girl," Chanelle said, going towards the door.

Rosa had escaped the garden the previous night and hadn't come back for two hours. Chanelle had been worried sick, thinking she was lost for good. Kieron had brought her back and said he found her wandering around the grassed area opposite the shopping centre.

Had she chased something away? If so, what?

She was frantically pawing the patio door still and barking. Chanelle had no choice but to let her out if she wasn't to cause any damage. As soon as she opened the back door, Rosa shot down the garden. It was a bitter night, and a dense fog covered the ground in fog. She could no longer see Rosa in the garden, assuming the dog had chased something into the shrubbery near the fence that separated her garden from the house behind hers. Then, there was a break in the fog, and Chanelle saw something quite large scramble up and over the fence. Rosa couldn't follow but frantically pawed at the wooden fence, barking like mad.

"What the fuck was that?" Chanelle cursed. "Rosa, come back now!" she shouted. "Rosa!" But she'd gone. "Rosa! Please!"

Silence. She stood at the patio door for a moment, listening, and then closed and locked it, hoping Rosa would return soon. Whatever she'd caught a glimpse of out there, the dark silhouette terrified her.

The previous nights, Chanelle hadn't seen a thing. And she wished that tonight she had seen nothing, too. She had always thought it was a fox or badger, and yet...

She shivered and moved away from the patio door. In the second before it had disappeared, she could have sworn it was human.

* * *

I'd done it again and got too cocky. That stupid fucking dog had chased me for the second time. But it was worth it—worth every second and worth every minute.

I needed to know exactly where she was and when. That way, I could formulate a plan in my mind that would get rid of the stupid, stuck-up bitch!

So last week, I spent hours watching Chanelle Cummings, studying which way she walked home from work. This helped me map out her schedule. From watching her, I knew that Chanelle got home at 5.15 pm Monday through Friday because she consistently clocked off at 5 pm and lived just around the corner.

I also knew she threw on some joggers and a hoodie and took her stupid fucking dog out at 6.30 pm after eating her tea. She ate alone during the week and sometimes at the weekend when her sted head boyfriend worked overtime at the gym.

What was it with pretty girls and muscle men? Poppy had been the same...

Chanelle's route took her out of her street and onto Town Street before she headed up Town Street towards Miggy Park. I don't know why we say Miggy instead of Middy, but that's the only nickname I've ever known for where I was born and raised.

Chanelle then turned right and went into the park via the entrance between the witch's house, as I know it to be called, and St Mary's Church. Chanelle was a creature of habit, as most of us are. I could see as I followed her that she got comfort from walking the same route five days a week.

After walking down the path, one that's usually covered with dogshit, and hypodermic needles, Chanelle took her dog back up the hill as if heading towards the park gates. Then she turned right onto the overgrown golf course.

Then it was a matter of looping around the old course, being wary, I noticed, of not entering the groves of trees that lined the old fairways before heading out of the park gates and down Town Street, back home.

The walk usually lasted anywhere between forty minutes and an hour. But once she was home, that's when things usually got exciting.

I guess I realised why the chumps back in high school salivated over Chanelle. I hadn't really been interested in women or men and had to force myself to masturbate as a teen. But I'm not that guy any more. Now I understand. And I know why the guys used to fight over her. Why they'd brag about shagging her.

She was a beautiful, raven-haired goddess with curls that cascaded down her chest. After walking her dog, she always stripped for the shower, and I used my binoculars to see the perfect folds below her silk-black landing strip.

But it was her 32D-sized tits I enjoyed the most. I knew their size because I had taken a day's leave earlier that week and wandered around her home. It was during the day, whilst she was at work, and whilst I knew that it was dangerous, the danger added to my excitement. Chanelle hadn't been cautious with the security of her house, and there was only the slightest sound as my feet met the rim of the water butt. My gloved hand reached an upstairs open window, and I pulled myself up.

Chanelle's house was lovely—much nicer than mine, anyway. I sat on her sofa and turned on the TV. I hated that she watched it with the curtains drawn over the patio doors. It meant I couldn't watch a film with her as I did with Poppy.

Chanelle had filled her Sky box with reality shows, shit that I'm far too important and far too busy to watch.

Though if it helped me to get to know you more, Chanelle, then maybe I thought I should have started watching that shit, too.

Speaking of shit. I took a shit in Chanelle's toilet. I wiped my arse using her vanilla-scented soft toilet roll. The stuff I have at home is like a cheese grater. Chanelle's was like using feathers.

I considered having a shower and using the products I watched her use on my own body. But it was a risk. My hair could fall out and stay in the drain; at least I could flush my piss and shit away.

I slept on Chanelle's bed for a bit, but only after I stole a pair of her panties from the wash basket in the corner of her bedroom. They're at home now, in my bedroom. I've sniffed them every night. I think that probably made me a disgusting person, but I don't give a flying fuck what other people think. I also looked at the size of her bras to get her a present. Seeing her wearing something I bought would please me to no end.

Back in the present, her mocha-brown nipples stood to attention from the cold as she switched the shower on, and I lowered my hand beneath my waistband. I'd been going at myself all week, using the memory of her soaping those 32Ds. However, this time, I wanted to go at it in person, knowing it would help me commit the view to memory.

I almost didn't want to kill you, Chanelle. Almost. I thought maybe I'd fallen for you. Perhaps we'd be good together. That was why you belittled me, right? Because you wanted me, but

I'd asked Poppy out.

I'm sure I was right.

I was wrong, of course. Very fucking wrong.

Before I left the house, I looked at her iPad. There were pictures of me on there from the night I'd asked Poppy out on a date at work, Photoshopped into a clown.

Poppy Lavell and Ruby Kaur laughed at my expense, calling me a loser. But Chanelle's comments were like a stake to the heart.

I was done with her then. After seeing those pictures. She needed to pay.

So I set up my plan. It was going to be perfect. First, I'd follow Chanelle into the park, then hide in the woods and wait. Then I'd distract that fucking dog and manipulate her into walking into the large grove of trees that separated the park from the golf course.

And then I'd kill her. Stab her in the neck with the box cutter I use at work.

Fucking bitch!

Chapter Four

Chanelle walked briskly through the old golf course with Rosa not far behind. From morning until afternoon, the weather had been decent for October, but now the clouds were gathering, and Chanelle could feel a headache coming. That, and she could feel the temperature dropping. Leeds had been blessed with relatively mild temperatures in October in recent years. Still, the weather forecast predicted ground frost by the end of the month, which, mixed with the rain that was sure to come, would make walking Rosa unbearable. Her mum was already asking about Christmas, hinting that she would like Chanelle to spend it at home with them instead of her boyfriend, but her dad was allergic to dogs, and she couldn't leave Rosa alone.

"Come on, Rosa Parks!" Chanelle called. Like a child's parent, Chanelle only used Rosa's full name when she was pissing her off. "Come on, Rosa, keep up!" She kept stopping to sniff and forage in the foliage, densely wooded areas that separated the fairways of the old golf course.

"Come on. Good girl!" Chanelle called again and turned.

But Rosa was nowhere to be seen.

"Rosa!" she shouted. "Come here. Now!"

There was no sign of her. Chanelle stayed where she was in the centre of an overgrown fairway and listened for any sound suggesting Rosa could be close. But the park was eerily quiet. "Rosa! Come on. Here, girl!"

Still nothing.

Partly annoyed and partially worried, Chanelle retraced her steps, knowing Rosa liked children. The swings and climbing frames weren't far away, and Chanelle had often caught Rosa on her back, being petted by innocent children.

So, Chanelle went east towards the pond, watching for signs of other people.

Rosa had been following her the last time she'd looked, barely a minute ago, but now she'd disappeared entirely. Chanelle kept going, calling her name and zigzagging the fairway, looking into the woods on both sides, not daring to enter. She must have chased something, Chanelle thought. But which direction did she go? As Chanelle headed down the hill, there were trees to her left and right on both sides. She only hoped Rosa hadn't gone to her left because it was easy to get swallowed up in the dense Middleton Woods.

"Rosa!" she shouted at the top of her voice. Then she heard a rustle. It came from her left.

Great.

She turned and looked into the woods where the noise had come from, just in time to see Rosa burst from the foliage and run flat out towards her. But what was that behind the dog?

It looked like somebody else was running there, too— somebody dressed in all black. Chanelle only managed the briefest glimpse before whatever it was disappeared into the woods. With it being all black, it was just an outline, but she was sure it was the size and shape of a man, similar to the one she thought she'd seen in her garden recently. Was somebody following her? Surely not. And yet...

Rosa was hard to spook, and truthfully, so was Chanelle. But here she was, shaking, just as the heavens opened.

Thick globules of freezing water hammered down on Chanelle as she clipped the lead to Rosa's collar and ran towards the play area, hoping for the comfort of people milling around, her thoughts spinning. She kept her eyes straight ahead and didn't look into the woods to her left for fear of what she might see. Rosa was running flat out beside her, her legs working hard to keep up.

On the short sprint, Chanelle could only think about the man's silhouette. Was he trying to keep low, possibly to avoid being seen? That thought alone made her more afraid. Were they following her? If so, why? What did they want with her?

Inside a long grove of trees separating a fairway from the play area, Chanelle paused for a moment, sweating and out of breath.

And that was all the chance Billy needed.

* * *

Rain fell on my head as I crouched down, watching, waiting. The thought of murder highlighted my every sense. I'd always wanted to kill something bigger, and now I had my chance.

Chanelle Cummings—my old enemy, my high school nemesis—stood alone, weak and frail. Chanelle had made my life a living nightmare, and now I'd become hers.

I pulled the Stanley box cutter I used at work from my hoodie and, from behind, drew it quick and hard across her throat.

She let go of the lead, and her best friend abandoned her.

Our eyes met as I twisted her to face me and pushed her to the ground.

And she recognised me. She said my name. My real name.

I grinned.

"Why?" Blood bubbled from her mouth.

Power coursed through my veins, charging my very soul. I felt—Godlike. There was no other way to describe it. "Because I've always hated you, you stupid, stuck-up bitch!"

Watching Chanelle Cummings bleed out was one of the best things I'd ever seen. Ever. But something was missing. The kill had been too quick. I'd wanted to savour in the murder, yet a quick brush against her throat had finished her.

The dog had run off, and I heard a voice in the distance say, "Where's your owner, girl?"

I glanced around, making sure nobody saw me and removed the friendship bracelet, a match to the ones Chanelle had given Ruby and Poppy for Christmas, pocketing it before standing back up. It would make a nice trophy. Then I glanced down at myself and laughed. The black clothes had come in handy. Whilst Chanelle's blood covered my hoodie and joggers, it looked like I had sweated through them. As for my trainers, it looked as if they were just wet from the jog.

I removed her mobile from her pocket and switched it off. I could see myself in the reflection on the screen. My face was spattered with blood, and I thought I looked like a demon. I scrubbed my face with my sleeve until the blood vanished into the black fabric. The heat had flooded through me during the attack, but now, cold gnawed at me as the adrenaline faded.

I needed to go. The longer I lingered, the higher the chance someone would discover me. That, or I'd be close enough to be placed at the scene by any potential witnesses. That would not be good.

After dragging her deep within the grove and stealing her

keys, I looked down at Chanelle Cummings, my old enemy, savouring the sight of the stunning ebony goddess lying in a tangled mess. I took delight in seeing her unseeing dark eyes staring up into the canopy of the trees. I took great pleasure in knowing that her chest would never rise and fall again. She looked even more beautiful in death. I nearly used a hand to touch her face, desperate to feel the heat leaving her body, but I stopped myself. I wasn't wearing gloves, and whilst I was a lot of things, I wasn't an idiot. The less I contaminated the scene, the better. Police forensics were excellent.

I twisted and turned to make sure I'd left nothing behind— no prints, no items, no nothing. A part of me yearned to stay just a little longer. The thrill of the kill spoke to me. It excited me, but I didn't want to get caught.

And so, I ran.

* * *

Elated, I had run all the way home that evening without stopping, as though the kill had energised every step I pounded into the ground. I had finally done it! The power coursing through me made me feel invincible. I had covered my tracks exceptionally well, and as such, nobody would ever know what I'd done nor the brilliance of what I'd caused.

I was meant for more extraordinary things. It was obvious. I didn't want to go back to being a checkout boy at Sainsbury's Local any more, overlooked and ignored, so I wasn't going to attend work tomorrow. Fuck them. The lot of them. The energy coursing through my body was far too precious to waste on selling fags, booze and scratch cards and lottery tickets all day. I'd already decided to email in sick when I got back home.

Things were going to change. Poppy would see me now. She wouldn't be able to help it. She would no longer misjudge and reject me, especially with Chanelle out of the way!

I reached the park gates and sprinted past the primary school with my hood up, startling an older man walking his dog. The stupid little twat tried to nibble at my ankle as I bounded past it, so I gave it a little kick and put up my hand in a fake apology. I probably should have ignored the critter, especially as I didn't want to bring myself to anybody's attention, but I couldn't help myself.

And anyway, I was now invincible.

I sprinted past the takeaways, café, and charity shop on Middleton Park Road, turning left down Hopewell View, past the chippy, and then left up Mount Pleasant, where I lived in a small back-to-back terrace that I thought was perfect. It was just off the main road, and there were many different ways to get to it, meaning it was easy to slip in and out unnoticed.

I closed the door behind me, the bolt engaging automatically, and leaned my back on it, panting, pausing, taking in the relief of getting away with the crime. The more I breathed, the more the power buzzed through me.

Once I got my breath back, I noticed the weight of the Stanley in my hoodie pocket. I pulled it out delicately, looking at the blade—which still bore traces of that bitch's blood—reverently.

My hoodie was sticky with blood, and I was glad I'd worn black. The T-shirt I wore underneath was cold and stuck to my skin, the blood clinging to the hair on my belly.

I removed my trainers on the doormat and stepped into my tiny kitchen, pulling off my hoodie and peeling off my T-shirt. Chanelle's blood now stained my once-white T-shirt a deep, dark red. I removed the rest of my clothes, standing stark bollock naked in my kitchen, and threw the clothes into the washing machine. Then I realised I'd left behind my trainers, so I fetched them and shoved them in.

In haste, I'd forgotten to retrieve Chanelle's phone from my pocket. So, after pulling it from the washing machine and throwing it on the table, I poured some detergent into it and set the washer on a hot, fast wash. I knew that would get rid of most of the blood, but I'd run a second one later to make sure.

I glanced out of the small corridor window and saw the alley that separated the two sets of back-to-backs was deserted. So, I picked up the knife and headed to the kitchen, where the entrance to the cellar was.

I flicked on the light, noticing a red smear on the light switch from the contact. It sent shivers through my body at the memory of the kill. I would have to remember to clean that later.

The cellar was an empty, unused, cold and damp space with no natural light or heating. Luckily, it did have power, but the pull switch for the light was at the bottom, so I trod down the concrete steps with care until I reached the bottom, each step freezing on the bare soles of my feet.

I stored my toolbox on an empty shelving unit. It was where I was going to hide the knife and my other trophies. I thought being hidden in plain sight was always the best, so I buried the knife, phone, and friendship bracelet deep inside, being sure to cover them with tools. Then, I slammed the box shut, sliding it between the shelves to wedge the lid down.

I stood back to look at my handiwork, and a smirk creased the corners of my mouth. It was perfect. No one would ever know.

I strolled upstairs to the bathroom, a spring in my step, and squeezed through the door, which wouldn't fully open thanks to the wash basket filled with filthy washing, before slamming the door shut.

The man who looked back at me in the bathroom mirror was glorious. Blue, powerful eyes stared back at me as I took in the view. A slight sheen of sweat glimmered in the bathroom light atop my forehead. I took in the evidence of the crime and saw Chanelle's blood—dark smears—hidden in the cracks at the side of my nose and between the hairs of my brows. There was also a bright spot below my ear.

I held up my hands, which were ingrained with Chanelle's crusty, dried blood, clinging stubbornly to every fold and crack of my skin. The sticky liquid that had nearly fused the T-shirt to my skin and stuck to my chest hair darkened my chest and stomach.

And whilst I'd attempted to clean my legs after the kill, the blood had doggedly remained, with a long line that stretched from my knee to my ankle, where it must have soaked down into my sock.

I looked fucking glorious.

And that look, and how the kill made me feel, was addictive. So arousing. And I knew then, deep within, that I couldn't just be done with one kill.

I needed to kill again.

Chapter Five

George followed the group out of the small chapel in Beverley into the misty rain. The gentle breeze attempted to knock the remaining leaves from the trees, and George's toes, stuffed into wet shoes, were going numb.

It was 9 am, and the service had been short, both the early hour and shortness due in most part to how and why Henry the 'Cross Flatts Snatcher' Davidson had died. That's what the papers had dubbed Davidson before he fell to his death from the Humber Bridge. His assumed death, anyway. The coastguard had never found a body, so Henry's parents had been forced to get a declaration of presumed death.

The Humber Rescue, based out of Hessle, searched for Henry's body for weeks after the jump. It was clear to George and the Government that Henry Davidson was dead, primarily because out of two hundred incidents, only five people had ever survived the freezing water of the estuary.

And if Henry had survived, he hadn't been seen since his jump in June, and it was now October.

Reaching the grave, the pallbearers—made up of Henry's father and uncles—laid the casket in place. The lack of any human remains had not deterred the family from having a coffin; the symbolism of the act of laying Henry to rest was what mattered to them, despite what he had done.

At that moment, as the priest delivered her final blessing, George pondered his reasons for being at the funeral. What Henry had done was wrong, but George understood why he had done it. As a father, George understood why Henry wanted to take Benjamin away from the dangers in Beeston. He understood wanting to take him away from an unfit mother and Benjamin's paedophile biological father.

That was the critical element in his decision. Biology. Despite being a murderer, which Henry was because he had killed Andrew Morris, Henry had been Benjamin's father for five years. Five years of memories. Five years of relationship building.

George thought about his own son and how he had been Jack's father for twenty-two months. He couldn't even come to terms with the heartbreak and anguish he would feel if Mia tried to take Jack away from him or deny him his rights as a father.

The reason Henry and Claire snatched Benjamin was positive, but he wished Henry had done it differently.

"I'm pleased to see you here, Detective Inspector Beaumont, if that's the correct word to use," Mrs Davidson said. George could see the gravediggers waiting patiently for the signal to start their task.

George looked towards the vast crowd of people who stood around the grave. Claire wasn't here; she was incarcerated at HMP New Hall at Flockton in Wakefield, awaiting her trial.

"It's a good turnout," George replied.

"For a murderer and a child kidnapper, you mean?" Mr Davidson said as he came over and put an arm around his wife. "You shouldn't be here, detective."

"That's not what I meant, Mr Davidson."

"So why are you here? To laud in your capture of our son?"

George looked down at the grave marker, just a temporary wooden cross until the family were allowed to put down a headstone. "No, sir. Henry and I were much alike. Whilst I disagreed with his decisions, it felt right to come here today. I'll leave if that's what you want?"

"There's no need." Mrs Davidson looked up at George, smiled, and placed a hand on his arm. "You tried to save my Henry, to stop him from jumping, and for that, you will forever have my thanks."

Mr Davidson huffed and pulled his wife away, back towards the grave.

George thought back to the moment on the bridge. "Let me go, Inspector," Henry had said whilst George held on tight, grimacing at the pain tearing throughout every muscle. "I mean it, George. Dangling here, I realise this is the only way out."

Henry had desperately tried to twist his wrist to free himself from George's grasp. "Keep a hold of me, you idiot. Reinforcements should be here any minute! We'll get the best outcome for you and Benjamin. I can promise you that!"

"That's your problem, George. You do everything by the book. You had me on the bridge, a child snatcher and a murderer, yet you pulled the car to the side, injuring yourself. Even after everything I've done, you still think I'm worth saving. I'm beyond saving."

"That's not why I did it," George had whispered.

"Then why did you save me before? Why are you trying to save me now?"

"For your son. Benjamin. And because I understand why

you did what you did. You were brave when I was a coward. Be Benjamin's father. Please."

A tear fell from George's eye as he remembered what had happened next.

Both men had met eyes, but neither man spoke. Henry nodded instead. George gripped Henry's hand tight, ready to take the weight of the man hanging from the bridge, but could do nothing when Henry opened his hand and released his grip on George.

And then Henry Davidson was gone, swallowed up by the water.

In the weeks after the incident on the bridge, George wondered whether he could have done more to save the man. The adrenaline pumping through his veins meant he could have held on for another minute or two. By then, the cavalry would have arrived, their boots pounding on the tarmac behind him.

But Henry had let go, and that haunted him.

George's phone began to vibrate in his pocket. He smiled an apology at Mrs Davidson and walked away, out of earshot. "DI Beaumont."

Detective Superintendent Jim Smith's voice boomed down the phone. "George, there's been a murder. Get back to Leeds. Now!"

* * *

Detective Inspector George Beaumont sighed as Mia's name flashed up on his phone. He took a deep breath, gritted his teeth and answered.

"For a moment, George, I thought you were ignoring my calls?" Mia snapped at him.

"Morning, Mia. I was driving. What's up?" He scolded himself for explaining, for feeling like he had to justify himself. He felt as if she had more power over him now than they did when they were together.

"Are you still coming over for tea tonight?"

George could hear the hope in her voice.

"About that—"

"What now, George? There's always fucking something getting in the way!"

"It's my job, Mia," he said, trying to keep the anger that flared through him from darkening his tone. "There's been a murder, and I've been made Senior Investigating Officer."

"Of course you have! Why do you always put your job before me..." George heard Mia falter. "Before Jack?"

George took a deep breath to force away the venom building in his voice. "Jack is the most important person in my life, Mia. But I'm a police detective. It's my duty. It should be an open and shut case, so once it's over, we can rearrange." George knew she would be pissed off about him cancelling, but she knew the type of man George was when they first got together. They'd been happy at first, but they'd become so detached since the breakup. And she'd become so bitter.

"It's a good job that Jack's not old enough to remember you are cancelling on him," Mia retorted.

She was being a bitch, and she knew it. Mia knew exactly which buttons to press and when. But George was used to it by now. Biting back would only make Mia more difficult, most likely ignoring her phone as George attempted to make plans with their son.

So he said nothing, swallowing everything he wanted to tell her.

After a momentary pause, she said, "You're busy, so I'm going. Ring me when you're not so busy, yeah? Jack misses his father." And with that, the line went dead.

George stared down at the black screen of his mobile and forced himself to take slow, deep, and calming breaths. Then, finally, he clicked the screen on, and a picture of Jack lit up his lock screen, his son's emerald eyes staring up at him in a smile. He loved that boy more than anyone—more than anything.

George remembered that Jack had been covered in chocolate cake not minutes later, having stuffed fistful after fistful into his widely grinning cheeky chops.

Pocketing his phone, George got out of the car, slammed the door, and locked it before stomping into Elland Road Police Station, home to the Homicide and Major Enquiry Team Detective in which Inspector George Beaumont served. George much preferred solving murders than dealing with Mia's bullshit.

"You took your time getting back, Beaumont," DSU Jim Smith's booming voice echoed down the hallway.

George grimaced. "Sorry, sir. The M62 was a nightmare."

DSU Smith pushed open the canteen door and crossed to the kettle. "DS Wood will be your deputy. She's setting up an Incident Room. CSI are on their way, but I want you down there now."

George nodded as he grabbed a thermos from the cupboard and began to prepare his own brew. It was going to be a long day.

When George entered the squad room, DS Luke Mason was sitting at his desk with a steaming mug beside him and an empty McMuffin wrapper.

"Morning, George," Luke said with a grin.

"Seen DS Wood?" George said with a grin before raising an eyebrow at the empty wrapper.

"Oh fuck off, George," Luke said defensively.

George shrugged. "Not my business, mate."

"I'm cutting down, but I've had a shit couple of days and needed the grease."

George snorted with laughter and clapped Luke on the shoulder. "The job does that to you, mate."

"It's not the job," Luke muttered.

George sat down in one of the office chairs. "Everything OK?"

Mason looked at him, a look in his eyes George had never seen before. "Me and our lass... We've decided to take some time apart. I've moved in with my mum."

"Shit, mate," George said, placing his hand on Luke's shoulder. "Anything I can do?"

Mason winced. "No, mate. But maybe stop taking the piss for a bit."

"No can do, Luke. You're an easy target." George grinned, but Luke looked sorry for himself. George knew Luke worshipped the ground his wife walked on, and it was probably not his idea to separate. However, seeing his mate that way was pretty sad, especially since Luke and his wife were teenage sweethearts. But if they couldn't make it work, then who could?

At that moment, DS Isabella Wood called George from across the office. She was wearing her coat, her bag slung over her shoulder. "Sorry to interrupt, George, but we need to get to Middleton Woods ASAP."

George turned back to Luke. "I'll ring you later, mate. Yeah?" Mason nodded as George shrugged his coat back on. Then, out of habit, he checked his pockets for his wallet, car keys, and phone before crossing the room to where Isabella waited.

"Morning, DS Wood." George hadn't seen her for a few days. Smith had put them on opposing shifts, and he was paranoid that DSU Smith knew about their relationship.

"How'd the funeral go?" she whispered as they walked out of the station and towards the car park.

George grimaced. "Difficult. Brought back memories of the bridge."

She placed a reassuring hand on his shoulder. "I told you it was a bad idea to go," she said.

After checking around for prying eyes, he winked and kissed Isabella on the cheek. "You were right." She grinned a perfect smile, a smile that melted him every time. "What have we got, anyway?"

"An IC3 female. A dog walker found the body in Middleton Woods this morning."

George frowned. Middleton Woods. Again. In the absence of any pool cars that day, he headed over to his new car, a silver Mercedes A-class. "Shit. Do we have any more info?"

"Not yet," Isabella said, allowing George to open the car door for her.

She squeezed his ass as he moved away from her towards the bonnet. Isabella could see from how his posture slackened that George had enjoyed it.

"I know I say this a lot," Isabella said as she slid inside, "but I like this car a lot!"

"Better than those disgusting pool cars, at least."

"At the very least." She pulled out her notebook to advise George of the details. "Police constables are on scene, and an ambulance is nearby."

George said nothing as he slid out of the car park and joined the main road.

Chapter Six

Ten minutes later, George parked behind the ambulance beyond the park gates, having flashed their warrant cards to the PC guarding the entrance. As the pair of detectives walked down the hill, they could see a hive of activity to their left, the section of trees separating the park from the old golf course positively heaving with white paper suits. Lindsey Yardley and her crime scene team had been there for an hour already and were doing their best to gather what evidence they could, which, from the call DS Wood took in the car on the way over, hadn't been much.

The suspected murder had taken place relatively close to the playground, George thought. That was risky.

"That's where the dog walker found her," Wood said. "Inside the line of trees."

George nodded.

"Sounds as if her throat had been cut. She bled out. The rain was quite bad last night."

"I heard the call, Wood. You had Lindsey on speaker."

"Alright, Mardy. What's up with you?" she asked.

George stopped and turned to his girlfriend. "Sorry. Murder in Middleton Woods." He shrugged his shoulders. "It always gets to me."

"It's fine. I understand." She blew him a kiss.

The grass hill leading down to the playground was like a swamp from the rain. Parts of the grass had been churned up by dickhead quad bikers who regularly decided to vandalise the park. "Do we know what she was doing in the woods?"

"By how she was dressed, it looks like she was exercising." She shrugged. "We don't have much to go on."

"Do we know who she is yet?" George asked.

"A SOCO took her prints using a lantern, but she's not on the system. No wallet, so no ID. I've got DC Scott checking for mispers."

"Good." The detectives flashed their warrant cards at the PC guarding the cordon. She gave them the usual protective gear, and they ducked under.

"Morning, Lindsey," George said. "Got much for us?"

"Morning, DI Beaumont. DS Wood." Lindsey Yardley pulled a frustrated face at the pair. "No. I can tell you she died last night, but it's tricky to ascertain an exact time of death. I'd say between 7 and 10 pm. It looked like an assassination."

"An assassination. What do you mean?" Wood said.

"From the angle of the wound, it looks like her attacker came at her from behind and slit her throat. Of course, I can't be sure until Dr Ross does the post-mortem, especially as we lack blood spatter because of this fucking rain! But this seems the most likely scenario."

George nodded. Neither detective was taking notes. They didn't need to.

"It was a sharp, thin blade—from experience, a Stanley knife or something. Again, Dr Ross will confirm. We'll send you a report."

George's eyes narrowed a fraction. "Easily available then?"

George said. Lindsey nodded. "Guess you haven't found the weapon anywhere?"

"Haven't found anything, really. Well, nothing but a partial print and some black fibres. I've had my team search the entire treeline for footprints, but we got nothing. My guess is it started raining just after the murder."

George cast his gaze around the park. He could see people hovering at the outer cordon, no doubt gossiping. "Do you know which side she entered the trees from?"

"No. We found nothing, and I mean nothing."

The sky was a shade of grey that suggested it hadn't entirely made its mind up, but the clouds rolling in from the north begged to differ.

"I'm as disappointed as you are, Lindsey." He turned to Wood. "Wood, get DC Blackburn to put out an appeal for witnesses. The park's usually busy between 7 and 10 pm. Hopefully, somebody saw something."

His mind wandered back to memory from his teens, him walking through trees that lined the fairways, their Border Collie, Ben, begging him to throw the ball. George chanced a look at the body. Wood was right; she looked like she was exercising, yet CSI found no water bottle. Could she have been walking a dog?

He turned to find Wood, who was fifteen metres away, on her phone. She gestured for him to come over, but he held up his hand and pulled out his mobile.

There was a vet just up the road. He thought that if she was walking a dog, maybe somebody found it and took it there. It's what he would have done. And he would have asked them to scan for a chip.

"Good morning, Melissa speaking; how can I help you?"

"Morning Melissa, I'm Detective Inspector Beaumont from the West Yorkshire Police's Homicide and Major Enquiry Team. This is a bit of a long shot, but you don't happen to know if any abandoned dogs have been brought in, do you?"

"Abandoned dogs?" The confusion was evident in her tone.

"Aye. Last night or this morning. Maybe somebody asked you to scan their chip?"

"Can you hold whilst I check?"

"Sure."

There was no hold music, so George made his way over to DS Wood. They stood together in silence, both listening and waiting.

"Hello?"

"Yes."

"Detective Inspector?"

"Yes."

"Weirdly enough, somebody called last night wanting us to scan a dog, but we told them they had to wait for us to open this morning."

"Right?" George tried to hide the impatience he was feeling.

"Well, he's here now with the dog. The vet has just scanned the chip, and we have the owner's name and address."

"So what are you waiting for?"

"I'm sorry, Detective Inspector, but my boss won't let me release the information. I believe you are who you say you are, but could you please come up and show us your ID?"

George clenched his fist tightly around the mobile. "Fine. Give me five minutes. Melissa, was it?"

"That's right. Sorry for any inconvenience."

George was about to hang up the phone when DS Wood gestured for him to stop. "Wait a minute, Melissa."

"Yes?"

"My colleague wants to speak to you."

"Hi Melissa, this is Detective Sergeant Wood. Does the dog happen to belong to Chanelle Cummings, who lives at an address on Avocet Garth?"

From the hesitation, Isabella knew that was a yes.

"I—I'm sorry, Detective Sergeant, but my boss has asked that you come in."

"We'll be there in five," Wood said, hanging up and handing the mobile back to George. On their way out, they removed their protective gear and gave it to the PC. She showed George an image of Chanelle Cummings that DC Jason Scott had sent.

"Looks like we've found our victim."

* * *

The two detectives were about to get into the Mercedes when George heard the shout. It was loud and sharp, a wail of despair that shattered the silence, scaring the birds from the tops of the trees.

"Please, I beg you! Just tell me what happened to my baby girl!"

"Aw, shit," George muttered as he and DS Wood both looked toward the sound. A broad-shouldered man with salt-and-pepper hair was gesturing angrily at a PC. "That's got to be Chanelle's father, right?"

Wood nodded. "Aye. Got to be. How the hell did they find out so quickly?"

"The vet?"

"The vet," Wood said with a nod. "News like this travels fast around here."

"For fucks sake!"

"Just get out of the way. I want to see my daughter, alright? I want to see where she was found!" the man ranted, his anger rising in his voice.

George felt sorry for the guy and even more sorry for the young female PC, who was clearly losing a battle and doing her best to calm him down.

"How do you want to handle this?" Wood asked.

George sighed. "Take the Mercedes and go to the vet. Take statements from the staff and the dog walker. I'll finish here and walk up."

Gravel from the road surface crunched beneath George's feet as he strode over to where the uniform was trying her best to calm the situation. At the sound of George's approach, the man's head snapped towards the DI, the PC immediately forgotten.

"You," the man said, closing the gap. "Are you a detective?" he demanded.

"Yes, I am," said George, nodding to the older man. The woman who had tried to calm him down trundled over to join them but hung back. "Detective Inspector Beaumont. I'm the Senior Investigating Officer. Who are you?"

"I'm Eddie Cummings, Chanelle's father."

"I'm very sorry for your loss."

The news physically deflated Eddie Cummings. Where before he was imposing and broad-shouldered, now he was tiny. "Thank you, Detective! I'm glad I can finally talk to somebody with a bit about them," Eddie said. "Please, Detective, I want to see. No, I need to. I need to see where she was found. I want to see where my little princess was found."

"I understand, Mr Cummings," George said.

"Do you have a daughter, Inspector?" George shook his head. "Then no, you don't! How could you possibly understand?"

George said nothing, knowing better than to engage. It was always best to just let the anger burn itself out.

"She was my—" Eddie began, but he choked on the rest of his sentence. Then, taking a deep breath and clenching his fists down by his sides, the dark-skinned man tried to compose himself.

The woman behind him—who George assumed was Eddie's wife—slipped an arm around his chest and squeezed. He seemed to deflate even more as if he couldn't keep the pressure inside him, as if the squeeze from his wife had let go of the neck of the balloon so that it didn't pop. "Eddie. Eddie. Just... Please. Come on, leave this to the police, alright? Come home, please?" she said, smiling, though George could see the effort was visibly taking its toll on her.

"All I wanted was to see—to see where they found her. That's all. I'm not... I don't—"

Eddie looked down, and George watched the muscles in Eddie's jaw tighten and relax, tighten and relax, over and over. Eddie was doing the same with his fists.

When he raised his head again, his eyes were flooded with tears. "I just need to see where..."

George glanced at the enormously relieved PC, who shrugged. If he allowed Eddie Cummings to see, he'd be going against every rule in the book. Plus, Eddie could have vital information that George needed to solve the case, and any good legal team would have any evidence Eddie provided thrown out if they knew. So he said, "In my experience, Mr Cummings, it won't help. In fact, sir, it'll only make things worse."

"That's what I said, Eddie," his wife said. "Let's go. Please?"

"Worse? Worse? How can things possibly get any worse?" Eddie demanded. "You tell me how I can feel any worse than I already do? She's been murdered! It doesn't get any bloody worse!"

But George knew better. It could always get worse. But he said nothing. The man was grieving. It was understandable. But because he was suffering, he was desperate. And a desperate man couldn't think straight. George knew from experience. Still, he said, "Whilst against my better judgement, very well, Mr Cummings."

The man looked shocked.

"But, it's still an active crime scene, so we can't get too close. The PC here will provide protective coveralls, gloves, masks and shoe covers for you both. Once you've put them on, I'll show you the spot where Chanelle's body was discovered this morning."

He gestured towards the trees that lined the barrier between the park and the old golf course. The woods stretched out at the back, deep, dark, and riddled with secrets.

Eddie Cummings didn't move; his feet remained planted on the ground as his gaze went in the direction George had indicated.

George had him. It was why he'd phrased his sentences so deliberately and why he said the words, 'Chanelle's body'. It solidified the idea in Eddie's mind and forced him to confront the finality he almost certainly wasn't ready to accept.

"Mr Cummings?" George asked. "Would you like to see where the body was found?"

Eddie's bottom lip trembled, and more tears fell from his

eyes. He took in deep breaths. Then suddenly, he shook his head, the movement sending more tears cascading down his cheek. His wife stepped in closer, sliding an arm around his waist.

"Probably for the best, Mr Cummings," George told him, putting a hand on the older man's shoulder. "Look, we're going to do everything we can to catch the person responsible for this, Mr Cummings. Whoever did this will be brought to justice."

Eddie nodded but said nothing.

"I realise this is a terrible time for you at the moment, but would you be both OK answering some questions?"

Mr and Mrs Cummings nodded.

"Can I borrow your car?" George asked the PC, who nodded and handed over the keys.

"It's just there," she said.

Once George was seated in front, twisting to turn and face the Cummings family, he began asking the hard questions. There was no point in beating around the bush.

"I'm recording this conversation. Are you both OK with that?"

They both nodded. George reeled off the usual spiel and said, "If you know of anyone with a motive, even at this early stage, please tell me. Did Chanelle have any enemies or anyone who might have held a grudge? Had she fallen out with anybody recently?"

"How did she die?" Mrs Cummings asked.

"The post-mortem is yet to be carried out, Mrs Cummings, but preliminary results suggest a stabbing."

Mrs Cummings moaned, twisting her body and face into her husband's chest.

"Why? Why would somebody stab her?" Tears carved rivers down Eddie's cheeks.

"We don't know that yet, Mr Cummings, but we're doing everything we can to understand what happened and bring the person responsible to justice."

Eddie shook his head, wide-eyed, staring out of the car as though he saw none of it. He tightly wrapped his arm around his wife's shoulder, holding her close. "To answer your question, Detective, no. Chanelle is a good girl. She always has been. She loves her job, has plenty of friends... She loves—" Eddie winced. "Loved living in Middleton. It's far enough away from us in Lofthouse for her to do her own thing but also close enough if she ever needed us. Or if we ever needed her. At our age, it's probably more the latter these days. The house is too quiet without her." He smiled sadly.

Anger and hatred cut through Mr Cummings' heartfelt comments as Mrs Cummings said, "It was that—that dickhead boyfriend of hers!" Her hand trembled as she covered her mouth, and her eyes flickered. "Oh, Christ the Lord, what did he do to our baby?" Her hand fell to clutch Eddie's.

"Boyfriend?" He nodded at the PC to start taking notes but realised she was already scribbling away in her notepad. She had potential.

"Yes," Mrs Cummings spoke again, glaring at George, desperation in her eyes. Desperation blinded you. "Kieron Swithenbank. He's a vile creature, one of those giant men who spends all his time building muscle in the gym. He has an ego and likes to make everyone else feel small. Kieron is a nasty, spiteful, and immature man, and I don't know what she ever saw in him."

"So they were still together?" Eddie nodded. "Does he know

about Chanelle?"

"He knows she's missing because he phoned us last night. She was going to break up with him not that long ago because she'd finally come to her senses."

"What makes you think Mr Swithenbank is involved?" George asked.

Mrs Cummings shrugged. "She says he never did anything to hurt her, but he was controlling, and they argued all the time. She was as stubborn as her father," Mrs Cummings said, straightening as pride took her. "She deserved better."

"What caused the attempted breakup?"

"She didn't say, and we didn't ask," Mr Cummings added. "He kept her away from her friends but made promises to change. Men don't change. You know as well as I do that all we do is lie."

George raised his brow but didn't comment. "When was the attempted breakup?"

"About a month ago, the man took her away from us or attempted to, anyway. So her visits to us slowed down when they got together," Mrs Cummings admitted. "When she was considering splitting with him, she came 'round for Sunday dinner and stuff. It was nice, like we were a family again."

"So you're saying you think he could have held a grudge against her for the attempted breakup?"

She nodded. "Nobody else would have wanted to hurt her." Once more, Mrs Cummings broke down into tears.

"I'm sorry to have to go through all this at such a delicate time, Mr and Mrs Cummings, but do you have his contact details?" George said.

"No."

"Do you know if she had any problems where she worked?"

Eddie shook his head. "As with all jobs, she didn't get on with everyone, but I can't imagine anyone wanting to..." he trailed off and pressed his face into his wife's head as she embraced him.

The red-headed PC took down the details for Chanelle's place of work for further enquiries and quietly interjected before George spoke again, "What about any friends? Or arguments with friends?"

George turned to the PC, who jumped back, embarrassed. "Sorry, sir. I don't—I don't know where that came from."

"No problem, constable," George said with a grin. "I was just going to ask that question myself." He turned to the Cummings'.

"She had two good friends here in Middleton. They went to school together. They were always chatting, going out for drinks and the lark." Eddie let out a mirthless chuckle. "Poppy and Ruby were all she would talk about during our dinners together."

Once more, George nodded to the PC, who took their full names, and Mrs Cummings provided her with contact numbers.

"Finally, does Chanelle have a mobile phone?" George asked.

"She does," Mrs Cummings advised. "Why?"

"It's currently missing. Could you please provide her number so we can get in touch with the provider?"

Mrs Cummings provided the young PC with Chanelle's contact number, and George ended the conversation by asking, "Did you come here by car, Mrs Cummings?" She nodded. "Are you OK getting home?"

"We're fine, Detective," the wife said, shooting George a

brief smile. "Thank you for... for everything you..." Her voice failed her, so she cleared her throat and tried again. "We'll be on our way home. Thanks again."

He nodded and handed her his card. "I'll come and see you later, but call me if you think of anything I need to know ASAP, alright?"

She smiled, and George watched as Eddie allowed himself to be led away slowly and unsteadily. Despite being in his late fifties or early sixties, George knew the clumsy gait was most likely through shock and grief rather than any ailments or old age.

The gravel crunched as the PC walked up to stand at the DI's side.

"Nicely done, sir."

"Those poor people," George muttered.

Chapter Seven

DS Isabella Wood picked up DI Beaumont from the park and drove to Chanelle's workplace whilst DC Blackburn worked his magic tracking down Chanelle's boyfriend, who George had moved to the top of the suspect list.

She explained that a local man, Sean Parker, had found a collie last night in the park around 8 pm. He contacted the vet last night and asked them to scan the chip, and as the receptionist had already mentioned, he was asked to come back this morning. So Sean kept the dog at his place overnight and brought her in at his first opportunity.

The vet had scanned her and confirmed she belonged to Miss Chanelle Cummings.

Isabella had interviewed Sean Parker extensively whilst George had been speaking with Chanelle's parents but received nothing of value from the man. He heard and saw nothing. Wood did, however, call Lindsey Yardley to ask whether her team could take samples from the dog in case she encountered the murderer. The young American, Hayden Wyatt, was there now.

After managing to park in a cramped car park, they entered the pharmacy—a typical layout consisting of a long till, with medicines and medical supplies lining the available space.

Various posters on the walls advertise the disposal of unwanted or out-of-date medicines and advice on treating minor health concerns and healthy living.

"Can I 'elp you, love?" an older woman said brightly, standing tall from behind the front till—a few years older than his mother, George thought, with short, grey hair cut into a bob, wearing a smart white tunic and matching white trousers.

"I'd like to speak to the manager, please. I'm Detective Inspector Beaumont, and this is Detective Sergeant Wood." The detectives showed their warrant cards.

"OK, love," she replied after a pause, looking between them, a curious but apprehensive look in her eyes. "Priya?" she called, retreating to the back, where the pharmacists were dispensing medication.

They followed her once she gestured and filed past her into the private room, where two chairs sat opposite a tiny desk. A middle-aged woman with sharp brown eyes rose from behind it. "How may I help you?"

"I'm Detective Inspector Beaumont, and this is Detective Sergeant Wood." The detectives showed their warrant cards again. "We need to ask you some questions about one of your employees, Chanelle Cummings, Miss..."

"Mrs Priya Singh," the woman stated as George paused. "Anne, please, would you close the door on the way out?"

"What can I do for you, Detectives? I'm afraid Chanelle isn't in today. In fact, we've struggled to get in contact with her. Is something wrong?"

George cleared his throat. "I'm afraid Chanelle's body was found early this morning, and her death is being treated as suspicious. It appears she was killed last night."

Priya stared, her thin mouth wide open.

"I appreciate Chanelle's death will come as a bit of a shock to you and her colleagues here, Mrs Singh. We're investigating to understand what happened to her and bring whoever is responsible to justice."

"I—I just can't believe it," Priya said, shaking her head and staring down at her desk. "She finished work last night and went home. We didn't suspect anything was wrong. What happened?"

"I'm afraid we can't comment on an ongoing investigation. We're here to build a picture of Chanelle's everyday life and relationships at this stage. How long did Chanelle work here for?"

"She's been here for two or three years and was working her way up the chain. I expected her to become the manager here."

"So she got on well with everyone here?"

"Yes, of course," Priya said. "Well, except for Anne, the woman you just met. They weren't unfriendly, but Anne... How do I say this? She disagreed that such a young woman should be above her."

"What do you mean by not 'unfriendly'?"

"Well, they were either thick as thieves or fighting like cats. Anne may not look it, but she is ultra-competitive, you see. Chanelle was the same. In fact, they fell out this week." Priya pursed her lips.

George said nothing, inviting her to continue.

"A GP prescribed medicine for a patient with ingredients in it that the patient was allergic to. Anne hadn't noticed the warning when she dispensed the medicine, and just as Chanelle was going to hand the medicine over, she noticed. We trust the GPs, but even they're not infallible. As you can imagine, Chanelle was extremely cross, and in the end, I had to step in to salvage it." She shook her head.

"Salvage it?" George shrugged. "What happened?"

"A slagging match across the pharmacy, which, let me tell you, is not acceptable in my eyes." Priya's voice rang out sternly, and George did not doubt that she had stopped Chanelle and Anne's conflict. "It was settled. Anne should have double-checked the medicine, and Chanelle should have come to me about it."

Wood and George shared a glance. "So you think Anne took it personally?"

Priya's eyebrows rose. "You think—Oh my goodness, no. Anne was fuming all week because of the embarrassment, and yes, they only just started speaking again, but no, Anne wouldn't do something like that."

"Thank you for your honesty. Is there anything else you can think of, anyone else that might have wanted to bring harm to Chanelle?"

Priya's lips thinned into a line. "Only that arsehole boyfriend of hers. They had a big fight over a month ago, and he spent every night dropping by the pharmacy. I had to threaten to call the police on him to get him to leave. He's a big guy with an angry demeanour. Not much scares me, to be honest, but he does."

"Do you know where we can find him?"

"He works at a gym in Middleton, but there are a few of those. Sorry."

"Would you mind if we spoke to Anne in here for a few minutes?"

"Sure," Priya murmured. Then, after a moment, she stood. "I just can't believe it."

At Priya's request, Anne entered, her expression wary.

"Please, sit." Anne drifted to Priya's chair, the only free one, and perched awkwardly on the edge of it.

George could see she felt uncomfortable. Good. Put her on edge. If she had anything to hide, perhaps the pressure would make her spill.

"Where were you last night between 7 and 10 pm, Anne?"

Anne swallowed. Her mouth opened, about to ask why it mattered, George assumed, before she thought better of questioning the two detectives before her. "At 'ome."

"Where do you live?" Wood asked.

"Morley." A market town just over two miles to the west.

"Do you have anybody who can corroborate that?"

"Mi husband, Phil."

George nodded. "Thank you. Unfortunately, this morning in Middleton Woods, we discovered the body of your colleague Chanelle Cummings."

Anne's mouth fell wide open, and her hand flew to cover it. "W—What?" Once she composed herself, she added, "What 'appened?"

"We can't comment on an ongoing investigation, but as you knew Chanelle, we need to ask you some questions." She nodded. "Did you get on well with Chanelle?"

"Yeah," Anne said, glancing between the detectives, bewilderment they had seen a thousand times before at the impossibility of the news they'd delivered on her face.

"Always?"

Anne hesitated. "Well, not always." She shrugged. "Mostly."

"Did you ever argue?"

She winced. "Yeah. Last week. Most colleagues argue. I'm sure you two do, yeah? Anyway, I'm guessing Priya told you, love."

George ignored her question and asked one of his own. "What happened?" It was one of the best interview tactics he'd been taught—never give but always take what they offered. And then, when needed, stay silent to get them to reveal more than they intended to.

A momentary flash of anger flickered across Anne's face, which she quickly suppressed. She told them the same story as Priya.

"And how did that make you feel?"

"How did what make me feel?"

"Your boss took your colleague's side, right?" George let the phrase linger.

"I wa' fuming at first!" Anne spat out and then stopped. "But Chanelle was right, and I should have checked for allergies. I might 'av been mad, but that doesn't mean—that doesn't mean I would ever hurt 'er! It's only work, and Priya sorted it. I didn't kill 'er." Anne's voice had fallen to a whisper as if she would be guilty just by saying the words.

"Did you do anything together outside of work?"

Anne shook her head, then shrugged. "The occasional drink now and then. Birthday meals together wi' other colleagues, like. Work stuff, really."

"Do you know of anyone who would have wanted to hurt her?"

Anne shook her head. "No. She was a nice girl."

"Thank you, Anne, you've been very helpful, and we are sorry to bring such terrible news." He stood, and then so did DS Wood.

Anne nodded, her eyes sliding to her hands in her lap.

"Just one more thing," said Wood, turning back to her. "You

said you two sometimes went out after work. Do you know of her boyfriend and happen to have his contact details?"

"No, why would I have his details?" Disgust curled Anne's lip. "I already told you we were just work colleagues. However, I do know all about him. And I do know where he works. Across the road at the gym in the leisure centre. You'll probably find that arsehole pumping himself full of steroids or admiring himself in the mirror. Probably both."

"Thanks." With a glance at Wood, they left, thanking Priya on the way out for her time. George gave both his card and asked that they call if they thought of anything else that might help them. They left as Priya began taking each staff member into her office to share the unexpected news.

"Who next, then? Best friends or boyfriend?" Wood asked. She'd received a text from DC Blackburn, who had found the boyfriend's home details.

George chewed his lip. "Did Tashan get a hold of the friends?"

"Just one of them for now. Poppy Lavell. She works for a solicitor just up the road."

"Let's try her first, then. We don't want to spook the boyfriend until we know more. I reckon her friend will be best placed to grass on anyone with a motive."

"You're hoping it'll be the boyfriend, aren't you?" Wood asked.

"Aye," replied George, a grim look on his face as they stepped across the car park. They had zero evidence and had no idea who might have killed Chanelle. Their only suspect was a conveniently placed giant of a boyfriend with a temper. The friend would hopefully confirm what Chanelle's parents and colleagues had already advised, allowing George and his team to draw the net closer around Kieron Swithenbank before he realised the police were onto him. "Should be open and shut this case. It means we get the answers quickly for the family and swift justice for Chanelle."

Chapter Eight

DI Beaumont and DS Wood pulled into a car park on Middleton Park Circus. Across the road stood a solicitor firm where Poppy Lavell worked.

A slight brunette woman in reception ushered them quickly into a private area, where a young blonde woman in a white blouse and navy pencil skirt greeted them. "Hi, I'm Poppy. Poppy Lavell." She stuck out a hand, shaking George's first and then Wood's as they both introduced themselves. "Please, follow me." Her accent was local, George thought. He and Wood followed as she led them into a small room and closed the door.

"Mrs Cummings called me." She'd been crying; her eyes were puffy and bloodshot. "How can I help?"

"You were one of her closest friends, is that right?" George asked.

Poppy nodded. "That's right." She closed her eyes and grasped her hands tightly together. "I just don't understand. What happened? Why would anyone do anything like this to Elle?"

"That's why we're here. It looks as though Chanelle was killed on her evening dog walk. A dog walker found her this morning," George replied. "Can you think of anyone who might have wanted to hurt Chanelle? Anyone who'd she'd argued with or held a grudge against her, or threatened her, that kind of thing?"

"No. Elle was the life and soul of the party. I guess she could be a bit abrasive if you didn't understand her, but she normally didn't have that problem." Poppy wiped away a rogue tear. "She had a minor spat with a woman named Anne at work last week, but they sorted it out."

He didn't think Anne was involved, so he said, "Aha," inviting her to continue.

"There was not one person she didn't get on with."

"What about Kieron?"

She frowned and furrowed her brows. "They were in a relationship. They must have got on."

George smiled. "Go on?"

"What is there to say? Their relationship wasn't any of my business."

"But you didn't approve?"

"What makes you say that?" She grinned, flinching momentarily before a look of disgust settled back in.

George said nothing, adopting his favourite technique.

"Fine, I didn't approve," Poppy said. "Unfortunately, Chanelle and Kieron met through my ex-boyfriend. Kieron and Kai work together at the gym. Kai got her a trial membership, and she met Kieron there. During the trial, he was her personal trainer."

"And?" Wood said.

"And they hit it off, somehow. Kieron charmed the literal pants off her, which was impressive because Chanelle was always fussy about men. She'd never gone for a bulky guy before but was always complimentary about Kai, so perhaps she wanted to see what all the fuss was about, if you catch my drift. Things were great for a while, but he soon showed his true colours. Kai warned me that Kieron was a complete dickhead."

"What happened?" Wood asked.

"Well, as I said, he's a dickhead. He showed his true colours, similar to Kai, and Chanelle didn't like what she saw. In the end, though, she caved and stayed with him. She liked the extra attention. Kieron showered her with bunches of flowers and took her out for drinks and dinners. It seemed to make her ignore the fact that he had a short temper."

"A short temper?"

"Yes. When Kieron got mad, he got loud and would smash stuff up. I don't think he ever laid a finger on her, though, not that I know of, anyway."

"So tell us about the threatened break up? Did he take kindly to that?"

Poppy cocked an eyebrow and said, "What do you think? Before he charmed her again, he was so angry with her. He showed up at her work, and they called the police."

"Her boss, Priya, mentioned it. He sounds immature to me." DS Wood rolled her eyes, and Poppy smiled.

"He was an absolute psycho, his mentality like a yo-yo. Up and down, then up and down. He'd get angry with her, then text her a love letter. It was like the guy was chemically imbalanced. But Chanelle told me he was better recently. Calmer. She shouldn't have told me, but the doctor prescribed him meds. With her being a pharmacist, they'd discussed his options."

"Do you think he'd hurt her?" George added.

Poppy fell silent and started chewing her lip. She knew what the detective was asking, what he left unsaid. Did she think that Kieron could have killed Chanelle? "I'm unsure." She met George's eyes, and every word was carefully weighed when she said, "To my knowledge, he has never hurt her before. But he was always angry. So volatile. And I hate to think about what he would be capable of if he lost his temper and couldn't find it again."

"That's extremely helpful." In damning the boyfriend, at least, George thought. "Do you know where we can find him?"

"Sure. I don't know Kieron's home address, but I know he works at the leisure centre gym."

"Thanks. Is there anything else you can think of, Miss Lavell?" George asked.

"I don't think so. Sorry." Her green eyes were grave as they regarded the detectives. "Did—Did Elle suffer?" She clamped her lips together, and George could see more tears glistening in her eyes.

"I can't answer that yet, I'm afraid," he said quietly, getting up from his chair. Wood followed suit. "The post-mortem will happen later today."

Poppy nodded and sniffed, and then her eyes bulged. "Actually, there was one other thing." Poppy looked troubled as George turned to look at her. "It's probably—probably nothing."

"Even the smallest thing can help," Wood said, smiling.

Poppy hesitated. "Look, I'm sure it's nothing. Just... Chanelle thought somebody was... I don't want to use the word she used, but I'm going to... She thought somebody was stalking her. But it's the only other thing I can think of."

"Stalking her?" George said.

"It sounds silly, doesn't it? That's why I say it's nothing. I shouldn't have mentioned it."

"Go on."

"She heard noises coming from her garden, and her dog, Rosa, used to go mental as if somebody was outside."

"Did she ever see anyone?" Poppy shook her head. George handed her a card. "Right, we'll look into it. It could be nothing, but it could be everything. If you think of anything else, please ring."

Poppy took it and stared at the card for a second. Then, quietly, she said, "Please find out who did this to my friend."

Wood answered before George could speak. It was like an unspoken sisterhood, woman to woman sworn to protect each other. "Don't worry, Poppy; we will."

* * *

George and Wood drove in silence down Middleton Ring Road before turning right into the leisure centre car park, which housed the gym where Kieron Swithenbank worked. George reversed into a gap and thought about the last time he was here. Probably when he was a kid learning to swim; they had a pool back then, but not now, despite the petitions still going around.

"Let's see what this prick has to say for himself," Wood said. George looked at her, a smile on his lips and an eyebrow cocked at her words. She was on a mission, and he would not get in her way. He let her lead as they approached the entrance to the leisure centre, the sign for the gym emblazoned above the reception.

George opened the door to a large room where a collection of huge weights was stacked against one wall in front of the wall-to-ceiling mirrors that sweat-slicked men and women were grunting into as they pumped iron.

Beaumont was in shape, but nothing compared to these people, and he instinctively sucked in his small gut. Maybe I'd better start doing press-ups on a night, he thought. His youth was fading, after all, and whilst the job took too much out of him during the day to go to the gym, perhaps Isabella would appreciate a harder, firmer body.

"Can I 'elp ya, love?" a buff man said, wiping the sweat from his chest with a towel. He was talking to Wood, a grin on his face, his height towering over her, his bulk swallowing up her slender frame.

DS Wood flashed her warrant card and introduced them both, and the man's attention flicked to George. His eyes narrowed, and his muscles tensed.

"Is Kieron Swithenbank here?" George asked. "We need a word."

The noise of the gym suddenly dissipated, and the patron's eyes were suddenly drawn to one man.

Kieron Swithenbank.

Then, a blur crossed George's eyes through the gym and towards the exit.

George moved quickly, darting past a giant of a man to give chase. He caught a brief glimpse of tanned skin, bulging muscles, and short, spiked platinum blond hair before the door slammed shut behind him.

George crashed through the same door a few seconds later, the door bouncing against the wall from the force, the sound echoing like a gunshot down the long hallway George had traversed many times as a child. George turned right, gave chase, and reached the exit just as it crashed shut.

"Police! Stop, and get on the ground!" a voice roared, and George saw that somehow, DS Wood was already outside and flanking Swithenbank, cutting the man off.

Kieron halted, his neck twisting, and his head swung towards the beautiful brunette. DI Beaumont closed in behind him in the car park.

"Kieron Swithenbank?" George bellowed.

"Yeah? Who wants to know?" the man spat, looking around for a way to escape.

George eyed him warily. And George was no fool. Kieron towered over him and would crush him like a fly if George tried to take him down. But George wasn't about to let the love of his life in harm's way, either. George couldn't arrest him—not without any evidence, and all he had was speculation. Plus, George didn't fancy trying to detain the enormous guy and cause a scene. Still, he said, "I do. I'm Detective Inspector Beaumont, and this is DS Wood." He pulled out his warrant card. "We need to talk. Why don't we go back inside and have a civil chat, or we can keep doing what we're doing now, and you end up in cuffs? Yeah?"

George could see Kieron's mind whirring as he looked between Wood and George, who were getting steadily closer and flanking him on either side. "Yeah," Kieron said.

"Yeah?"

"Yeah, let's go inside."

Kieron led them through the still-open fire door that Wood had burst out of. The door rattled against its frame with help from the wind. Wood pulled it shut behind them, cutting off the outside noise with a clack that echoed down the quiet hallway.

"This way," Kieron murmured, opening the door of a small,

dark room. The two detectives walked in, and George almost recoiled from the smell of stale sweat, the popular scent of Lynx Africa and Dettol. Then Swithenbank flicked the light on to reveal a small desk pushed up against one wall. There were no chairs. He shut the door behind them and folded his arms. "What d'ya want, Detectives? I didn't do nuffing."

The fluorescent tubes overhead flickered, and a tanned-skinned, chiselled giant with short, spiked platinum blond hair and a nose ring stood before them. He could see the appeal, but he hoped Isabella Wood would not.

"Then why did you run?" George asked, meeting Kieron's eyes and folding his arms, too. Besides George, Wood stood with her feet planted, exuding quiet confidence even in the face of the giant before them. He could quite probably tear them both apart if he wanted to. It was George's job to stop that from happening.

The massive man just stood and did not offer George an answer.

Two can play that game. George took in a deep breath and said nothing, maintaining eye contact.

"Why are you here?" Kieron spat.

"Why did you run?" George said.

Another pause. Another stalemate.

"I'm guessing you thought we were here about steroids?" DS Wood said.

Kieron's venomous gaze bore through Wood as he gritted his overly white teeth and planted his enormous feet. She had clearly struck a nerve.

"Don't worry, Kieron. It's not why we're here. What you choose to do with steroids, even if it's stupid to take them, is up to you, as long as you're not dealing the stuff. You're not a dealer, are you, Kieron?" George left the question hanging.

As before, Kieron gave him nothing.

George waited a full minute before he let out a chuckle. The guy was more intelligent than he looked—for now, at least. "OK, Kieron. Where were you last night between 7 and 10 pm?"

"Why?"

"Answer the question, Kieron."

"Home."

"Do you have anyone who can verify you were home?"

Silence. Kieron gritted his teeth. "No. Why?"

"That's not good. Is it DS Wood?"

"No, it is not," she said.

According to DC Blackburn, Kieron lived on Newhall Road, near Manorfield Hall at the bottom of the park. It was easy to enter the park from there, and close enough to the golf courses. And without an alibi, the man was fucked.

"Do you ever go into Middleton Park, Mr Swithenbank?"

"Eh?" That caught him out. "Middleton Park?" George nodded. "Yeah, sometimes. Why?"

"Do you walk around the old golf course near the children's playground?"

Kieron stared at him blankly, then shook his head just a fraction. The man looked confused, and that wasn't a good sign.

"So you wouldn't have been there last night then? Between 7 and 10 pm."

Silence again. Kieron's jaw clenched.

"Mr Swithenbank?"

"Last night between 7 and 10 pm?" George could hear the frustration in Kieron's tone.

It sounded as if the giant of a man was hiding something.

"No. I told you I was home, and I was. Look, I dunno what you're on about. What the fuck do you want from me, eh?"

"Easy," George warned him. "This is about Chanelle Cummings."

"What? What about her? Stupid bitch is ghosting me, man. Did she report me or something? I didn't do nothing!"

"That speaks of a guilty conscience to me, DI Beaumont."

"I agree, DS Wood. When did you last see her or contact her?"

Kieron shook his head, scowling. "A week ago. We've not been too good recently." His voice caught in his throat. Perhaps he had genuinely cared for her. Maybe he still did. If so, what the detectives told him next would crush him.

"Did you ever want to hurt Chanelle Cummings?" George asked.

Kieron's attention snapped back to George, and he took a step closer. "What the fuck? Nah! Never. Not me. Did that silly cow say that?" George said nothing. "Look, I know I get angry, but I wouldn't lay a fuckin' finger on her."

George stepped forward and stood firm. "I'm sorry to have to tell you this, but Chanelle Cummings was found dead in Middleton Park this morning," George said, watching Kieron for his reaction.

The bigger man seemed to deflate in size, no longer the overbearing giant. "What'd you just say?" he murmured, his eyes blinking rapidly. "Tell me again what 'appened to Chanelle?"

George nodded. It was always better to say nothing during these situations.

Kieron stared right through George for a long moment. "I don't—I don't understand. She can't be," he said before pausing. "That's why you're 'ere. You think I did it?" he asked slowly, his focus returning to George. The man's hackles were up.

Shit.

But still, George again said nothing.

"I din't. I wunt never hurt her. I love her, man! We were sorting shit out," Kieron insisted, his hands shaking, his eyes closing as his face contorted in grief. "Nah…"

"You have no alibi, a known temper, and, according to your record, a history of violence. Plus, you fled from us," George said, his voice firm.

Kieron wiped away a stray tear with a sausage finger. "I get that. But Chanelle…" his voice was surprisingly soft, a slight snarl with no bite. "I'd never harm a hair on her beautiful head. What 'appened?"

He looked at the detectives, pain evident in his eyes, the anguish seeping into the creases in his face. He wanted answers, answers that George could—but wouldn't—give him. Kieron was their only suspect, so he reeled off the usual line. "I can't comment on an ongoing investigation, but, Mr Swithenbank, we may need to speak to you again." George laced each word with a threat.

But Kieron didn't rise to it one bit. It was as though he had been rendered mute from the news as if it had knocked all the fight from him. He stared at the wall behind them, unaware the detectives were still there. "I said some nasty shit to her the other day, you know? Real nasty shit." Tears fell from his eyes.

George had lost count of the number of grieving partners, parents, or children whose final words with their loved ones had been said in anger. He'd held mothers who wished, more than anything in the world, that they could take back the last thing they'd said to their child before never seeing them alive again. He'd watched husbands and wives break down, stricken by the lack of love and affection they'd shown their other halves in those final days, only to become haunted by some of the things they'd said or done.

"Come on, Wood," George murmured, and the pair left Kieron alone. As they left, a guttural roar of grief and pain, plus the sound of fists against a wooden door, reverberated from the room behind them.

"What do you think, Isabella?" George asked. His fingers drummed on the Mercedes' steering wheel as he appreciatively inhaled fresh air through his open window, a far more pleasant aroma than the stench of the gym.

"You want the truth?" she asked.

"Always."

"It looked real to me. I think he's too emotional to be able to act that well."

"I agree, and we have nothing to connect him," George added.

"Nope. Nothing. Just that temper of his, which by itself doesn't make him a killer."

George sighed. "Fuck."

"Fuck, indeed. Now what?"

George glanced at the clock on the dashboard, shook his head, and blinked his eyes. "How is it past five already? Shit." Wood placed a hand on his shoulder. "I think we have more digging to do before we can discount him, Isabella."

"Agreed. Let's check Kieron's phone records and search his home address."

"Good thinking. Currently, he's the only suspect in the

picture." George sighed.

"I'll get on a warrant to search his property right away, George."

"Good." He smiled. "We've stayed late enough for now and done the rounds for today. Let's get back to the station, write all this up, and see if Lindsey has managed to find anything else for us yet. Then, we can check in on DC Blackburn to see if any of his work has paid off. Hopefully, someone back at the station has done better than us, anyway."

Chapter Nine

"Look, I don't have to tell you how big this is, George. I never usually do. But look at this." DSU Jim Smith handed him his phone, which showed a message from the popular social media reporter, YappApp. "The media has caught on already, but we've put in a gag order. A local woman was killed in a public park." He shook his head. "It's terrible news, and to tell you the truth, it reminds me of the Miss Murderer case. And like then, if we don't get to the press first, there will be a frenzy."

"I agree. When are you giving the parasites a statement?" George asked.

A sly grin appeared on his face. "That's not my job now, Beaumont," he confirmed. This is not your first case. You're the SIO. Juliette Thompson has organised a conference in half an hour. Go and see her."

"Cheers, sir," George said and got up, pulling out his phone to call Juliette.

* * *

"Good afternoon, everybody. My name is Detective Inspector Beaumont, and I'm the Senior Investigating Officer on this case. The body of a local woman was discovered in Middleton

Woods shortly after eight this morning. I can confirm that she is Chanelle Cummings, aged twenty-six, from Middleton. It is believed she was walking her dog in the park when she was attacked and subsequently murdered."

"Was she the victim of a sexual assault?" A male reporter shouted from the front row.

Why was that always the first question when a woman was murdered, George thought.

"No, she was attacked by a bladed weapon."

The energy changed from one that was calm and solemn to a ripple that became frenetic, and every member of the press began firing questions at George all at once.

"Do you know the identity of the killer?"

"Do you have any leads?"

"Are there any suspects in custody?"

"Is this an isolated incident, or should we be warning female dog walkers?"

George didn't feel like a deer in headlights any more and maintained his composure, lifting his hand and drawing silence from the press. He kept his voice firm, showing confidence and competence. "Reassurance patrols are out in the area, and uniformed officers are conducting house-to-house enquiries."

George waited for silence.

"Anyone with information is asked to contact me, or DS Wood, at the Leeds District Homicide and Major Enquiry team quoting reference 17819726377 or online via live chat. We are currently pursuing all lines of enquiry. That's it for now. Thank you."

* * *

DI Beaumont stood, massaging his neck and shoulders and wincing at the pain. What the hell was I thinking, chasing after a man ten years younger than me? He grabbed a coffee from the canteen and returned to his desk to open the post-mortem report, which was waiting in the shared inbox from Dr Ross, who had finished the report only minutes before. George was grateful that the man had worked hard to help the HMET where he could.

He scanned the report. Chanelle Cummings had died from exsanguination, blood loss caused by the severing of a major blood vessel. Ross had also noted the lack of defensive wounds, suggesting that, as Lindsey Yardley did, Chanelle had been taken by surprise.

Because of the angle of the single wound, Ross had managed to establish that the killer had been taller than Chanelle. Chanelle was quite tall, which ruled out the dog walker who found her and the dog walker who found Rosa. However, it did not rule out Kieron Swithenbank, who was six foot six. He would have towered over Chanelle and was strong enough to restrain her easily.

George leaned back in his chair. He was waiting for the search warrant to be approved for Kieron's property.

Ross also noted that the victim and attacker were likely in extremely close proximity and that because of the attack from behind and the single strike, the culprit must have been extremely strong. In George's eyes, that was another tick against Swithenbank; the huge, muscled man exuded brute strength.

The weapon was something that used a carbide blade, probably a Stanley knife, Ross reckoned, because of the wound measuring only 60 mm. Microscopic shards from the sharp blade were left embedded in Chanelle's throat.

Besides brown hair with no follicle, CSI also found a partial blood fingerprint on Chanelle's arm and black fibres on Chanelle Cummings' body. Next, they'd check for a match against Swithenbank's clothes.

Hayden Wyatt had also taken samples from Chanelle's dog but also found nothing.

George scanned the information reported and collated from the press conference, but there was little to go on. However, George hoped the information would start to come in soon, as all they had currently was a dog walker who complained of a young man kicking his dog while jogging.

When asked if the young man was covered in blood and wielded a knife, the elderly man blushed and said, "No."

DS Wood knocked on the door and entered. "George, I've got Yolanda on CCTV. She's looking for Chanelle as we speak. There are plenty of cameras on Town Street. There are no blind spots now." George nodded. Phone records should be back in the morning."

"Excellent. Can you get Jay to liaise with Yolanda? Perhaps they'll find something more we can sink our teeth into."

"I'll chase the search warrant for Kieron's place, George."

"Brilliant. I've arranged with Chanelle's parents to meet them at her house tomorrow to hand over their spare key. CSI will be heading over, too, to see if they can find her phone or anything else, especially after the 'stalker' story Poppy Lavell mentioned. The records will be helpful tomorrow, but it'd be better if we could find the handset."

"Agreed. You really think Swithenbank's involved?"

George was unconvinced but didn't have any other lines of enquiry. "He's worth a look, Isabella. The profile of this attack fits him perfectly, so that warrant is vital because we need access to his home to search for any evidence."

"That's if he's not already destroyed any evidence," Wood said.

Like him, she had seen the man's show of grief, which seemed so raw and honest. But she also knew that didn't mean Kieron hadn't done it deliberately or in a momentary lapse of control.

They just needed to prove it.

* * *

I'd spent the entire Thursday reliving the high, smoking weed and ignoring calls from work. The buzz from the weed and the kill made it hard to concentrate on scrolling through YorkshireFlirt.com as my alias, a catfish made up of my favourite Harry Potter character and the actor who played him.

Matthew Longbottom.

I'd merged a picture of me with the actor and was pleased with the result. I'd also made up a description which suggested Matthew Longbottom was just shy of thirty and worked for Yorkshire Water in Bradford.

With his chiselled chin and dimples, no woman alive could resist him.

I already needed to scratch the itch that my act of murder had caused, but I wouldn't be hasty in choosing my next victim because I wasn't stupid.

The problem was that every time I scrolled past someone who looked like Poppy—a woman with long, wavy blonde hair, pale skin, and green eyes—it stopped me dead in my tracks and reminded me of the humiliation she had caused me with her rejection. Then I thought about Chanelle Cummings, and a mix of euphoria at my kill and anger towards her rejection surged within me.

I needed another release. And quickly.

There were three candidates on the app—but only one seemed keen to meet me so quickly.

From her pictures, Harper Verril was a twenty-four petite blonde with fat in all the right areas. For a small woman, she had a nice, round arse and big tits, and whilst she wasn't my usual type, she'd do. From behind, she would look enough like Poppy to fulfil a need. All I wanted was a quick shag, and then we could go our separate ways.

Well, that's if I could control myself.

* * *

Harper must have lost weight since posting the photos because she looked more like Poppy than I'd wanted. Petite like Poppy. Thin like Poppy. She even wore the same perfume as Poppy. Despite that, Harper's pale body was beautiful, especially with only a nearby streetlight outside illuminating my bedroom. I'd already had my cock inside her mouth, fast and rough, and she'd swallowed like a good girl, but it hadn't been enough.

Now she was on all fours and at my mercy.

She moaned as I inserted my full length, sliding inside her slowly, thrusting deeper, crushing her under my weight. I raked my fingers up and down her back as I continued an even rhythm with my hips, pulling at her blonde curls with my left hand and gripping the back of her neck with my right.

She was fingering my scars. The ones I'd cut into my skin. Roman numerals.

When I clenched my fingers around the back of my neck, I felt power like I never had before.

And I liked it.

I let go of her blonde curls and traced a line around the sides of her throat before grasping and squeezing tighter as I thrust, my abs screaming from the exertion. Finally, a moan escaped her, and her arms buckled under our combined weight as she came.

I had a decision to make then. Did I let Harper go to survive another night, or did I strangle her?

"You're crushing me, Matty," she said, grabbing the headboard, her neck muscles taut. "Move back; I can't move."

Then I decided. I made up my mind. Killing Harper inside my home would only cause a mess I wouldn't quite know how to clean up. I'd watched enough true crime to know getting rid of a dead body was an absolute nightmare. And so, because of that reason and because I'd enjoyed her company, Harper Verril deserved to survive.

Until next time, anyway.

It had been a satisfying second round and much better than masturbating. Gone was the arousal, for now, but an itch remained. It burned a hole through me, made my heart thump rigorously in my chest, threatening to burst out of my chest like something I'd seen in a film, and I wasn't sure it would ever be satiated.

My heart hammered so loudly that I could barely hear Harper's breathless laughter next to me, her husky voice babbling on about God-knows-what as I struggled to control my breathing.

I wanted to throttle the Poppy-imposter. Adrenaline surged through me.

I was still so angry that Poppy had rejected and humiliated me. And as Poppy's imposter, Harper needed to pay. And soon, before Harper rejected me as Poppy had.

"Are you alright, Matty?" Harper said, breaking through my trance. I was sat on the edge of my bed, elbows propped up on my knees. I pulled the condom off and tied it up, inspecting for leaks as my dad had taught me.

"Matty?"

"What?" I glanced at her, though not really seeing her.

"You look as if you're miles away, gorgeous." She nibbled my ear and giggled again. I realised the laugh irritated me, so different to Poppy's, whose laugh was calm and soothing. Harper's giggle seemed to screw right into my nerves. I glared at her again, hoping she would see the fury in my eyes and shut the fuck up, but she'd already turned away to pull her skirt on. "I really enjoyed tonight. You wanna do it again sometime?"

I stood but didn't answer and chucked the condom into the bin before pulling on my boxers, aware of Poppy's—no, Harper's—eyes boring into me.

"I could stay over, you know. It's getting late, after all," Harper said. I turned to find her smiling suggestively. "I'm sure I'm not the only one who'd like that kind of wake-up."

As I said "No," a little too harshly, I saw the hurt and anger flash across her face.

"I start work early tomorrow," I muttered. It was a lie, and I wasn't sure why I was sparing Harper's feelings because I couldn't give a shit how she felt. But, if I wanted to fuck her again, I'd better not piss her off. I put my hand on her shoulder and said, "Sorry."

Harper's face softened as she blew a stray blonde curl from her face. "No worries. Can you walk me to the bus stop?"

I shook my head and held the bedroom door open. She squeezed past, brushing her ample chest purposely close against my own, a sultry grin on her face. There was nothing wrong with Harper, nothing wrong at all, and if Poppy Lavell hadn't come back into my life six weeks ago, I'd have thought Harper was girlfriend material.

But Harper wasn't Poppy Lavell. And she never would be.

I opened my front door and grinned at her.

"Well, see ya, Matty."

She pulled my face towards hers, and then her tongue was in my mouth.

After she had gone and I had closed the door behind her, I stood in my dark hallway, my head bowed, my eyes shut, as I took deep breaths in and exhaled slowly. No matter what I did, that anger was still there. It was as if a beast had awoken within, feral and bloodthirsty.

Killing Chanelle hadn't been enough.

Chapter Ten

That morning, the overnight rain battered the sad little pile of flowers that mourners had left inside the line of trees. I stretched and drank my water as I surveyed the scene.

Crime scene tape fluttered in the wind, though no one staffed it. Aside from that and the flowers, there were no other signs of what had happened. It was as though all traces had gone in just a day.

There was no way the police could have found anything related to me in the area, and if they did, like hairs and stuff, then I'd explain how I jogged that route regularly. It's why I was there now. I nodded at people so they'd recognise my face. I wore bright red running gear so they'd remember me.

It was all part of the plan.

I also wasn't on the system. Until killing Chanelle, I'd never done anything wrong. Not really. Not unless you counted all the animals I'd killed.

I stood out in the rain, letting it drench me as it had done Chanelle. I knew it was fortuitous that the heavy rain had started just after I slit her throat. The rain was my saviour. It had washed away my sins.

I wondered for a moment whether the heavens cried for Chanelle and then looked at the flowers again. They made me fucking angry. She was a bitch, a stuck-up cow who didn't deserve to be remembered. To be loved.

I wondered whether they knew what Chanelle was honestly like. If they did, they wouldn't have sent flowers. Instead, they would have stood there like I did, glad she was no longer alive.

I can't believe I nearly fell in love with her.

It was strange to think I had been here with her just a day and a half before and what had transpired in this quiet, beautiful place. I breathed in the damp, earthy scent and wished I could bump into Chanelle Cummings once again so I could cut her down more in a more satisfactory way.

More people arrived as I continued to stretch and take in water. Truth be told, it was morbid curiosity that had drawn me back, though now I wasn't sure whether it was a good idea. It was probably better to leave now, so I turned and ran up the grass hill before turning right, up a steeper incline to reach the park gates. It was better not to linger in case private CCTV cameras saw me. As I crossed the road and jogged past the Catholic primary school, I passed a dog walker and a pair of female joggers—all of whom I smiled at so as not to arouse suspicion.

When I got home, I was drenched, but it was OK because I needed a shower before work.

I desperately hoped that Poppy Lavell would come into the shop today.

* * *

DS Wood stood in front of the Incident Board, ready to give a presentation on the information she had pinned to it regarding Chanelle Cummings' death. The presentation was mainly for the DI's benefit, though a recap wouldn't harm the others, either.

The map took up a third of the board, and another third was currently empty. The space between these was mostly filled with photographs of Chanelle Cummings. There were four in total, but only one of them showed her alive. A few reports and lines of enquiry had been stuck around the photographs by magnets to the board's shiny white surface.

There were two other photographs to the left of Chanelle's pictures; both joined her by lines of red marker pen. Poppy Lavell, and Kieron Swithenbank.

"Do we know much more about these two?" George asked.

"Nothing much about Poppy. No priors, no nothing. She's clean," DS Luke Mason said.

"And Swithenbank?"

Luke scratched his chin. "Same as what we told you yesterday, really, though we did find out he has a history of domestic call outs."

"With Chanelle?"

"No, boss. Kieron's ex."

"Interesting."

"Aye, it is, boss," Luke said. "She's made a couple of complaints against him over the years since then. Swithenbank is from Bradford. He has a history of harassment, mostly. No charges ever pressed."

"So, nothing concrete to tie him to the murder?" George asked.

There was an uncomfortable silence, so George nodded for DS Wood to start her presentation.

"Chanelle Cummings. Aged twenty-six at the time of death," Wood stated. "She was last seen Thursday evening by her colleagues when she left the pharmacy where she worked to go home. DS Williams and DC Scott have trawled through CCTV footage from Town Street in Middleton, which shows Chanelle taking her dog for a walk around seven-twenty, and that's the last trace of her until her body was discovered in the early hours of yesterday morning."

"Was that the same on previous days?" asked George.

"The same routine Monday to Friday, sir," DC Jay Scott said. "Home. Then a dog walk." He shrugged. "It was like clockwork."

"Any CCTV from the park?" asked DC Tashan Blackburn. The others were standing through Wood's presentation, but he'd taken a seat and was taking notes on a tablet.

DS Wood shook her head. "None that we can use. The Visitor Centre near the pond has CCTV, but it's nowhere near where Chanelle's body was found."

"Seems a bit stupid," Jay remarked. "You'd think the playground would have CCTV around it, especially as it's always getting vandalised."

"It's all about budget cuts," DS Joshua Fry told him. The council can't afford to put up and maintain cameras in the park."

"No, I get that; it's just—"

Jay felt George's stare burning into him before he saw it. Jay smiled sheepishly, then motioned to Wood. "Sorry, Sarge."

"Thank you for allowing me to continue, DC Scott," she replied, with her usual degree of sarcasm that always impressed George. "Yolanda stayed late last night and looked at CCTV from each entrance to the park two hours before and after the time of death Lindsey Yardley gave us. We're still checking for private cameras."

"And?" George asked.

"She has a long list of people who were in the park during those hours," Wood said. "With my help, we've cut that list down. We excluded people who entered and left before 7 pm."

"How many people are on that list, DS Wood?"

"Fifty-six." She winced.

"That's a lot," said Tashan, tapping away. Shall I post images of people on social media and ask them to come forward with any information?"

"It's a good idea, Tashan, but resource-intensive. I doubt the Super will allow it," George said. The booming Geordie had been relatively quiet, but that wouldn't last long, especially as George had no leads. He turned to Wood. When you looked through the footage, did you see anybody who looked like Kieron Swithenbank?"

"No. Swithenbank wouldn't be easily missed, not with his size. If it was Kieron who killed Chanelle, then he must have entered the park using an entrance without CCTV."

"Which is still a reasonable assumption, DS Wood." George looked at the board. "We can't discount the fifty-six people because they may have seen something. They might live locally if they entered on foot via the entrances. I have uniform on the streets today, partly as reassurance patrols and partly for house-to-house enquiries. Who's in charge of that?"

"Sergeant Greenwood, sir," Tashan explained.

"Right, DC Blackburn. Good," George said. "Get in touch with him and send him the list. Two birds with one stone. Or three, if you want." He grinned, but nobody laughed at his joke. They were reeling from the murder, and so they should be. "Anything else, DS Wood?"

"No, George," Wood reported. "Nothing new."

There was a moment of silence as they all contemplated the lack of any leads. It was broken only by the sound of Tashan's fingers tapping on his tablet.

"What about her phone records?" George asked.

"I've got them, sir," Josh said. "I'm waiting for more, but this covers the last couple of weeks."

"Anything decent come up?" George asked.

"Possibly, boss. Four numbers stood out. I've been able to identify two of them," Jay said, consulting the notes he'd been making on his tablet. "Kieron Swithenbank's the one you'll be most interested in," the DC continued. "I counted seven-hundred-and-fifty-three texts, plus thirty-two phone calls."

"Over what period?"

"Just under a fortnight, boss."

George whistled. "Right. Sounds like a bit of a stalker to me."

Jay nodded. "The last message he sent was on Friday morning," Jay said. "He texted her and tried to call a couple of times but got no response."

"Aye, well, we know why now, don't we?" George said. He didn't say the words, but his team knew what he meant. George took a step closer to Jay to get a better look at the phone records. "Was that message from Kieron to her the last one she received?"

"No, boss. That would be another of the numbers that might be of interest. Poppy Lavell," Jay said. "I looked her up. She's pretty fit." Jay caught the look of disapproval from the room of senior officers and then quickly moved on. "They're best friends from the look of it."

"Aye, we've met with Poppy," George said, "which, if you'd

been paying attention yesterday, you'd already know."

Jay's cheeks turned red.

"Why's Poppy of interest, then?" George asked. "Other than her being 'pretty fit'?"

George smiled as Jay grimaced. It used to be Jay taking the piss out of George, but recently, the balance of power had swapped. "Poppy messaged Chanelle about a lad she'd taken the piss out of. Apparently, Chanelle had gone a bit far, and Poppy didn't like it. So they argued all day about it."

"Any idea who the lad is," George asked.

Jay consulted his tablet again. "No, boss. We haven't got the content of those messages."

"I think it's odd that Poppy didn't mention the argument when we spoke to her yesterday. Do you think she's hiding something?" Wood asked.

He shrugged. "How much message content do we have?" George asked.

"Just the day of her murder and the day before, boss," DS Fry said. He smiled at DC Scott as he said it.

"The phone company's being an arsehole about it," Jay said. "We're having to go through the—" He made air quotes. "—proper channels. DSU Smith has provided a warrant for Chanelle's entire records. If only we had the phone—"

"No surprise there, then. The operators can be pedantic bastards when they want to be. Anyway, thanks, lads," George remarked. "What about the trace on Chanelle's phone? Do we know where it was last switched off?"

"Waiting on the warrant," Josh interjected.

"OK, well, I'd like you both to keep doing what you're doing," George said. He passed the paperwork to DS Wood to stick up on the board and then sat back down. "You're doing a good job on this," he said.

Jay winked. "That a compliment, boss? Thanks."

"Was it?" George turned to DS Luke Mason. "Did I just compliment DC Scott?"

"Not that I heard, boss."

"There you go, Jay. You must have been hearing things. Right," he said, standing up and clamping his hands together. "DS Wood, I want you with me. We're going to Chanelle's house. Josh, you're Office Manager, which means you're also in charge of Exhibits."

Josh blinked in surprise. "After all the time I spent off sick, sir, I'd like to be in the field."

"I get that, Josh, I do," said George. "But you're only just back. I've been there before, you know, and from experience, it'll take some time to get back in the swing of things."

Josh shook his head and said, "With respect, sir, that's bullsh—"

"I can run the office and Exhibits," DS Luke Mason explained. "Think of it being like the hair of the dog. Yeah?"

George smiled and rubbed a hand across his bearded chin. "Are you sure about this, Luke?" he asked, dropping his voice to a low whisper. It was unusual for Luke to challenge him, but George respected Mason's decision as his senior. Moreover, Luke had been George's sarge when he was a Detective Constable.

"Sitting on my arse with a nice cup of tea, DI Beaumont? What's there to be unsure of?" Luke asked with a laugh. "Add a biscuit, and it's right up my street, is that."

George raised his brow.

Luke nodded and smiled before looking at DS Wood. "It'll be good for him. Right, Sarge?"

Wood nodded, and then George sighed before he turned to Josh. "Fine. Josh, you're out and about. Liaise with Sergeant Greenwood."

Josh exhaled slowly through his nose. "Thank you, sir. I appreciate it. And I'm sorry for the bad language."

"Jay, keep putting pressure on the phone company."

"OK, boss," Jay said, rubbing his hands together, playing up his excitement.

"Do we all know what we're doing?" George asked his team.

They all nodded and began filing out of the Incident Room.

Chapter Eleven

George pulled up behind the CSI van outside Chanelle's home, a decent development of modern detached and semi-detached houses that a cousin of his lived in before his untimely passing.

A grey Audi was also parked outside, and Chanelle's parents, Mr and Mrs Cummings, got out. He slipped out of his car and raised a hand to greet them.

"Morning, Mr and Mrs Cummings. Thank you for coming," George said, making no attempt to comfort the red-eyed, waxen couple. They looked as if they'd aged a decade overnight from their grief. I'm afraid you won't be able to come inside until our SOCOs have gone over everything, just in case there's anything relevant to our investigation. When we're finished, I'll return the key to you, and you're free to make whatever arrangements as necessary."

Eddie nodded, and his wife Camilla sniffed loudly beside him. They looked at the house for a long moment in silence before Eddie took a deep breath. "Here you go, Inspector." He handed over a key with a keyring attached—a picture of Chanelle hugging Rosa.

"Thank you."

"We'd best go, then," said Eddie, though he dithered. George understood why as soon as Eddie spoke his following words. "I'm going to identify her now. Formally," Eddie said, his voice hollow and lifeless. George didn't blame him and sympathised with the man. He wouldn't enjoy the prospect of attending the hospital to confirm the death of his only child, either.

"I'm so very sorry for your loss," DS Wood said.

Mr and Mrs Cummings drifted back to the car and drove off, not seeing George as he raised his hand in farewell.

While he waited for Lindsey and her team to finish their work, he and Isabella organised a weekend date. During his last case, when he apprehended the 'Cross Flatts Snatcher,' the two detectives had barely any time together outside the job, which was not ideal.

Luke Mason texted him that they'd got the warrant for Swithenbank's home address, so he was clear to search.

George desperately wanted to drive there now but knew it was better to wait for Lindsey and her CSIs to finish. His stomach flipped at the thought of searching Kieron's once he'd scoped out Chanelle's. Kieron wouldn't be happy with George searching his place, and he didn't like the prospect of the giant man becoming aggressive. He only hoped he wouldn't need backup.

Lindsey slammed the CSI van door shut, and George jumped. He got out and went to speak to her. "Good afternoon, DI Beaumont."

"Is it the afternoon already? Christ..."

"Yep. You want me to walk you through the house?"

He didn't reply but started rummaging around the boot for a coverall, gloves and shoe covers. George had asked Wood to stay in the car and get updates from the team. There didn't need to be two detectives in an empty house.

George stepped inside; the fresh spiced apple scent of a diffuser plugged in at the bottom of the stairs lingered, reminding him of his mother. For a moment, George looked around, picking out the little details of the still, silent house. Brown carpets lined the stairs and upstairs landing. Light-coloured laminate covered the living room floor, with a chocolate-coloured leather sofa and chair nestled in the corners. A sleek brown bookcase that matched the colour of the furniture stood against the feature wall, housing a variety of romance titles Mia liked. In the final corner was a TV on a unit. Between the TV and the armchair were glass patio doors.

They swept the property in silence together, Lindsey saying nothing. She beckoned for him to head upstairs, where they entered Chanelle's bedroom. A tunic and trousers, similar to the ones Anne from the pharmacy wore, were laid out on the floor in front of an overflowing wash basket.

As they searched more rooms, George couldn't see a phone anywhere, but he saw a charging cable next to the bed, plugged into an extension that snaked behind it. The bed was made, ready for her, though she'd never returned to it. It lay still and undisturbed, with no sign that anyone else had been there. The second bedroom only had a single bed frame and a mattress.

There was nothing in the bathroom besides a folded towel on the sink. George assumed she usually showered after walking her dog. Unfortunately, she'd never gotten home to use the towel.

In the kitchen at the front of the property, Chanelle's tea awaited, a piece of salmon marinating in a bowl and veggies in a colander in the sink. The kettle was heavy with un-boiled water, and rice sat in a pan on the stove. An empty water bottle with Chanelle's name on it stood nearby. George thought it was probably organised precisely how Chanelle liked it, ready for her to return from her walk and start cooking.

There was no obvious sign of a disturbance anywhere. It was like a show home that was cold and lacked personality.

Lindsey's paper suit rustled as she headed toward him. "I'll drop the key off at the station when I'm done. You don't need to be here."

George turned and raised an eyebrow at her. "Nothing suspicious?"

"There are some footprints in the garden and a couple of hairs in the bedroom. There are no follicles, but we might get lucky. To tell you the truth, I don't think the killer was here or with her when she left the house. And from HOLMES, it seems your CCTV validates my opinion. There's nothing else I can see, but I will go over things with a fine-tooth comb before I leave. We haven't checked the bins yet.

"Aye," George said. "It's always better to double-check, then there's no doubt later."

"Exactly, DI Beaumont."

"Alright, thanks, Lindsey. I'll speak to the neighbours before I return to the station to see if anyone heard or saw anything. Chanelle's friend mentioned something about somebody being in the back garden. So maybe somebody saw something."

Lindsey adjusted her surgical mask. "I'll send you a report on the footprints. We'll take casts. Hopefully, your somebody in the back garden wears unique shoes."

"We can only hope."

"Oh, George, we know that the site where the victim's body was found was the kill site, purely from the blood analysis there. Unfortunately, we didn't find much because of the rain, but there's no trail."

"So she wasn't transported there and dumped already dead." Shit. That had been one of their theories. George pursed his lips. "Anything else?"

"Only to say we capture a partial fingerprint from the attacker. It was left in Chanelle's own blood on her arm. We know he slit her throat from behind and then turned her to face him. It's possible he accidentally caught a blood drip with a finger—"

He already knew about the print, so he said, "Which helps us."

Lindsey smiled smugly. "Exactly. He wasn't as careful as he thought. I have someone working on inputting that; then we can begin comparing it to any suspects."

"Might have one for you. The boyfriend. His prints are already on the system."

"Brilliant," Lindsey said. "Send them over, and we'll take a look as a priority."

"Great. Anything else?"

"No. You're very welcome."

"Thank you, Lindsey." Then George nodded at her and left to speak to the neighbours to see if anyone had heard anything.

* * *

The neighbours in the quiet street revealed little. Clearly, it wasn't like where he grew up, where everybody knew everyone's business. Half didn't even know who Chanelle was by name or even which house she lived in. However, the neighbour directly to Chanelle's left complained vociferously to George about Chanelle and her boyfriend, about the shouting and the summer weekend parties on the patio.

George thanked the older man for his time, not wanting to hear much more of the rant and the man's lack of empathy regarding the dead. It did him absolutely no good to complain about Chanelle now. But it wasn't the first time he'd heard such callous comments, and nor would it be the last. Human beings never ceased to amaze George with their ignorance and cruelty.

Chapter Twelve

George and DS Wood raced down the hill to Kieron Swithenbank's home in Belle Isle. He wasn't sure the goliath would be home, considering it was mid-afternoon and didn't relish the prospect of having to batter down the door. So he rang Kieron from the car as he left Chanelle's, knowing it would only take a few minutes to get to the flat on Newhall Road.

"Who is this?" Kieron asked.

"Kieron, it's Detective Inspector Beaumont. We met yesterday. Are you home right now?"

"What? Nah. I'm at work."

"Can you get home, please, Kieron? I have a search warrant for your address, and I think we need to talk."

"You fuckin' what?" George heard deep breaths reverberating around the car. "You're not fucking going inside my house!"

"Yes, I will, Kieron, because I have a warrant. I can either enter with you or without you. I'm calling to give you the courtesy of letting you know so you can come and open up; that way, I won't have to batter the door down."

"I share the flat with my mate, so you can't—"

"I can and I will, Kieron," George interrupted. "So, I'd get home quickly if I were you."

"But I have clients. I can't just fuckin'—"

Expecting a string of expletives fired down the line, George cut off the call and took deep breaths of his own.

Shit.

He'd wanted to do this calmly. He turned to Wood, who smiled. "Do you need me to come in with you?" she said with mock sweetness.

George said nothing and shook his head. She would if he asked her to, but he didn't want to put her in any danger. He'd also decided not to call for backup, reasoning that by the time anyone from the office arrived, he'd be most likely to have been beaten to a pulp anyway.

Shit.

George pulled up at the kerb beyond a bus stop, outside a large block of maisonettes. He'd seen these maisonettes a thousand times before but had never been inside. Kieron had told George it was a flatshare, and George wondered who else lived there. He'd soon find out, as the warrant gave him the right to search with or without Swithenbank.

He knocked on the door, and a man as big as Swithenbank answered. He looked a similar age to Kieron but white-skinned and streaked with fake tan, wearing shorts and a vest and messy blond hair not dissimilar to George's own mop.

George showed his warrant card. "I have a search warrant for this address concerning Kieron Swithenbank." The man tensed. "I'd like to come in." George put on shoe covers and pulled on a pair of gloves, the material snapping satisfyingly against his skin.

"I'll need to search any communal living areas and his private room."

The man's eyes narrowed. "Not my room then?" the man

questioned.

"Not unless you've got something in there you shouldn't have, mate," George replied, cocking a brow.

"Nope," he said, holding up his hands. "Nothing to hide, officer."

"Detective. Detective Inspector, actually."

The blond man stood aside and let George in. He detected the faintest smell of weed inside, and George sniffed loudly in mock jest and cocked another eye. But he wasn't here for that; he was here to try and solve a murder. So, personal possession of a bit of weed was the last thing on his mind.

"Which areas does Mr Swithenbank have access to?" He glanced into the living room stroke dining room next to the entrance hall and noticed a small kitchen at the back.

The blond man hung back in the shadowed hallway beside the stairs. "His bedroom upstairs and a shared bathroom. And all the rooms down here."

George nodded. "How many people live here?"

"It's a three-bedroom, but um, just Kieron and me at the moment. It's a flatshare."

"Who owns the maisonette?"

"Our landlord."

"Anybody else stop at this property in relation to Mr Swithenbank?"

"Nope."

Talking to the man was like watching paint dry. Fuck me...

"Right, I'll take a look down here first, then head upstairs to Mr Swithenbank's room and other shared areas."

The house was messy, as if students lived in it, with used cups and plates scattered about every available surface. Joggers and hoodies littered the sofas. They must have enjoyed gaming, as they had the most recent PlayStation and Xbox behind their TV. A cabinet was filled with DVDs and games.

The old roller blinds were pulled down, which caused it to be dark inside the living room. Nothing jumped out at George as he finished sweeping the ground floor.

The kitchen was surprisingly tidy, though George thought that was because of the tiny size and not to their credit. Large tubs of protein dominated the countertop. George noted there was no toolbox under the sink, but that didn't mean Kieron didn't have a Stanley somewhere.

"Who do these belong to?" George jabbed a thumb at the tubs.

"Both of us. We work together in the gym. I've just realised you don't know my name. It's Kai."

Kai? Poppy's Lavell's ex? Probably. George said nothing but carefully opened each tub, checking the contents. The protein powder inside lingered in the air, releasing chocolate, strawberry, and vanilla scents that were a pleasant break from the tang of weed permeating the air.

The bin was empty. Lindsey and her team would check the communal bins outside.

"Take me to see Kieron's bedroom, please?"

"It's locked, Detective. We each have a lock on our doors, you see. Only he has the key for his."

"Fair enough." George would either have to wait for Kieron to return, which he suspected would be soon, or batter the door down. He preferred the former, and probably so did the big man. "The spare bedroom and the bathroom, then, whilst we wait for Kieron to return home."

The man nodded and led George up the stairs. George looked around the small bathroom, finding nothing, not that he had expected to find anything, of course. Kieron didn't appear stupid enough to leave things out in plain sight, but George wondered what Kieron had hidden behind his locked bedroom door.

The two lads appeared to be fitness addicts, as the third bedroom was a weights room. Free weights, resistance bands, kettlebells, and smaller gym equipment littered the room.

The front door crashed open downstairs with such force that George winced. "Kai?" Kieron bellowed.

The blond-haired man also winced. "Up here, K. Police are 'ere, man."

Kieron thundered up the stairs like a bull, nostrils flaring.

George stood his ground. "I'm glad you're here, Mr Swithenbank. I need to look in your room, that's all."

Kieron looked between his mate and George. George didn't think he could take on Kieron, let alone Kai and Kieron, together. He was regretting coming in alone when Swithenbank did something completely unexpected.

"Whatever clears mi name, Detective." He opened the door with a key, his hands shaking. A keyring was attached—a picture of Chanelle kissing Kieron on the cheek. "I've nothin' to hide."

"Thanks for being so accommodating, Mr Swithenbank."

George entered the bedroom, and because the curtains were drawn, he flicked on the light. They were blackout curtains that had cut out all the light apart from a thin crack that crept in through the middle. The tiny bedroom was unexpectedly tidy and only just managed to contain the double bed that was neatly made. He wondered whether Kai was the culprit for the downstairs mess. George checked underneath the bed and found only boxes containing expensive trainers and some brica-brac he assumed were from Kieron's childhood. A third box was filled with a collection of trophies.

"Be careful with them. I used to play rugby for Parkside. So those're precious to me." Behind him, Kieron stomped the tiny upstairs hallway like a jailed beast, the floor creaking under his weight with every stomp.

George nodded and smiled. He'd played rugby himself for the Middleton Marauders and had similar trophies to Kieron. However, considering the age gap, they would never have played each other. In fact, most of George's mates who played rugby in the Super League were beginning to retire. The hooker for the Castleford Tigers and the stand-off for one of the Hull teams.

George found clothes hung up in the wardrobe and dress shoes on the bottom. A chest of drawers next to it held underwear, socks, and gym gear.

George approached the bed but decided to leave it for Lindsey. However, he did check the corners of the mattress for any bulges.

"What you looking for, anyway?" Kieron said, bursting into the room angrily.

"Evidence," George said, a grim look on his face. "And finding a lack of it."

"You really think I—" Kieron let out a scream of anguish. "You really think I killed her?"

George looked up and met eyes with a monstrous beast.

"As I told you yesterday, I can't comment on an ongoing investigation. However, I wouldn't be doing my job if I didn't explore all possibilities." George stood and met the man's eyes. "Chanelle deserves my best."

"You're right, Detective, she does. But you're wasting time.

I didn't do it. I couldn't. Hurt her. That is. I never could!" The words burst out, and it was like Kieron couldn't stop. "I loved her more than anything. I just—I just went a bit far sometimes. With my temper, I mean. Hitting holes into walls. That kind of stuff. Never her. Never. We were working on it. I was working on it. My anger. And our relationship. I promise." His last words came out as an indignant whisper.

George saw actual raw pain in his eyes and knew then that Kieron was telling the truth. Yet that temper was nasty, and George knew it would take very little for Swithenbank to lose control and do something he would regret. George wrestled with his instincts. His mind was telling him the loud, angry boyfriend was the killer, and once Lindsey managed to match the bloody fingerprint to Kieron, they could take him in. But his heart was telling him otherwise.

He only had one more place to look, the bedside drawer, and as soon as George went to open it, the shadow of Kieron Swithenbank engulfed him.

George tensed, sure a blow was coming, but Kieron reached across him and opened the top drawer. "Steroids," the man muttered, pointing at the pills that rattled in a clear tub. "For personal use."

George raised an eyebrow at Kieron, then nodded. "Fine. I won't lecture you again, even if I think you're being stupid." Kieron was certainly big enough and ugly enough to take care of himself. If he wanted to put stupid things into his body like that, it was his choice. It wasn't illegal to own them for personal possession, at least, and there weren't enough in there for George to charge Kieron with intent to supply.

Inside the bottom drawer was a half-used pack of condoms and a tube of water-based lube. George cocked his brow again, a grin on his face when a small black box caught his attention right at the back of the drawer.

George drew it out and pulled the box open to find a diamond engagement ring nestled inside.

Tears flowed freely down Kieron Swithenbank's face as he saw George handling the box.

Fucking hell...

"You were going to propose to Chanelle," George whispered. It wasn't a question.

Kieron nodded.

George's heart sank. Despite being suspect number one—his only suspect, really—George couldn't help but pity the man and his predicament. George thought about the love of his life and wondered how he'd feel before putting it to the back of his mind. He didn't want to tempt fate.

Those thoughts helped, in George's mind, diminish Kieron Swithenbank's guilt. What had been a sure bet before was wavering because a deliberate attack seemed unlikely. And that's precisely how Chanelle died. From a planned, deliberate attack. Swithenbank was capable of a momentary lack of control, but the murder hadn't happened that way. George looked at the ring in the box in his palm, and he wasn't sure any more. He was even more unsure as he slipped the box shut and placed it back where he'd found it in the drawer.

George stood up and gazed around the room again, checking he hadn't missed anything.

He hadn't.

There was nothing to find

Nothing at all.

Well, nothing but an engagement ring that Chanelle Cummings would never wear and her boyfriend's crushed and broken heart.

Chapter Thirteen

"Where were you yesterday?" Afzal hissed from the checkout while serving a customer when I came through from the staffroom. The young, chavvy woman he'd sold cigarettes and scratch cards to scoffed and left without a 'thank you'. "You fucking dickhead. I had to cover your shift and ended up missing my mate's birthday meal!"

I shrugged. "I was ill, mate, soz."

"Yeah, right, dickhead," muttered Afzal as a haggard older woman pointed at a bottle of vodka, or paint stripper, as I liked to call it. "Hungover more like."

The day passed excruciatingly slowly between my breaks, though I had snuck my phone onto the shop floor to try and contact Harper Verril again. I wasn't sure whether I wanted to fuck her or kill her. Either was good, though I knew I wanted one more than the other.

I'd hoped for a hook-up and a body all in one, but that would mean meeting her at her place, and that was risky.

The only break in the grind that was work was the quiver of fear and horrified excitement that passed through the village at the murder of one of their own. It sent shivers down my spine with each passing person that mentioned it. I'd caused this, and I'd never been so proud.

I'd have to kill something bright and pretty again, something young to keep the village talking.

I gleaned what information I could from each passing customer who brought the murder up. The police were investigating. I knew they would be, but I didn't realise they'd already spoken to someone about the murder. It was a pleasant surprise. Rumour was it was the boyfriend, which means they weren't even looking at me—not that they would have known where to look.

Perfect.

So, I decided to pass on that helpful rumour about the boyfriend to each customer I spoke to.

From what I'd heard about Kieron Swithenbank, the dickhead had it coming. Despite how Chanelle treated me, I felt protective of her for some strange reason. The stupid sted head had treated her like shit. And so I decided he had it coming, even though he didn't do it.

* * *

I was shocked when the beautiful Poppy Lavell entered Sainsbury's Local that evening, ten minutes before my shift ended.

She smiled at me when she entered, though it was a sad smile that didn't quite meet her eyes. The sadness was all my fault. I'd killed one of her best friends. Remembering how I slit Chanelle's throat made my heart hammer. I fucking loved the feeling her smile gave me. It made me hard—harder than I thought possible. I wanted to go through the back and pump furiously until I came, but I couldn't. Something was telling me to stay still. And watch.

Poppy came to my till and handed me her basket. Our fingers

touched, and there was a spark.

Of course, there was.

It was fate. I always knew. We were destined to be together.

"Hey, how are you?" I asked.

She nodded, and that same smile adorned her face. "I'm OK. And you?"

Did I mention the murder or not? I didn't want her to see me as insensitive, but... I couldn't help myself. "I'm so sorry for your loss."

She looked up from the floor, shocked. "Oh, you knew Chanelle, didn't you?"

I nodded.

"I'm sorry for how she treated you last time we were here. I..." She took a deep breath. "I told her off, you know, that night. She had no right to do that to you. You know? But now..." A glorious tear fell from her eye. "Now I feel guilty. Because I told her off."

"Thank you. And I'm so sorry." I smiled.

"That's..." Another tear fell. "Thank you. I'm sorry, I don't remember your name."

"Understandable, after what you've been through. Billy." I offered my hand, and she took it. It was warm and moist. I wondered what her hands would feel like roaming my body, pulling at my cock, and squeezing its tip as I came. I wonder what her tongue would taste like or what her lips would feel like as she sucked my dick. The thoughts sent shivers through my body.

I wanted her.

No, I needed her.

Poppy Lavell was the reason why I killed Chanelle Cummings. She was the reason I existed.

"Poppy, isn't it?"

"Yes."

She tapped her card against the hub, and as she was about to leave, it looked as if my luck was changing. "I understand the hell you've been through. I lost someone very close to me. My mother." I could see the compassion in her eyes. She was so beautiful. "Do you fancy a drink? Maybe some food? We could chat about..." I smiled. "About Chanelle. If you'd like?"

Poppy began to nibble at crimson nails.

"Or we can just drink and eat. Might take your mind off everything?"

"You're asking me out?" She questioned.

"Yes, I am. Tonight. We can go wherever you want?"

"Give me your number, and I'll think about it."

* * *

My mum died when I was five, and I miss her. I would never admit it to anybody, but I do. I miss her beating heart; I miss burying my face in her freshly shampooed blonde hair, inhaling the scent of her perfume. I also miss the softness of her lips on mine. I've heard of the Oedipus complex, alright, so fuck off and stop lecturing me.

One morning, I was outside my house when a girl caught my eye. My chest clenched so tightly that I could barely breathe. I recognised those cascading blonde curls anywhere.

I was convinced my mum was back.

But it was Poppy.

Her resemblance to my mum had initially taken my breath away, but as I studied her, I saw differences. Poppy was far more beautiful than my mum, with green eyes and perfectly pink lips.

I remember seeing her the day she left me. We went to high school together, and I cried that night. The image of her heart-shaped face and thick lashes, mixed with breasts that swelled beneath her blouse, had regularly made my mouth fill with saliva and heat surge through my body.

That was the image I had of Poppy until she entered my life nearly two months ago.

In those early days, I binged on Poppy, taking in her adult form that reminded me so much of my mum. I kept my eyes on her Facebook and Instagram and followed her wherever I could. She was sweeter than my mum had ever been and funnier, too. I learned what she was listening to, reading, and watching. Then, I devoured every morsel of herself that she shared.

Lucky for me, that was pretty much everything. It was too much, especially for a paralegal. But that was her problem, not mine.

My favourite image was her standing on a beach, her porcelain skin contrasting against a navy bikini. Poppy was partially turned to the side, her body angled to show off her tattoo on her hip, her eyes looking straight through the screen and boring into mine. Both arms were stretched high into the sky, crossed above her head, framing her flowing blonde locks.

That image was forever burnt into my wank bank, replacing that of my mother's.

* * *

Poppy texted me an hour later and declined my date. She didn't want to see anybody. I was fucking fuming. No matter how often I messaged her back, she didn't respond. When I tried calling, it wouldn't connect, and I quickly realised she'd blocked me.

My mood spiralled from there.

Chapter Fourteen

He reached behind her porcelain skin and attempted to unhook the bra, but he froze when loud banging from the front door interrupted them.

The sound was so sudden and so violent that Poppy gasped, her heart pounding in her chest. Their eyes meet in stunned silence. Another pound forced Kai to look out of the window. "Expecting a visitor?" he asked, shaking his head, seemingly frustrated by the interruption. There was nobody there.

"No," Poppy said, quickly putting her blouse back on and rushing down the stairs. She took a moment to check through the peephole, but the front porch was empty.

Kids playing knock-a-door-run?

Poppy stepped back from the door, her brow furrowed. She felt as if the night was closing in on her and jumped as she felt Kai's breath on her neck. "Dickhead kids. Let's go back upstairs and continue where we left off."

I should have known better, Poppy thought. Kai was only ever after sex. The prick!

She was in no mood to continue. The aggressiveness of the knocking had thrown her. Whoever knocked had been angry. Chanelle's murder had affected her in ways she never thought possible. Instead of trying to seduce her, Poppy thought Kai should have offered to open the door for her and check outside for the culprit.

Especially after what happened to Chanelle.

Instead, Kai ran his fingers through Poppy's blonde curls and snaked a hand down her front, glancing at a nipple through her blouse.

She brushed his hand away, feeling irritated by her ex's presence. If he weren't brave enough to look outside, I'd have to go out instead.

So Poppy unlocked the door and threw it open. But she saw only the same sight she had seen through the peephole.

She stepped onto the porch, and cold air buffeted her blonde curls, sending shivers racing across her skin. Goosebumps rose as she stepped forward, the slabs freezing under her bare toes. Poppy checked to the left first and, after seeing nothing, went and checked to the right where the bins were.

No one was there, but she thought that somebody could have been, of course. With it being so dark, someone was watching her without her knowing. She considered putting on some shoes and a coat and conducting a proper search, but as much as she loved horror films, she didn't want to star in one.

Kai joined her on the porch and said, "Bye, my love. I'll come round tomorrow so we can sort stuff out, yeah?"

Poppy shook her head. "Tonight was going to be a one-off, Kai. I don't want to sort stuff. You messed up."

"I know. But—"

"Go on. Leave. Now!"

As Kai stormed off, Poppy could feel someone watching her. Who it was, she wasn't sure, but she could feel it. Poppy was as sure of it as she was about the existence of gravity. She couldn't see it but knew anyway. A chill ran down her spine, accompanied by a burst of adrenaline. Poppy hated the feeling, the same feeling she got whenever she watched a scary movie. It always began with the heavy beat of her heart, and then a heavy weight settled deep, crushing her stomach, sinking into her core.

Poppy Lavell shifted from one foot to the other, looking left and then right before turning back to her house. She was not entirely comfortable with the feeling deep within her gut.

When she returned to her door, she saw a small, cellophane-wrapped box waiting on her doorstep.

* * *

Poppy's hands shook as she picked up the package. As she ripped off the cellophane, she realised it was a bottle of her favourite perfume and a scribbled note.

Her breath caught in her chest with panic as she scrutinised the box and re-read the note. She closed her eyes, wishing the note and box would disappear when she opened them again. But no, they were very real.

Poppy, I'm so sorry we got off on the wrong foot. Please let me make it up to you. My offer still stands for a chat over drinks and dinner. Perhaps we could even go dancing? I really like you, and I don't want to screw this up. Please give me a chance. Billy x

She opened her door once more and looked around the dark street. The streetlights illuminated the area, and it was deserted. The aggressive knock on the door was ingrained in her mind. It must have been Billy. He must be hiding now, or he must have legged it. Either way, Poppy went back inside, locked the door, and bolted it. She considered calling Kai back, but all he wanted was her body, and that was the last thing she wanted right now.

Now, further paranoid that she was being watched she threw the box to the floor, hearing it shatter and inhaling the sweet almond and jasmine notes she once loved. Poppy felt sick and nearly threw up in the kitchen sink. That sadistic pervert was getting to her. She ran around the house, turned on all her lights, and closed all the curtains.

A whimper escaped her. How the hell did he know where I lived? Poppy had always thought he was weird. She'd noticed him staring at her from the first moment she stepped into the shop those two months ago. It was very creepy how he made a point to call her by name and how he tried to engage her in conversation every time she shopped, even when other customers were waiting. It had felt so awkward, her receiving all the attention. She hated it. It made her cringe. Even more so now. It was disturbing.

And to think, I felt as if we'd been too hard on the man. I'd even apologised for Chanelle's behaviour, she thought. It was difficult because it wasn't his fault she had a specific type, a type that clearly wasn't Billy from Sainsbury's Local. But for him to go that far was ridiculous, absurd.

It was clear she'd dodged a bullet. Poppy was glad she'd cancelled on him. She stomped to the front door again to ensure it was locked, and then she checked all the other windows and doors. They were all secure, yet her racing nerves would not steady.

Poppy retrieved her phone from the kitchen table and, with shaking hands, unblocked Billy and typed a WhatsApp message.

STAY THE FUCK AWAY FROM ME, BILLY. I've given you the

wrong impression, so to be clear, I don't want anything to do with you. If you contact me again, I'll report you to the police. So delete my number, and FUCK OFF!

She hit send and then re-blocked the number. Poppy then grabbed the box from the floor and the note from the table and threw them in the bin.

* * *

At that moment, I realised how wrong I'd been about Poppy Lavell. I'd been desperately trying to prove I was worthy of her, and as such, I'd put so much time, care, and effort into getting to know her and understanding her.

On Friday night, six weeks ago, a week after she first entered Sainsbury's, Poppy Lavell was in the bar with her friends, being her usual social self. No worse place existed to meet a woman than in a bar. The floors were always sticky with spilt drinks, and the music drowned out any chance of meaningful conversation. That, and the air of desperation hangs heavy. Everybody in that bar was out to get laid, me included.

She was so pretty, so glamorous. I'd followed her and her friends from the wine bar in Morley she frequented. Without fail, bars and drinks were part of her weekend life now, or at least it has been whilst I've been following her.

Her Instagram feed was the same, chronicling one party after another. The wine bar and its decadent cocktails frequented her feed with images of a rotation of creative craft cocktails, tall glasses of luminous liquid, and rocks glasses with enormous round ice cubes. The photos were so innovative and brilliant that she could have been an influencer. Poppy was certainly beautiful enough.

I hated it when people posted food and drink on their socials, but when Poppy did it, I didn't mind.

In fact, I rather enjoyed it.

I enjoyed it because Poppy was the brightest light in the room, the sun around which everybody orbited.

I watched her standing at the bar that night, her slender, manicured fingers sliding up and down the stem of her empty wineglass. The up-and-down motion was turning me on, and I knew I shouldn't stare; I knew it would be all over if she caught me, but I was powerless to pull my eyes away from her. I just wished the stem was my cock; that was all.

The beautiful blonde had tried something new that night, her skin glistening in the light as though she were covered in a million tiny diamonds. Poppy Lavell was stunning, and it took all my strength not to wrap my arms around her dainty waist and push her lithe body against the bar as passion overtook us both.

I ached for her.

I swallowed hard and then turned away from her to take my pew in the corner, where I watched her for the rest of the night.

I'd have her soon, I promised myself. Soon.

Yet, it had been painfully evident in Poppy's actions tonight; it had nothing to do with whether or not I deserved her. No. Poppy Lavell had never deserved me—and I needed to fucking punish her for it.

Those thoughts and feelings festered, and I couldn't sleep that night. I couldn't cope with the embarrassment, shame, anger, rejection, humiliation, and hurt any more. All those feelings gnawed at me until there was nothing left.

I'd do the same to Poppy. I'd keep going until there was nothing left of her.

And she'd never turn me down again. No. I would make sure of it.

So, that very same evening, when she had rejected me and taken in her ex-boyfriend, I swiped through Yorkshire-Flirt.com until I came upon Poppy. I tapped the thumbs-up icon on her again, but it wasn't my profile; it was my alias, Matthew Longbottom, the one I'd used to seduce Harper Verril.

I wanted to see how she'd act, and I wasn't disappointed.

I grabbed a burner phone from my drawer. I'd purchased a fair number of burners and prepaid SIMs from Tesco in Batley.

The ping came barely half an hour later.

As expected, Poppy and I had hit it off. We chatted in the app until late, and I lost track of time before she agreed to meet with me on Sunday night. Poppy had even suggested the wine bar in Morley, precisely as I had asked her the first time. It was fate.

But I couldn't sleep. Anger still seethed deep within. I hated that she would say yes to a catfish but not to me. I was myself whilst we talked over the app; the only difference was the profile picture and the description. That fact alone infuriated me, especially as I had spent weeks following her, watching and waiting, so that I could understand her as a person, who she was, and what she liked and disliked.

Yet all Matthew had to do was say, "Hey."

Chapter Fifteen

Poppy Lavell suddenly felt a sensation, and for a moment, she wasn't sure what it was. It was odd and different; something about the change in the air around her—a suffocating atmosphere.

She stood on the corner, staring at the Merrion Centre, watching shoppers cross the road at the lights. The cold air swirled around the back of her head, her neck, and between her shoulder blades. An intensity so freezing that it cut through the warmth of her exertion, tingling her skin. Every nerve was on fire, and Poppy became acutely aware of her blonde curls and heavy coat, the tug of the Loungefly bag, her dress, tights, the rain patter, and everything else touching her.

There was something else, too—something that was not touching her but was there just the same. The cold air felt as if a presence was breathing down the back of her neck. Poppy closed her eyes against the fear that flooded through her. Then, she took a deep breath, opened her eyes, and dared to turn around.

There, on the corner of Albion Street, perhaps twenty metres away, stood a man dressed in all black with his hood up. He stood very still, watching, even as Poppy turned around and stared at him.

After a short moment, he turned around and walked down St Anne's Street, disappearing from her view.

Poppy stared at the empty corner where the man had been standing, watching, waiting. She wanted to see if the man would return if she turned, so she took a step towards the Merrion Centre and looked around, scanning corners, streets, doorways, and windows.

The man had gone. She turned just to make sure. How silly. The man had just been a shopper or was possibly waiting for someone. It was cold and wet, so why wouldn't he have his hood up? What an idiot, she thought. But then, she was positive that someone had been watching her. In fact, Poppy could still feel the lingering feeling of the intense stare aimed directly at the back of her head.

And the man was the only person she was sure had been watching her.

She was conflicted.

Poppy then hurried towards the centre's shelter, shaking her head and smiling at her fanciful imagination.

* * *

Poppy Lavell turned her attention to her muffin. As she sipped her coffee, she absently watched people coming and going on the street outside. Office workers and shoppers were heading home, walking up and down Merrion Way, waiting for taxis or heading into the Merrion Centre to pick up tea on the way back.

Unfortunately, Ruby had cancelled on her. Somebody had covered her car in dogshit. How minging.

Poppy finished the muffin and pushed her plate aside as she

watched a woman walking the most adorable chihuahua.

As Poppy watched the chihuahua trot away with its owner into the distance, she spotted a man standing outside the bank's glass doors, looking directly at her, and she felt the strange chill she'd felt earlier.

Icy fingers clawed at her neck, absorbing all the heat from her body.

Was it the same man from earlier? Surely not.

But he was definitely looking her way. She could feel his gaze lingering on her.

Poppy squinted, desperately trying to make the man out in more detail. Could it be Kai?

No. The man was shorter than Kai and not as stocky. But still tall. Thinner, though. Like the man from earlier. That thought disturbed her, and she shuddered.

Poppy looked back at the figure, hoping he'd turn away, embarrassed. But, unfortunately, it wasn't unusual for men to stare. The last ten years had taught her that men couldn't help themselves. Hopefully, he was just one of those who appreciated her looks, and she could forget about the whole incident and write it off as nothing.

Yet the lingering stare unsettled her. He sort of looked familiar in his dark joggers and dark hoodie. The man's eyes stayed on her, unapologetic, staring intensely into her. Did she know him from somewhere? Perhaps an old school friend who recognised her but didn't want to commit to a wave. Just last week, Poppy waved at a woman at Middleton Circus who didn't wave back. On closer inspection, the woman was a complete stranger to Poppy but looked like Cara, who was from high school.

So Poppy smiled and gave a little wave, trying to show the

man she wasn't bothered by his staring, showing him she wasn't scared. Hopefully, it was the attention he wanted and would soon piss off, so she turned her attention to her phone and scrolled through Instagram.

Ruby had posted a picture of her car for the entire world to see. She hadn't reported it to the police, despite people commenting, telling her to do so. A few people had tagged their friends, asking them to check for any CCTV.

Poppy added a message of support, finished her coffee, and glanced up to see that the tall, thin man was still standing outside the bank. This time, he watched the increasing traffic heading into the car park. There was no doubt a show or concert in the arena across the road that night.

But then, as if sensing her attention, the man turned and faced Poppy, his hooded head cocked to the side. They stared at each other, and she again tried to figure out where she'd seen him before, but it was impossible in the waning light.

It can't be Billy. He didn't seem that tall at Sainsbury's. And anyway, she knew he worked Saturdays because she had seen him there every weekend since moving back to Middleton.

But it wasn't Kai, either. So who was it?

A stranger? Probably. Hopefully.

It was time to go home and get away from hooded strangers in the city. Her phone buzzed, and it was Ruby apologising again.

When Poppy looked up from the text, the hooded man was gone—finally disappeared into thin air. On her way out, she looked up and down Merrion Way but couldn't see him.

He must have gotten bored and moved along. Poppy shuddered again—what a creep.

* * *

Poppy saw the bright white, yellow, and lavender flowers attached to her gate as she walked towards her house. The number 13 bus had dropped her off on Town Street, and as she turned right down her street from Moor Flatts Road, there they were.

She was confused.

As she drew nearer, she was greeted by flowers—a gorgeous bouquet bursting with white, yellow, and lavender chrysanthemums fastened to her front gate.

Carefully, Poppy untied the bouquet and turned it over in her hands, looking for a card. But there was nothing.

She wasn't sure who would have sent them. Kai, probably. She was such an idiot, inviting him over and then getting spooked by Billy. She'd led him on. It was obvious. But not her intention. She didn't want him back. Not now, not ever. He had been a short fling who had become obsessed with her.

Maybe, she thought, Ruby sent them to apologise for standing her up. It was undoubtedly something Ruby would do to try and cheer her up. But then Ruby would have left a card.

As she fingered the beautiful blossoms, she suddenly remembered a conversation she'd had on the phone with Ruby just last week whilst she'd been in the queue at Sainsbury's. 'I just love chrysanthemums.' So Billy could have heard her that day.

Was that why there was no card? Because they were from Billy? No, definitely not. She'd threatened to call the police. He wouldn't be so stupid. Would he?

But only Ruby and Billy knew how much she loved chrysanthemums. Kai didn't, not unless Ruby had given him the idea.

She still wasn't sure who sent the flowers as she unlocked her door.

Inside, she bolted the door, closed all the curtains, and turned on the lights. You can't be too careful.

Regarding the flowers, she thought it didn't really matter who sent them, pressing her face into the bouquet and inhaling the floral scent as she carried it inside. Never look at a bouquet of gifts in the mouth.

She laughed at her own joke.

* * *

Later that day, when I finished watching Poppy—fucking fuming at whoever had bought her those incredible flowers— and returned home, morbid curiosity drew me down into the cellar to look at Chanelle's belongings. Stupidly, I took them up into the kitchen and used a dampened cloth from the sink to wipe off the traces of blood that had found its way into the cracks in the phone case and the silver links of the friendship bracelet.

As I contemplated, I passed the phone from one hand to the other for a few minutes. It was stupid of me to bring it out and even more foolish of me to think about turning it on, but I was too curious not to. First, I needed to know more about Poppy and now Ruby. Ruby was sure to have recognised me.

I was being stupid because I knew about cell towers, but I also knew how imprecise they were.

A flicker of adrenaline rushed through me as I switched on the phone. Chanelle had been a silly, silly girl.

No password.

That was good for me.

As I walked into the living room, the phone buzzed in my hands. A few concerned messages popped up, wanting to check if she was OK. There were also plenty of notifications from social media feeds that Chanelle Cummings would never see.

Totally absorbed, I flicked through her phone, the screen's backlight the only illumination in the living room as the sun set quickly that autumn night. I was cautious only to read the notifications of the messages, not wanting any read receipts or blue ticks to be sent to friends and family. After all, it would've been impossible for Chanelle to have checked her phone after she'd died. And I didn't want to push my luck, already knowing that switching on the phone was already a taunt to the police.

A challenge.

After reading the notifications, I added Poppy's and Ruby's numbers to my phone and scrolled through Chanelle's camera feed. Amidst the selfies, many of which I had already seen on Chanelle's Instagram, were the images she'd taken of me at Sainsbury's when I'd asked Poppy out. The ones where she had turned me into a clown.

The fucking bitch!

I continued scrolling until I found what I was hoping for—pictures of her naked ebony skin contrasted against white lace, pictures of her marvellous tits and the treasure between her legs. I'd have liked copies of my own but had to make do with taking images of her screen with my own mobile. They would do. For now.

That boyfriend of hers had been a lucky boy. Christ. I took the phone in my left hand, my cock in my right, and I came over an image of her face. As I finished, I felt the need for power and control and the desire to kill again.

Then I wiped my cum from her phone.

Chapter Sixteen

"George." Isabella sat up, and from the tone in her voice, George shot up and rushed over to her desk. "The network provider has sent the info through."

He placed a hand on her shoulder before quickly removing it. "Go on?"

"Chanelle's phone disconnected from the network Wednesday night." George nodded. "Well, according to them, it reconnected last night."

"Nice. Did they send across a location?" George tried to search through the ream of data on Wood's screen—but realised he was looking only at a call history—a pain in the arse to cross-reference.

"Yep." Isabella clacked the keys, and a small screen popped up over the call record. "Middleton area. Somewhere between Town Street and the Ring Road."

"That's a large area." George could see the blue overlay on the map.

"It's something to go on, I suppose—"

"How come it's not more accurate?" interrupted DC Scott over Wood's other shoulder.

"This isn't a film, Jay," George said. "They have to triangulate regarding location, which means three cell towers. They then use signal strength to make a reasonable guess at the location," George sighed. "But that's all it is, a reasonable guess. The only way to get an accurate location is to have the handset itself."

"Well, that's shit," Scott said, shaking his head. "How can we access the location history on a device when we don't know where it is?"

George scoffed. "Exactly. Did they not teach you this at the academy?"

Jay shrugged, and Wood chortled. It was lucky Luke wasn't here; otherwise, he'd have taken the utter piss out of the young DC.

* * *

To no avail, the trio spent the rest of the afternoon combing through Chanelle's phone records for any clues. DC Scott matched numbers to Chanelle's parents, friends, colleagues, and boyfriend and various places like her bank or local take-aways for the calls made and received. There were a few calls from numbers he couldn't match, but when DC Scott looked into them, it seemed they were cold callers.

Another dead end.

DS Williams continued to comb through the CCTV, and George waited on further Forensics from Lindsey.

* * *

Later that evening, the forensics results finally arrived in the shared inbox, and he opened them eagerly. As he read, his shoulders fell. The partial fingerprint they'd found in blood was no match for the ones they had on file, not even Kieron Swithenbank. It didn't mean it wasn't his because it was a partial and smudged, so there was room for error, as Lindsey had noted, in such an instance.

After searching Swithenbank's flat, he didn't think the man was guilty. And that was even more assured when George clicked on the following attachment. Lindsey's team had searched Kieron's home after he had and had confiscated items of clothing that they hoped would provide a match to the microscopic black fibres found on Chanelle Cummings' body. Still, the fibres didn't match any of Swithenbank's clothes. So that meant one of two options. One, Kieron Swithenbank hadn't killed Chanelle or two; he hadn't worn any of the garments found at his home address as he slit her throat.

The fact that Yardley had found nothing they could match to Kieron meant George believed the former.

Damn it!

He'd worried as much after leaving Kieron and his engagement ring, but to see it in black and white was a massive blow to the investigation. He'd wanted an open and shut investigation, as had his superior, DSU Jim Smith.

Smith, like he, had desperately hoped the forensics would confirm beyond doubt that Kieron Swithenbank had murdered his girlfriend in cold-blooded revenge. Or, at the very least, it would prove someone else, another serious criminal on file, had killed her.

Unless new evidence came forward, like finding her phone, the murder weapon, or perhaps a sighting was reported, then George had precisely fuck all.

George groaned and closed his eyes for a moment, only to be interrupted by his ringtone.

"Afternoon, DSU Smith."

"An update, George," Smith said. "I've just read Yardley's report."

George straightened, knowing this conversation was always going to happen. "Doesn't sound like the boyfriend, sir," was all George could say.

"So, who is it, then?" Smith's Geordie voice boomed.

"We don't know yet, sir. We're fifty hours in."

"I won't accept excuses, Beaumont. You know that. Find the culprit before I give the job to somebody who can."

The line went dead.

George stared at his phone for a moment. They had nothing to go on, and he was truly lost.

* * *

Poppy Lavell awoke with a start, uncertain what had roused her. As she blinked her eyes open in the dark, she strained her ears, listening for something amiss. But instead, she heard nothing other than the suffocating sound of silence.

Convinced she had awoken over nothing, she closed her eyes and rolled over, sheltering beneath the soft new sheets she'd treated herself to. Poppy breathed deeply and methodically to slow her heart and get back to sleep.

Her eyes flew open. What the hell was that? She was sure she had heard footsteps in the ginnel and laid still as a corpse in her bed, listening intently. But this time, Poppy heard nothing—which made her skin prickle rather than reassure her. Someone was out there, and they weren't moving. No, they had stopped right outside her window. The window that looked up to her bed.

With her pulse thundering in her ears, Poppy crept out of bed and peered down out of the glass after moving the pink and white curtains. In the space where they gapped, she saw the outline of something dark. Something was looking up at her. She caught her breath—a dark figure wearing a hood.

She blinked, and then the figure was gone.

It was late, and there was no reason for someone to be in that ginnel. Poppy understood it provided access between Middleton Park Road and Moor Flatts Avenue. Still, many of her neighbours were elderly, and the neighbour on the opposite side of the ginnel had obvious cameras up.

Perhaps it was somebody trying to take a shortcut. Yes. That was it. It was late and cold, hence the hood.

Poppy smiled and tried to calm her breathing. She remained perfectly still, watching the ginnel and waiting for movement.

She saw nothing.

Don't freak out, she told herself.

But it was too late. Poppy thought about Billy and the bottle of perfume. Then the flowers.

Her first thought was to call the police, and she smiled as she imagined flashing blue lights pulling up outside, catching Billy in the act of stalking her. He certainly deserved it, but what if it wasn't him?

Or could it be Kai?

When they'd split, he'd spent a whole week of evenings out in the ginnel, throwing stones up at her window. And she had invited him over. Perhaps she'd made a mistake.

Yes. A mistake.

And what if it's not Billy or Kai? she challenged herself. What then?

What if Chanelle's killer was standing outside, waiting?

Watching? Kieron Swithenbank said it wasn't him, and she believed him. The police hadn't charged him, either.

She pictured herself calling the police, reporting a suspicion that someone was outside her window. How long would it take them to respond to a non-emergency like this? By the time they arrived, whoever it was could be long gone. Or what if the officers arrived and found it was nothing other than a homeless person looking for a safe space to sleep? She would feel awful. She saw the officers rolling their eyes, thoughts about silly women who lived alone, losing their pretty little minds over any passers-by, running through their heads.

So she talked herself out of calling the police, slipped her feet into slippers, and headed down into the kitchen to pour herself a large glass of Riesling.

Poppy heard another noise and grabbed the unopened bottle by the neck, gripping it tightly, hoping she wouldn't have to use it. It wasn't the most conventional of weapons, but it would give her something to swing threateningly should Billy—or whoever it was—attempt to assault her.

Quietly, she went through her front door and gate, not wanting to alert whoever lay in wait. The night air was cold and damp; still, a shiver ran down her spine.

Come on, Poppy, she scolded. You can do this.

Keeping as close to the house as possible, Poppy crept to the corner, where she paused and listened. She was sure she heard someone heavy breathing—panting, really, a disturbing sound that convinced her this was no innocent person. But there was also something else. Material on material. A wet sound?

Poppy jumped around the corner, brandishing the bottle, and shouted, "Oi! Fuck off!"

A shadowy form turned her way and pulled up its trousers before sprinting down the ginnel away from her. Poppy lowered the wine bottle as she processed what she had just seen.

Was he masturbating? She thought back to the panting and the sound of material rubbing.

The dirty bastard!

Trembling with rage, Poppy ran back into her house, immediately bolted the door, and turned on all the lights.

Had that really been Billy? Or was it Kai? She couldn't tell. It had been dark, and the figure had been quite far away.

She called Ruby, who said she'd come and pick her up straight away.

Chapter Seventeen

Holy shit! Is this what a heart attack feels like? I wondered what the fuck was wrong with me as I sat on my sofa, head between my legs as I struggled to breathe. My entire body felt sore, and my head was clammy. My pulse throbbed in my throat and chest. As it did in my cock, which was still hard. Fuck! How could I have screwed things up so completely? Had Poppy seen my face? Did she know it was me?

I knew that I shouldn't have been outside her house. I told myself I was only there to ensure she liked her gift, but that was a lie. I knew she liked the flowers because she had Instagrammed the bouquet earlier that night, captioning the image:

Surprise flowers are the best!

I wondered whether she knew how open her social media accounts were.

The truth was that despite her rejection, Poppy was a drug to me. The way her small, ruby-coloured lips turned into a cute smile as she picked up the surprise flowers was a high I couldn't stop chasing, as was the pale porcelain of her exposed collarbone that I so desperately wanted to kiss.

I had entirely fallen off the wagon.

I wanted to touch and lick the folds between her legs, then

give her every inch of me. It's all I thought about as I became hard in the ginnel, and I had no choice but to provide myself with a release.

But Poppy had interrupted me. I'd spent hours standing outside her window in the freezing cold, my stomach rumbling and my legs cramped.

Earlier, I'd broken in, using the spare key she left under the toad—the one I saw her leaving for Ruby Kaur in my first week of watching Poppy—and watched as she slept, mesmerised by the rise and fall of her chest.

Poppy was so perfect, so dizzyingly, heartbreakingly perfect, that part of me longed to wrap my hands around her delicate throat and take her life away, lovingly, so she would stay looking so heartbreakingly peaceful like that forever.

I wouldn't. Not yet, anyway. I'd decided to give Poppy another chance.

Because, as Matthew Longbottom, Poppy had given me another chance to prove myself to her.

I'd watched her for as long as I could before she began to stir as if she sensed my presence. And so I escaped into the ginnel to watch and wait, and then disaster struck in the form of a drunken dickhead, using it as a shortcut.

"Alright, wanker? Fuck you doing out here in the cold? Having a slash?"

Repulsed, I'd ignored the drunken fool until he spat and lunged at me. I jerked out of the way and hit Poppy's fence, the resulting sound like a firework on a silent night.

Fuck.

The knobhead laughed at me and strolled down the ginnel towards Middleton Park Road.

But the sound I'd made made me freeze. The hit against the

fence was as loud as any I'd ever heard. So I moved closer to her fence to try and hide and looked up cautiously to see the light of her lamp and her shadow stirring.

I should have run right then, fled before she could see me, but I was caught in the moment. The thought of wanting to be seen turned me on, and so I remained in place, a voyeur. Go! I screamed at myself. There would be no happy ending if Poppy found me outside her house. But I chose to lower my joggers instead.

It was Poppy herself who snapped me out of my trance. Her shout—"Oi! Fuck off!"—had broken through to me, brought me back to earth. So I pulled up my joggers and ran.

* * *

I was a bag of nerves that Sunday night. I'd splurged about two hundred quid on a new outfit; to be fair, I'd never felt as sharp. New Nike trainers and jeans from JD, topped with a Superdry shirt and a squirt of Dior Sauvage aftershave, were all bought at the White Rose Shopping Centre.

I swung by Sainsbury's for a bunch of flowers on the way into Morley. Afzal whistled at the sight of me. "You look sharp, Bill. Nice one, mate." I barely spoke to the prick as I paid for the bunch of flowers—white, yellow, and lavender chrysanthemums—a bouquet as beautiful as Poppy herself.

I took a deep breath before entering the wine bar in Morley, and my heart hammered as I saw the breathtakingly beautiful Poppy waiting by the bar. She wore a little black dress with matching black stilettos. My eyes were fixed on her long porcelain legs, taking in her calves. Already, I wanted to slide my hands up and down those shapely legs. I hoped she was wearing lace beneath that short dress. White, in contrast. I shook with anticipation. Her hair fell in luxurious blonde waves over one shoulder, leaving one shoulder bare, her collarbone exposed. I could be kissing it tonight. And other parts of her body.

As I moved closer, I saw that Poppy had her eyes on the door, taking in every man who entered, weirdly still oblivious to me. She looked nervous. I liked the way she'd darkened her eyes with makeup and desperately wanted to kiss those ruby-red lips. Arousal surged in me again. Fuck me; she was hot. I once again imagined sliding her out of that little black dress later.

So, before my nerve deserted me, I quickly strode over to the bar and greeted her, flowers outstretched, a massive smile on my face. "Hi, Poppy."

Confusion spread across her face, and her brows lowered into a frown. "Are you following me, Billy?" Her gaze swept to the door again. "I thought I was very clear in my text. I will call the police, you know?"

I ignored her. "You waiting for your date?"

Poppy's eyes flicked to me, widening slightly. "How'd you know?"

"Because I'm your date, Poppy. I'm Matthew Longbottom. It's my online alias. Your date is with me." I grinned and held out the flowers once more. "These are for you. You look so beautiful. Can I get you a drink?" I gestured to the bar.

But Poppy's look of confusion turned to one of horror. "What the fuck, Billy? You catfished me?"

"Catfished? No—No I..." I was confused.

Poppy shook her head and tried to leave, so I grabbed her by the arm and drew her into me—Christ, I never wanted to let her go. She smelled of the perfume I had bought her. It was fate—a sign. Or so I thought...

As she pulled away, I felt the fabric of her dress slide between my fingers and her muscles tense beneath my other palm.

"I warned you what would happen, Billy," she said, pulling out her phone. "You sick bastard! What kind of muppet catfishes a person into a date?"

"There's no need for that, Pops," I said, stepping on the flowers I'd dropped when I caught her. "I'm sorry, OK? You wouldn't give me a chance as Billy, the checkout boy, but you did, Matthew. But I'm Matthew, and Matthew is me. You really liked Matthew, Pops, which means you like me too. Right?"

"No. And stop calling me Pops!" Poppy's face contorted as she moved out of my reach, and her lips curled in disgust, one hand still clutching the mobile. "No, I fucking don't, Billy! I can't believe you tricked me, you fucking stalker!"

"Stalker? No, I..." I didn't know what else to say. I wasn't a stalker; I just loved her. She was gorgeous, clever, and funny, and I knew we'd hit it off if she gave me a chance. So I told her as much, leaving out the part about loving her.

Poppy, her lips pulled into a thin line, blushed with fury. "You're wrong, Billy! You know nothing anything about me. I don't want anything to do with you. Nothing at all! I swear that if you ever contact me again, I will call the fucking police!"

With those words, she stormed past me, dodging out of my way as I tried to cut her off.

Then she got lost in the crowd and was gone.

I remained there in stunned silence for a long moment, surrounded by the noise of the patrons.

She had rejected me again.

And for the final time.

This time, I'd make Poppy Lavell pay.

* * *

Poppy chucked a twenty quid note at the driver and told him to keep the change. She was shaking as she unlocked her door. Then she slammed it shut and bolted it closed.

He knows where I live, she thought. Would he really try to get to me after threatening him with the police?

She ran around the house, turned on all her lights and closed all the curtains.

He wouldn't be that stupid, would he?

Poppy made a drink and sat down in the kitchen. It was even worse that he'd found her on YorkshireFlirt.com. She groaned. Matthew Longbottom had quite literally been too good to be true. It was her own fault. The catfish was simply a rebound from Kai, one she'd enjoy, and if it became anything more serious, well, great. Perhaps she'd lowered her guard too far with everything that had happened.

Ruby had been keen to know how the date went, so Poppy fired off a message via WhatsApp.

You're not going to believe this, Ruby! The guy from Sainsbury's, the one Chanelle, turned into a clown. It was him. The fucker catfished me!

* * *

How fucking dare she? The thought taunted me. I was so kind to her, so compassionate. And this was how she treated me!

I'd followed her home and watched as she closed the curtains and turned on the lights. Did she know I was watching, or did she just suspect? Clearly, she had me on her mind, and it both pleased and annoyed me that she feared me. That feeling of power pleased me, feeding the wickedness within.

That fucking spoilt bitch!

There was only one way I could end this torment now: the torment of seeing her every day, knowing she would never be mine.

So I'd make sure she'd never turn me down again.

Chapter Eighteen

George yawned as he slid into his car. It was Monday, but it didn't matter, not really, because it was just another working day for the police, who didn't work a traditional Monday to Friday. George wondered when he'd last had a weekend off. He couldn't remember. His contracted working pattern of six shifts on—a mixture of two earlies and four lates, and vice versa—didn't really occur during a murder investigation, and if he were honest, he worked a hell of a lot of hours to get the job done. That was happening more and more each year as the government allowed ever-increasing funding cuts to the department. When he took it, his day off was entirely reserved for Jack, which meant he and Isabella had barely spent any precious time together.

Though they had last night. The couple watched the beginning of a documentary on Netflix called Crime Scene: The Vanishing at the Cecil Hotel, though they didn't get through the introduction as Isabella had stripped down to her underwear and beckoned him into his bedroom.

Today was allegedly a late shift, but he was still going in for 9 am. That was the problem with working in the Homicide and Major Enquiry Team, as he could never really leave his work at the station.

Whenever a new major crime happened, such as the murder of Chanelle Cummings, it followed him home, a spectre that sat in his living room, hovered in his kitchen or stood at the foot of his bed. Like the others, Chanelle had been there in his waking and sleeping hours, begging him to bring her justice.

Those who demanded justice followed him as he lived his life, sitting quietly in the corners of his mind, reminding him of his failures. Despite the therapy, the Miss Murderer was still there, taunting him. It was why he'd taken up boxing again. It gave him a much-needed release. And reprieve. As he took deep breaths to focus himself in the ring, his mind focused on one thing and one thing only. Winning.

"Morning all," George said as he stepped into the warm office, a welcome heat against the autumnal chill outside.

"Morning, son," Mason said from his desk, a giant yawn escaping his mouth. "You're upbeat today; you good?"

George laughed. "I had a good night's sleep for a change. That's all."

"Oh, did you now?" Mason winked suggestively.

He thought about Isabella and the way she looked in her black lingerie. "Get your head out of the gutter, Luke," George said with a laugh. "Like I have time for that." George and Isabella needed to keep their relationship a secret; otherwise, it could ruin their careers.

George pulled off his jacket and hung it up in his office. He turned on his computer and headed back into the squad room. "Do you have anything new for me on the Chanelle Cummings case?" George asked.

* * *

"Let's start from the beginning," George said, to which his team nodded. "We know that Chanelle Cummings was killed between 7 and 10 pm whilst walking her dog in Middleton Woods."

"We followed her from home, where she walked alone with her dog the entire time, via CCTV, where she turned into the park next to St Mary's Church," DS Yolanda Williams said. "That's where we lost her. DC Scott and I checked all the CCTV in and around the park. Calls are coming in, and statements have been taken from people willing to identify and alibi themselves. But out of fifty-six people, only thirty-two have called in."

"Some of those came in via house-to-house, too," Jay added. "We get a lot of people travelling into Leeds, so our appeals may not reach those people."

"Good work," George said. "Any witnesses?"

"No," DS Wood said, "except Sean Parker, who took Chanelle's dog home with him. He didn't see or hear anything regarding the attack, though."

"Lindsey Yardley described the attack as an assassination—quick and effective. Do we think the killer had a lucky break on the timing and location, or was it very well planned?"

"Planned, sir," DC Tashan Blackburn said.

"Why?" He agreed, but he wanted to hear Tashan's theory.

"The culprit brought a knife with him to a park. Whether he planned to kill Chanelle or somebody else, it was still planned."

George tilted his head. "Yes, I agree. But what I wanted from you was a decision on whether it was Chanelle's murder that was planned or just simply a murder was planned?"

Tashan smiled. "I don't know, sir, but we haven't found anything suspicious in her background checks." George nodded. In fact, she seems to be squeaky clean, well-liked, and popular."

"If I may, sir?" Jay asked, putting up his hand. George grinned. Being hard on the young lad had paid off. "If it was a random attack, I reckon we'd have caught someone by now. No one commits a random act like that and gets away without leaving a massive evidence trail."

"Point to DC Scott," George said. "Exactly. The lack of evidence, plus Chanelle's squeaky clean background check, make it certain this was a deliberate attack, hence why we wasted hours on Kieron Swithenbank. But to be honest, I'm not convinced it's him." George scratched his beard. "But this doesn't scream 'crime of passion', either. It's not frenzied enough."

"So, an assassination?" Wood said.

"Got to be. But why? The background checks suggest nothing untoward." This was what was confusing George. Crimes of passion were violent and frenzied. There were usually feelings there. Strong feelings. Yet Chanelle's murder was cold. A single slit to the throat. Why?

"From the evidence we have, Yardley suggested the killer was taller than her because of the angle and force of the wound inflicted," Wood interjected. George was glad for the interjection. She was keeping the team motivated.

"What else do we have?" George asked.

"There was a partially smudged, inconclusive fingerprint on her arm. No match to Swithenbank or anybody on the database," DS Josh Fry said. "Anyway, the blood is important. The culprit would have gotten blood all over their hands. They also put Chanelle on her back. I just don't understand how he could have melted into thin air, covered in blood."

George nodded. "A good question. He probably wore black, which, from a distance, you wouldn't be able to see any blood as it would blend into the dark fabric. At worst, it'd say it'd look wet."

"But he couldn't have gone far, right? Not like that. His hands would have been covered. He wasn't wearing gloves."

George licked his upper lip and examined the map printed of Middleton. The entrances were circled: "Middleton, Beeston, Belle Isle. Those are the three areas surrounding the woods. Then we have Tingley, Morley, Churwell, East Ardsley, Stourton, and Lofthouse further out."

"I think we can discount the latter ones, George," DS Wood said. "If we consider what Josh said, he'd have to live locally."

"I agree, DS Wood. I think we need to concentrate on Town Street, the Manors, and the Ring Road in Middleton, the Southleighs in Beeston, and the Winroses and Newhalls in Belle Isle." George knew all the areas well. They'd already checked the CCTV around the John Charles Centre.

"We only have Kieron Swithenbank as a suspect at the minute, and that is only because of his lack of alibi and not through any evidence. Everybody else has been discounted." George stroked his beard before he continued. "Kieron has a history of anger management issues, and their relationship had suffered a recent breakdown. Even Chanelle's friend, Poppy, disagreed with the relationship. And when we attempted to speak to him, he fled—a reaction that does suggest innocence."

His team nodded, and DS Wood added, "That gives him a potential motive, but I'm unsure about means or opportunity. Plus, he's a big guy and easily identified by those platinum locks. Lindsey and her SOC team found no potential murder weapon—a toolbox with a knife missing, for example."

"That doesn't mean anything, though," George countered. "Could have bought one just for this purpose." He paused before saying, "I don't think DSU Smith will like this, but Josh, Tashan, I want you both to check shops that sell Stanley Knives in Middleton, Belle Isle, and Beeston. Then, get the usual and bring it back here."

By the usual, George meant CCTV, the inventory log of all knives bought within the last two months and any card details if used to purchase said knives.

The two lads nodded.

"Any other info?" George asked.

"Yes, more details from the phone company. The triangulation of Kieron's signal at the time of the murder shows his phone was switched on and present at or around his home address. And, due to the high concentration of masts in the area, there's a very low margin for error on this," Wood said.

"Shit." George sighed and shook his head. "He might have left it at home."

Wood shrugged. "The fibres on Chanelle's body don't match any of Kieron's garments."

"Anyone with half a brain knows if they don't want to get caught, they have to dump, hide, or destroy the clothing they used."

"Then where is it, sir?" Jay challenged.

"Fuck knows, DC Scott," George admitted. "We're getting nowhere with Swithenbank, are we?"

"No, sir."

"OK. Guess the last thing we need to do is search for known offenders in the area." He turned to Isabella. "Can you get on that now?"

* * *

George and his team worked hard for the rest of the day, only stopping at 7 pm when George told his team to go home.

From their knife hunt, Tashan and Jay had an extensive list of people they were calling up, but they had nothing yet.

Wood had chased up any known offenders in the area with no luck on any likely candidates. She'd checked all of Middleton, Beeston, and Belle Isle, which were strong areas that suffered from anti-social behaviour, so there were plenty of drugs-related, drunk and disorderly, and violent offenders thanks to the poverty in the areas. However, there were no known hardened criminals they would consider assassins. George knew from experience that whilst there were lots of problems in the areas, there was also a strong sense of community.

He was, after all, part of that community of Middleton. He always had been.

Was it Kieron? No. George doubted very much the gym bunny was guilty. But if it wasn't Kieron, then who?

They weren't any closer to solving the mystery of Chanelle Cummings' killer.

Chapter Nineteen

I, or rather my alias, Matthew Longbottom, had managed to charm Phoebe Widdop into a date that evening. I was glad of it, too, for I needed a release. Harper hadn't been enough to fulfil me, and adrenaline rushed through me on the way to my date, a swagger in my step.

I'd used a burner and created a new YorkshireFlirt.com profile using Matthew Longbottom and the same cover story—a Yorkshire Water manager working in Bradford but living in Middleton.

Phoebe was well out of my league, and I needed to charm the pants off her, quite literally, if I were to stand any chance. And anyway, the lies wouldn't matter to Phoebe Widdop in a few hours because she'd probably be dead.

I stepped out of the taxi, checking out my reflection in the window before it sped away. I flicked up my brown fringe and scratched my freshly shaved chin. I wore the same outfit I'd bought for my failed date with Poppy, and whilst it filled me with bad memories, it also gave me purpose.

I also carried a bouquet of chrysanthemums.

Phoebe was outside the restaurant in Rothwell, a beige blazer highlighting her thin, lithe figure. So naturally, I wanted to see what was underneath, as, from behind, her arse looked spectacular.

She turned to me, and I was reminded of Poppy Lavell all over again. Yet, as I drew closer, I saw subtle differences. Phoebe was taller than Poppy but less athletic. Her glossy blonde hair was shorter, her skin more tanned, and Phoebe had a smattering of freckles across her cheeks. Her lips were a pale pink, which parted in a smile as she saw me. I preferred crimson.

"Hi, Matthew." She extended a hand.

I took it, pulled her forward and kissed each of her cheeks before pulling the flowers out from behind my back. "For you, beautiful lady."

She blushed as she took them. "Thank you, Matthew. You're such a gentleman."

"This place good for you?" I asked as I gripped her hand and kissed the back of it. I then laced my fingers between hers and gently pulled her into the doorway, not waiting for an answer.

I charmed her all night, plying her with wine and compliments, exchanging stories, though mine were all lies, preparing her for what was to come. The cost of the bottles made me wince, especially as I ordered more to keep her pliable. Before ordering my next, I made my beer last as long as I could.

I needed to be clear-headed but needed an edge and more courage. I needed Phoebe to last longer than Chanelle Cummings did. I needed to remember everything as I took her life from her.

So I smiled as she drained her glass and offered her another bottle as our eyes locked. Phoebe wasn't nearly as pretty as Poppy, but she was pretty enough and friendly enough, too—a bit like Harper. She was girlfriend material. If only I weren't in a relationship with Poppy Lavell.

And for a slight moment, I felt guilty. It was a shame Phoebe had met a monster like me. It was the luck of the draw.

"Fucking hell!" she giggled as she stood up, stumbling down from her stool.

I caught Phoebe under her arm, glancing against the side of her ample breast. I laughed and said, "Are you OK, babe?"

"I am, especially with you being here. My hero." She grinned as I helped her back onto the stool, and our eyes met. "It's the wine. It's good. I don't normally drink this much on a first date, but you—you're special. I think you're lovely."

The bill came then, and I paid for it, adding a decent tip. It was all part of the plan for Phoebe to take me back to hers. She lived alone, which would be perfect for what I had planned. Phoebe had talked all night about living with her friend, who was in Ibiza for the end of the season. "I think you're lovely, too," I said.

"I'm sorry; I shouldn't be making such an arse of myself on a first date, should I?"

"Doesn't matter to me, babe," I assured her and winked. I placed my arm around her, and she melted into my side comfortably. It was a shame she'd met a monster like me—the luck of the draw. I know I keep saying it, but it's true.

I led her outside and along the pavement towards the taxi, pushed her into the shadows, and kissed her. She submitted and opened her mouth to me, her tongue tasting of wine.

After a long kiss, she pulled away, her cheeks rosy. I planted teasing kisses on her neck, getting steadily lower and lower. "Can I come back to yours?" She said nothing, so I added, "I promise to be good. Well, unless you want me to be naughty."

She moaned from the kisses. "Oh, I don't know. I'm not that type of girl, Matthew!"

I continued kissing her neck, and a frisson of excitement that had nothing to do with shagging her spread through my body. It was evident that I wanted sex, but she was oblivious to my darker intentions.

"You don't want to?" I murmured, my breath hot on her neck. I kissed just under her ear then. Then I pulled away and smiled. "But tonight's been excellent, and I'm not quite ready for it to end."

I paused a moment. "But it's up to you." I stepped forward, planted a small kiss on her lips, and then pulled back. Dad explained that women were taught to tease men and leave them wanting more.

Bitches!

She stepped forward and coiled her arms around me. "Fine. As you say, tonight's been amazing. But I don't want it to end here, either."

I kissed her deeply and then asked her to call a taxi.

When it arrived, she told the driver, "Please take us to Back Mount Pleasant, Middleton."

The taxi driver nodded in response and set off up the A654. The journey wouldn't take long, so I decided to warm Phoebe up, laying my hand on her leg and sliding it slowly up her skirt.

We got out of the taxi outside her home, and I paid with cash. It was strange that she lived so close to me, yet I'd never seen her before. She pulled me into her front door, where we collapsed together in a heap in the living room. The cold air and the taxi home seemed to have hastened her inebriation.

She pushed me to the floor and climbed on top of me, expertly placing me inside her, where we rocked together until we came together.

But that wasn't enough for her, nor was it enough for me.

One minute, we were on the floor, panting; the next, she was manoeuvring us upstairs, one step at a time, shedding clothes on the stairs from the bottom to the top.

For a moment, the arousal had steered my brain in a different direction to murder, which was fine until later. I had no intention of coming this far, only to give up. My body needed to feel something for a change. So I pushed Phoebe onto the bed, where she fell in a giggling heap, her fit, tanned, naked form tempting me to enter her once again. It was a good job I'd taken a pack of condoms out with me. I knew that the police could forensically identify my semen, and I had no intention of being caught.

Her blonde curls bobbed as I fully entered her, and she groaned, clutching at her sheets.

"Harder," she moaned, pushing her sex against mine, forcing me deeper.

I wondered just how hard she wanted me to go.

In the dark, I closed my eyes and pretended it was Poppy I was fucking. But it did nothing to alleviate my anger at her rejection; in fact, fucking Phoebe that way only made me want to wring her neck.

"Matthew," she moaned, pulling me closer, her hands traversing me, fingering my scars, eliciting pleasure I hadn't expected. And so I made sure we both came before my hands found Phoebe's slender neck.

Phoebe retched; she tried to breathe as she tried to speak. She was drunk and lacked the strength to push me away, so she beat against my chest, gentle at first, then harder, as she realised that I wouldn't stop. Then the bitch's nails clawed at me, tearing into my chest, each sting burning me as my euphoria and power grew.

Pinned under me, Phoebe struggled fiercely as I squeezed, and squeezed, and squeezed.

Then, her fist struck my nose, sending stars dancing across my vision. Blood poured as she hit me again and again whilst I squeezed and squeezed.

And then it all ended.

Phoebe grabbed a porcelain lamp from her bedside table and smashed it against the side of my head.

She was already calling the police on her phone when I came to, so I ran, collecting my things as I sprinted out of her front door and west up Back Mount Pleasant.

I sprinted into the ginnel by the side of my house and put on my clothes. I'd left blood behind. And flesh under her fingernails.

I needed to be fucking careful from now on.

Chapter Twenty

The ambulance and squad cars' lights flashed across the front of Phoebe Widdop's house, illuminating the cracks in the upstairs curtains of all the neighbouring windows. George shot dirty looks up at many of them and watched them melt back into the shadows in response.

DC Tashan Blackburn stepped out of the car's passenger side, yawning, before hurrying after the DI who approached the front gate.

A uniform was stationed just outside the small, gated garden. George didn't recognise him, but the police constable nodded briskly and said, "She's at her mother's house next door. They live next to each other. CSI have taped it off."

"Thanks," George said. They met a second PC who opened the gate between the two front gardens as he and Tashan approached, then quickly closed it behind them.

Before George could knock, another officer opened the door. He vaguely recalled seeing this one at the Cummings crime scene, although he couldn't recall her name.

With a low and melancholy voice, the constable said, "She's in the living room, sir."

"How's she doing?" he asked as they entered the kitchen.

"As you probably can imagine, sir." George nodded. "Not

great, but her mum's with her, sorting her out. Paramedics are here, too, checking her over."

George's eyes were hurting from the flashing lights through the window. "Turn the lights off, constable. Neighbours are watching. It's like a bloody circus out there."

"I'll sort that, sir," Tashan said, exiting the house. From the window, George saw Tashan tap the officer guarding the gate on the shoulder. They then both chose a different car and headed for it.

George glanced past the young PC, assuming where the living room was located, and said, "Do you think she's ready to talk?"

The lass considered the DI's question. "She's been talking to us, but we haven't gotten much from her. The mum's been demanding a detective, so you'll probably have more luck, sir."

"Yeah, OK," said George, stepping past her. "Thanks."

Phoebe looked up briefly when George entered the living room. Her eyes were red and blotchy, and there was a faint rim of bruised skin around her neck. She was dressed in a gown and sitting on a sofa. A woman in her fifties—her mother, George presumed—was pressed tightly against Phoebe, her arm around Phoebe's shoulder.

Mrs Widdop looked like an older clone of her daughter, with a lifetime of laughter lines at her eyes, her head more ginger than blonde.

"And you are?" she demanded, glaring at George. She stood up defensively until he produced his warrant card, at which point she returned to her daughter's side on the sofa. By the fire, the paramedics were in the process of packing up their kits.

"Detective Inspector Beaumont. Miss Widdop, I came as

soon as I heard," George told her as Tashan entered the room. "That's Detective Constable Blackburn; he's with me." He turned to the older woman. "You must be Phoebe's mother."

"Yes, I'm Alison," she confirmed. "Hi."

"Hi," George began as one of the paramedics came closer. George pointed at them. "How are your wounds, Phoebe?" Her hands went to the purple-blue patch around her neck.

She said nothing, and the paramedic spoke. "We're just heading off. CSI has been."

George knew Lindsey had been because he'd spoken with her on speaker on the way over. Phoebe had sex with the culprit twice, using a condom both times, but she'd managed to punch him in the nose, drawing blood, and scratch him. She'd also smashed a porcelain lamp over his head. It had led to some incredible forensic evidence. But only DNA and no prints, which wasn't ideal as they wanted to try and connect the murder of Chanelle Cummings and the attempted murder of Phoebe Widdop. That, or the culprit could've been on the DNA database, and George hoped this case would be open and shut because he had enough on his plate as it was.

"They've taken some swabs, but they've asked that Miss Widdop come to the station for a more... rigorous examination," said the older of the two. She smiled down at Phoebe. "You sure we can't take you down?"

Phoebe shook her head firmly. "No. I'm OK, thank you. Mum will take me soon," she said, although a shake in her voice told George she was certainly not OK.

The older paramedic gave her a thumbs-up. "Right, well, after you're finished at the station, just call the number on the card we gave you if you need us, alright? They'll get you straight in."

Phoebe glanced around as if trying to remember what she'd done with the card, and her mother held it up. Phoebe nodded. "Right. Thank you."

"I'll see you out," Alison said, starting to rise.

"No need, love," the younger one said as he smiled at mother and daughter.

George waited until he'd heard the front door close before asking her to relate what happened. He recorded the conversation on his phone.

Phoebe adjusted herself on the sofa, shrugged, and then adjusted herself again. Every time she adjusted, she winced. She opened and closed her mouth half a dozen times, too, as if about to start speaking but then deciding against it.

Finally, the words came to her.

"I met a man on YorkshireFlirt.com, a dating app," Phoebe said. "We met in Rothwell, had food and drinks, and I brought him home." George nodded but said nothing, inviting Phoebe to continue."

Phoebe's voice grew faint as her throat constricted. She continued to touch the bruise. Alison nestled in closer and then kissed her cheek.

"It's OK, love. You're OK now," she soothed. "Everything's going to be fine."

"We—We had sex. Twice. After we finished the second time, he tried to strangle me. First, I hit him in the chest, then I scratched him, and finally, I punched him in the nose. He released his grip when his nose bled, and I whacked him with the lamp. As I called the police, you lot, he got up and escaped."

"Did you see where he went?" Tashan asked.

Phoebe raised her eyes to meet his. "No. I was curled up in the corner, afraid he'd come back. So I didn't move until you lot came."

"Is she OK staying here until we've finished next door, Mrs Widdop?" George asked.

Alison's lips drew into a tight pucker. "Of course she bloody is. She's my daughter, isn't she?"

"Can you describe him to us?" Tashan asked.

"She can do better than that," Alison said. "Show the detective, Pheebs."

"Show us what?" George asked.

"Matthew Longbottom. This is his profile on the dating app," Phoebe said. "Though he looks different in real life."

George took the phone from Phoebe's shaking fingers and looked at the screen. "What am I supposed to be looking at, Phoebe?"

Phoebe quickly dismissed George's concern with a shake of her head. "A picture of Matthew Longbottom. Click the messages at the bottom. His'll be at the top."

"I can see the messages, but it looks as if the profile has been deleted."

"What?" She grabbed the phone from George and scrolled through. "That bastard! That fucking bastard! He's deleted it. What the fuck?"

"It's alright, Phoebe. We'll speak with the dating company." He nodded for Tashan to get on it right away. "This must've been a very traumatic experience for you," George said. "And I appreciate how hard it must be for you to talk about it so soon after."

Not meeting his eye but still looking down at the phone, Phoebe made a non-committal sort of noise.

"Can you describe him for me, please?"

"Brown spiky hair. Tall. Thin. Blue eyes."

"Thank you, Phoebe. And what was he wearing?"

"Nike trainers and jeans with a Superdry shirt." She described the colours in detail, and George took notes.

"So you said you had sex, and then he tried to strangle you."

Phoebe nodded her head.

"Did he say why he wanted to hurt you?"

Phoebe shook her head. "He was the perfect gentleman all night. And then, after we finished, he just grabbed me. Started squeezing..." She gestured to the bruise forming around her neck.

"Then you defended yourself and called us?"

Phoebe picked at her nails for a few seconds before confirming. "Yeah. He ran out, and I guess he picked up his clothes on the way out as they were gone when I came downstairs. I guess he panicked."

"OK. The PC outside will escort you to the station where we can do internal swabs in case the condom broke. CSI has already swabbed you externally, right?"

"Yes, they took the skin from under my fingernails and the blood-stained sheet."

"And she'll be staying here with me," Alison said. "No way she's staying there."

"That's good, as we may need to search the place some more." He offered Phoebe a thin-lipped smile. "Tashan is speaking with the company as we speak. Did he give you a mobile number or anything?"

"No, we had all of our conversations via the app."

"Anything else you can tell us?" George asked.

"Just that his body was covered with scars."

"Scars?"

"Yes, Roman numerals, I think. Hundreds of them," Phoebe

said.

* * *

Smith had a knack for press conferences, so George never argued with his boss to attend. It wasn't that George didn't want to attend; he hated the parasites. Smith didn't care for the parasites, either. He shared George's contempt for the media but managed to hide it better than the DI did.

Somehow, Smith had a talent for knowing when a camera was pointed at him and could slip effortlessly into the media training the West Yorkshire Police inflicted upon its senior officers.

George had recently been booked into one of the training sessions, a laborious three-day session at a hotel, where they had more tea breaks than actual seminars. Luckily, Isabella Wood had joined him, and despite Detective Chief Superintendent Mohammed Sadiq booking them into separate rooms, they'd spent every night together.

At 9 am sharp the following morning, Detective Superintendent Smith opened with a statement prepared by liaison officer Juliette Thompson, thanking the public for their interest in the case before revealing some less-juicy details about the attempted murder. The focus was on appealing for witnesses to come forward with any information.

With his elegant Geordie twang, Smith had turned the press from speculators to allies, forcing whoever had tried to murder Phoebe into a corner.

George watched Smith take a few more questions from the press, then turned the TV off.

"He's got a flair for that, boss," DC Scott said, turning back to his computer.

George nodded his approval. "He's better at it than any I've seen bar one."

"Oh eye, who's that, boss?" Scott called.

"An old DCI of mine. Came up from London. A joint op with the Met. He was one of the best detectives I ever worked with."

"Other than me, you mean, George?" Luke added with a grin.

George laughed but said nothing. It was better not to inflate the older Detective Sergeant's ego.

Chapter Twenty-one

The Italian Restaurant in Rothwell eventually provided the CCTV, and DC Tashan Blackburn was tasked to trawl through it for footage of Phoebe Widdop and 'Matthew Longbottom'.

Meanwhile, DC Jason Scott was putting together a social media campaign to complement the appeal from the press conference. He hoped that people would share it to become viral, thus leading them to their culprit.

"Sir." Tashan's voice rang out across the floor.

George rushed across. "What've you got, Tashan?"

"Footage of Phoebe and 'Matthew'," Tashan replied, gesturing to his screen.

George stood behind DC Blackburn. "Play it."

Tashan did and commentated. "OK, so we have them both at the bar area around eight. Phoebe's there on the right—" Blackburn pointed her out, "—next to a man with brown hair, wearing exactly what Phoebe described. So that's 'Matthew Longbottom'." George nodded and gestured for him to continue. "I jumped through the footage, and they move to a table shortly after getting drinks. They stay there for about ninety minutes and then leave. At this point, the man pushes Phoebe into the shadows, where we lose them. Then, ten minutes later, we see them getting into a taxi, almost off-camera, and heading west, presumably towards Middleton, where they head to Phoebe's place."

"Right. Pull detailed stills of 'Matthew'. DS Wood is talking to the taxi firm. Do we have any private or public CCTV in the area around Phoebe's house?"

"No, sir. We have CCTV on Town Street and the Ring Road, where I identified their taxi, but we lose it as soon as it turns right onto Middleton Park Road. We see it again on the CCTV Jay got from the Old Village chippie but lose it when it turns left up her street. There're no private cameras on her street."

George stared at the image of 'Matthew Longbottom' for a long moment, nodding as the Detective Constable spoke. Who was he, and why did he want to kill Phoebe Widdop? He could have been investigating two murders if the man'd had his way.

Fuck.

Were the cases connected? Probably not. But you couldn't be too sure. It would be better to keep an open mind.

George thanked Tashan and headed toward DS Luke Mason's desk. "Did you speak to the staff on shift last night, Luke?"

"Aye, son. It was busy, so they don't really remember the couple. That suggests there wasn't anything unusual about their behaviour or their appearance."

"OK." It was what he'd expected, but it didn't mean he couldn't be disappointed.

"Right, you all know what you're doing?" George asked his team. They all looked up and nodded. "Good. Make sure the appeal goes out ASAP, including 'Matthew's' picture, Jay."

"Yes, boss."

George nodded. "DS Wood is speaking to the taxi company as we speak. DS Fry is chatting with YorkshireFlirt.com, the dating app, but from what he tells me, they're being pricks.

We're looking into an attempted murder, and they're asking for a fucking warrant. Once he gets one, we should get some info to go on. Luke's coordinating uniform on the streets with Sergeant Greenwood. They're acting as reassurance patrols and carry out house-to-house enquiries."

"Nothing so far, boss," Luke said. "It was late when Phoebe got home last night. Most people were asleep."

George grimaced. "Aye, they were until the nosey bastards started looking out of their windows."

* * *

Knowing this could be the key to catching Phoebe's strangler, DS Wood's heart pounded as she rang the taxi firm. She repeatedly tapped her pen against the desk while waiting for the call to connect.

"Middleton Cars," a man answered on the tenth ring, a local accent over a dodgy connection.

"Hi there, Detective Sergeant Wood from West Yorkshire Police; who am I speaking with, please?"

"I'm Rog, love. Roger Blades."

"Thanks. I need some details of a journey one of your cars made on Tuesday night. Can you help me with that?"

"Of course, love. What can I do for you?" the man said.

She provided the vehicle registration and said, "I need to know which of your drivers made a pickup in that car on the A654, Rothwell, outside Slice of Italy, last night." Wood provided the time from the CCTV.

"Right." Wood could hear the man tapping away at a keyboard as he searched for the information.

He replied after a minute, "Ahmed Patel, love."

"Thanks, can you give me Mr Patel's contact number? We have a few questions to ask him."

"Not in trouble, is he? He's one of our best."

"Not at the moment, sir. Just some routine questions regarding the couple he picked up last night."

"Well, Ahmed'll sort you out, love." The man provided a mobile number. "Need anythin' else, love?"

"Cheers, Rog, you've been very helpful."

As soon as DS Wood hung up, she dialled Ahmed Patel's number.

"Yes?" a stern voice answered.

DS Wood introduced herself. "Roger Blades passed me your phone number to speak to you in connection with a person we're trying to locate. I have a couple of questions about a journey you made last night."

There was a rustle on the other end. "Yeah, alright."

"You made a pickup after ten on Tuesday night from Slice of Italy in Rothwell, correct?"

"Correct."

"Who did you pick up, Mr Patel?"

"A young lad and lass. I think she was his bird. Pissed up. She was, anyway."

"In as much detail as you remember, can you describe them for me?"

"They were both in their mid–twenties. Local. She was tall and thin, with blonde hair. Blazer on. Short dress. I—" the man paused, no doubt wondering what words to use next. I saw him sliding his hand up her dress in the mirror. I told him to pack it in my car.

Nice. "And the man?"

"He wa' tall, with spiky brown hair. Jeans and a shirt, but

trainers, not shoes."

This is what Phoebe had already told them. "You said they were pissed?"

"No." Wood could hear the frown in the man's voice. "He wa' sober. She wa' drunk and giggly, but he wa' really quiet. I didn't like him. Gave off a weird vibe. You can tell the sort when you pick 'em up."

"What sort, Mr Patel?"

"Like the predator sort. Bird wa' pissed, and he had his hands all ov'r her. I see it a lot."

"Did you drop them off together or separately?"

"Together, in Middleton, on Back Mount Pleasant. He helped her out, and I watched her struggle to open her front door. Once they were in, I took my next job."

"What time was this?"

She heard more rustles as if Mr Patel was doing something else as they spoke. "Oh, I dunno. Between quarter past and half past ten? Check wi' the office; they'll have the time of mi next job."

It, again, matched the timestamp on the CCTV. "Brilliant. If I got you a picture of the young lad, would you be able to identify him?"

"Yer. Probably."

"Thanks for your help, Mr Patel. I'll be back in touch."

* * *

"Problem?" Frank, the plumber, asked me.

I shook my head. "Why would there be a problem?"

"Tell your face that."

I could feel the blood filling up in my ears. "Don't start."

CHAPTER TWENTY-ONE

"Don't start what?"

"Just tell me what you want; I've had a bad day, alright?" I masked a scowl with a smirk.

"Your face looks like a smacked arse. Someone bloody your nose?"

I gritted my teeth. "Something like that."

The atmosphere changed. I felt pressure. "Saw you out with your bird last night. Punching, ain't you?" Frank, the plumber said.

I let confusion fill my face despite knowing precisely what he meant. "What do you mean?" I asked, reaching into the cabinet for yet another scratch card. Fucking dickhead.

He shot me a look. "Last night. Saw you in Rothwell. Snogging that bird outside that Italian place. Did you fuck her?" Then a great big moronic grin filled Frank's face.

A flash of heat went through me. "What's it got to do with you?" I told him the price, and I didn't say please. Fuck him. Wanker.

"Just making conversation, mate. She looked hot. Decent arse. Honestly, I thought you were batting for the other team."

I raised my brow and ignored him as I pulled a bottle of vodka out of the shelf behind me. "It's none of your—"

"What, business?" Frank grinned. "You need to be a bit politer with your customers, mush," Frank said, stepping close to the Perspex that separated us. "Especially somebody with a big mouth like you." He stood up tall. "What time do you finish, dickhead? Maybe I'll come back and wait for you outside. See how big your fucking mouth is then, yeah?"

"Is everything OK, sir?" Afzal's voice rang out from my left. He was always like this with customers. We served people in Middleton, for fuck's sake!

"No, this little dickhead has a big mouth," Frank said, tapping his phone against the contactless hub. "You his manager?"

"No. The manager isn't in. But I can put in a complaint if you're unhappy, sir."

"There's no need for that, Afzal. The customer was just leaving." I turned to my colleague as Frank walked off, smirking. "Still trying to keep the peace, Afzal?" I asked.

"Someone around here has to."

I knew there was an appeal for information because I'd watched the press conference this morning. But, with Frank, my secret was out.

Frank, the plumber, needed to die. But did Afzal, too?

"How long were you watching Frank and me for?" I asked Afzal.

"Oh, not for long, mate. Just when he started getting close to the till and kicking off. Don't worry about him. He's no different to the usual dick heads who hang around 'ere."

I looked at the man and took his measure. "Close to the till?"

"Aye, mate. When he said he'd come back and wait for you outside, he won't, will he?"

Of course, he wouldn't. Because if he did, the guy was a dead man.

* * *

A quiver of excitement fluttered through me that night as I opened the YorkshireFlirt.com app to see that Frank, the plumber, had given me a thumbs-up. Or rather, on the catfishing profile I'd made pretending to be Poppy Lavell.

I smiled as we agreed to meet tomorrow morning in Middleton Woods.

It was like leading cattle to the slaughter.

169

Chapter Twenty-two

The following day, I awoke before my alarm. When I checked outside, the weather was dry but chilly. I headed to the park in my dark jogging gear—the same gear I killed Chanelle in—and waited in the stillness and silence. Fog adorned the surrounding trees, a welcome accomplice to the crime I was about to commit.

I'd had plenty of time to scout out the most deserted spots during my morning runs, so I picked a place where I knew no one would come across us. Poppy wouldn't be here for another half an hour, and I hoped she would be the one to find the body.

Frank was such a fucking idiot. So trusting. That was to be his downfall.

I smiled as I waited in the foliage, satisfied I'd planned this well. I savoured each moment, each breath, each rustle of the leaves that were beginning to fall to the ground as I gently fingered the kitchen knife. The thought of murder highlighted every sense. Killing Chanelle had been a disappointment. It had been far too quick. And then there was the disappointment of Phoebe Widdop.

Obviously, this wasn't the first time I had killed for Poppy Lavell, and I hoped she would see the symbolism of finding another dead body in Middleton Woods. That's if she found him, which I hoped she would. I knew the Rose Garden was part of her jogging route and what time she usually jogged.

Nobody would see me. Nobody would catch me. I would kill Frank and then disappear, just like I did when I killed Chanelle. To anybody who saw me, I would be just another runner on a morning jog, merging into the vastness of Middleton Woods.

At last, I saw the tell-tale blue polo shuffle along on the deserted gravel track ahead. I stepped out from the foliage and into the Rose Garden.

Frank faltered and stopped, a confused look on his face.

I stepped closer, contorted my face into a smile and revelled in the flash of abject fear that flashed across his face.

"What the hell are you doing here?" Frank asked, his voice sharp, echoing out in the silent woods, where it seemed not even animals or birds stirred.

"Oh, just running," I said casually. "What are you doing here?"

Frank backed away a step and looked around. "I'm waiting for somebody. Go on; you can fuck off now."

I closed the distance. Frank was fat but not very tall. We were also in a deeply wooded area surrounded by trees. It was too early for dog walkers. Too dark. Too cold.

"What the hell do you want? Why are you doing this?"

I sprinted towards Frank and pushed him away from the gravel track and against a tree. "Why? Because you saw me with Phoebe Widdop the night I tried to murder her."

"Phoebe Widdop?" Then I saw the realisation spread across his face. "So what, I'm a witness? Is that it?" The plumber grinned. "You're not going to hurt me, Billy, because you couldn't even kill a fucking little girl!" he spat at me. This close, Frank's breath rolled over me—garlic and cigarettes. I felt nauseous. "Fuck off, Billy, before I call the police."

I moved even closer, our noses nearly touching, his body pinned up against the tree—and, unknown to Frank, I caressed the knife in my hoodie pocket. I was bigger. Stronger. Able to dominate him. I'd always been big for my age, and with my anger issues, people didn't fuck with me. I was the psycho who thought about taking a knife into school an fucking killing everybody with it!

"Last chance, Frank."

He laughed at me, so I took a step back and pulled out the knife.

Frank's attention snapped to it, his eyes drawn towards the arc of the knife's movement. "W—Wait, Billy! Please? N—No!" Frank held up his hands in surrender. "I have a wife and kids. P—Please. Let me go, and you'll never see me again." Frank's eyes never left the stainless-steel blade—the largest I'd taken from the block at my house—whilst he babbled breathlessly. I'd sharpened it this morning, making sure it cut through meat like butter. Then, I'd carve that bastard up good with it. I'd take my time. Enough time to be satisfied this time. As Frank spoke, my hand tightened around the handle because I already knew the bastard was married. He was a leftie, so I could see the tan line where his wedding band usually sat as he paid for his goods.

"Put your wedding ring on, and shut the fuck up. Then I'll consider letting you go," I said.

Frank did as he was ordered and said, "Please, Billy. Let me go. I promise I'll say nothing. Alright? Think about my wife and kid."

"Did you think about your wife and kid when you agreed to meet up with Poppy Lavell for a fuck this morning?"

"How—How do you know about that?"

The fog continued to drop as the anger took hold. "Because I'm the one you were talking to, not Poppy Lavell. You fucking idiot."

"You're the fucking idiot." Frank stepped forward, ready to defend himself, his right hand up, palm out as if ordering me to stop. "Stop it, right now. You've taken this joke too far!"

But I was too quick. I'd planned for everything. That was the way my mind worked. So I stepped forward and thrust the knife deep inside the palm of his outstretched hand. It really was like slicing through butter. I pulled the knife back out and pushed Frank into the tree.

I could feel the pleasure of it, the tingling around my entire body.

"Last chance. Put on your ring."

This time, the fat bastard did as I told him. Then I struck, slicing off his ring finger.

He shouted out in pain, and I felt his knees give way.

Then I thrust the knife deep again, this time into his fat gullet. Then I thrust again and again, and I continued until I could no longer feel the vibration of Frank's body.

I stepped back and looked at the lifeless body of Frank Hinchcliffe, gazing at the fat plumber in horror as he slid and crumpled to the ground, his once blue shirt now black with blood.

Frank Hinchcliffe would never be able to disrespect me or Poppy Lavell again. And that made me smile. Power once again coursed through my veins, charging my very soul. I was addicted to the feeling of murder.

For a long moment, I took in the sight of Frank. The iron tang of his blood was heavy in the air. Then I pocketed the chopped-off ring finger. It would make a nice trophy.

I carefully slipped the blood-speckled knife into my hoodie pocket, admiring the droplets of Frank's life force, fascinated by just how much blood had spilt from him. Chanelle Cummings hadn't bled that much, that was for sure. I tried to wipe the blood from my hands on the inside of my hoodie pocket, but it was stubborn and refused to leave the cracks and crevices of my skin.

Then I heard footsteps in the distance, jolting me from my gaze. I blinked and checked my watch. Poppy would be here soon. In fact, that was probably her footsteps I could hear. I glanced around, making sure nobody saw me and searched through his pockets for his mobile. If the police found it, then they would go straight to Poppy. That's not what I wanted. Not yet, anyway.

The footsteps became louder, so I looked down at Frank once more, savouring the sight of the fat, bald plumber. Unlike Chanelle, he lay in a tangled mess, slumped on the ground, his eyes staring down into the grass, unseeing. Unlike in life, he was beautiful in death. My gloved hand went to touch his face. I was still desperate to feel the life leaving him, but I stopped myself.

And it was lucky that I did because Ruby Kaur, Poppy's other best friend, entered the Rose Garden.

Our eyes met as she stepped closer.

Fucking hell!

She'd seen me. Recognised me. She knew my face. I was sure of it.

And so, I ran.

* * *

George barely slept the night before, his mind working overtime, the spectre of Chanelle Cummings haunting his every move. He also had Phoebe Widdop on his mind. There were two men out there in Middleton with the potential to harm. Or kill. That, or it could even be the same person.

Not that they had any evidence to compare. They found no foreign DNA from Chanelle, so even in two or three days— once Calder Park lab finished DNA profiling the blood from Chanelle's sheets and the skin collected from under Phoebe's nails—they'd still be no further ahead.

He hated how long it took for the profiling to be completed but was amazed at the same time how they managed to take two different types of material and compare them.

"Where are we on YorkshireFlirt.com, DS Fry?" George asked.

"I've sent the warrant to them, so just waiting for them to provide the details we asked for," Josh replied. They'd asked for any images to be sent, alongside a full name, phone number, address, and any card details they held. A warrant had to be extremely specific, which often slowed the process down, especially when mistakes were made. Companies only had to follow what the magistrate had signed off.

"The taxi company gave me the driver's info, and I took a statement from him over the phone," DS Wood shared. Once the dating company has come through with an image, I'll add it to a six-pack and interview the driver." A six-pack was a set of six photos with five fillers and a suspect. DS Wood would ensure they contained images of detectives and officers who looked similar to 'Matthew Longbottom'.

"Anything yet from the appeal, Jay?" George asked DC Scott.

"No, boss. I had a dog walker call in who thinks the young

man who kicked his dog could be our culprit. Want me to look into it."

"Aye, take a statement. Can't be too careful," George said. "Anything from house-to-house, Luke?"

"Not a thing, boss. An older woman reckons she heard a door slam at about 11.30 pm, which is about the right time, but she is partially sighted and so didn't see much. A shadow ran west. That's it."

"Fair enough." George turned to Tashan. "Have you checked for private CCTV east of Back Mount Pleasant?"

"Nope, but I can do it, sir."

"Good. Get on it." George checked the room for the rest of his team. "Yolanda still off sick?"

"Aye, boss," Jay said. "Not doing good by the look of it. COVID."

"Always rife this time of year, she does right," George said. "Anything else for me?"

Before anyone could reply, there was a knock at the Incident Room door. A uniformed sergeant put his head around the door. He looked between the faces of the team, then settled on George.

"Sorry to interrupt, sir. There's been another murder in Middleton Park. The Super says you're SIO."

Chapter Twenty-three

Fifteen minutes later, George parked behind the ambulance outside the Rose Garden. They'd flashed their warrant cards at the PC guarding the black-and-white barrier and had followed the road north. He'd walked and cycled the path many times as a kid and an adult, but he'd never driven down that path himself. His grandfather had driven him down the road many times as a child, taking him to the clearings to fly kites, but Leeds City Council had installed a barrier whilst George was a teenager.

The morning fog was already lifting but only revealed more of the grey, drizzly, wet weather they had already had enough of that month. The scent of damp soil and decaying leaves hung heavy in the air. But George gladly breathed it in because he knew what he would soon smell. Death was never a welcome experience to any of the senses.

The pair approached the scene where police tape fluttered in the breeze, and a red-headed PC stepped forward, a grimace on her face. The tall trees overhead were slim, silent sentinels that guarded the hedges surrounding the Rose Garden. It was deathly quiet, as though all life had retreated from the woods.

This scene wasn't too far away from where the Miss Murderer had taken his first victim in the woods, and George felt sick to the stomach as he remembered being SIO on his first murder case.

George took a deep breath, and he and Wood held up their warrant cards. "DI Beaumont, SIO, and DS Wood. Who's in charge so far?"

The young, ginger PC nodded towards a woman George recognised. "PC Fletcher—her there."

"Cheers. Please keep the cordon and your scene log going." The HMET didn't have the staffing to take that over. Recent budget cuts had crippled them further. It was why George had two active murder cases despite being only a Detective Inspector.

PC Sally Fletcher stood with one of the ambulance staff and a miserable young, shivering woman. Sally looked up as they drew closer and made the usual pleasantries. George liked how organised Sally Fletcher usually was, and she didn't disappoint him as she went through a list of pertinent facts concisely and detachedly. Sally's years of service on the force were clear.

"This is Miss Ruby Kaur. At approximately 6.45 am, she, unfortunately, came across the deceased body of a man. She called for an ambulance immediately, but they pronounced him dead at the scene. That's when we were alerted. PC Willow and I attended, secured the scene, and alerted the HMET. Unless anything else is needed from them, the paramedics are about to leave."

"Thank you, Sally," George said and turned to Wood. "Can you get me an ETA on Lindsey and her team of SOCOs, please?"

"On it." Wood immediately turned away, her phone already to her ear.

George turned to the young jogger. "Miss Kaur, I'm Detective Inspector Beaumont, and I'd appreciate it if we could keep you a little longer as we'll need to take some details. Also, our Crime Scene Investigators will need to take fingerprints, DNA swabs, and shoe prints to ensure you're properly accounted for at the crime scene."

"I—I didn't do anything," the young woman said, her face going slack with horror as she misunderstood his intentions. "I just found the man." She continued to shiver, and George asked a paramedic for a blanket.

George smiled reassuringly and held up a hand. "It's just to exclude you from our investigation." He looked around at the scene."

George didn't think for one minute that the young woman was guilty, but it wouldn't be the first time a murderer had stayed close to the scene. It wasn't even uncommon for the culprit to call in the crime in an attempt to hide in plain sight to acquit themselves. Whatever Miss Kaur's position, however innocent, the young woman had important details DI Beaumont needed to know.

But first, George needed to see the body. It was inside the Rose Garden, and he was drawn closer to it by the same morbid fascination as usual. DI Beaumont didn't want to look, yet he couldn't look away. First, he saw black boots scuffed with mud, then legs covered by black and grey work trousers. Then, as George got closer, he saw the crumpled form of the dead man, his back against the tree, his blue polo shirt covered in dark blood.

The unpleasant scent of death floated towards George on a light breeze, thick and pungent. It defiled his tongue, a cloying taste that wouldn't leave. Without his protective gear, George was careful to approach the scene no closer because contaminating the crime scene was far too high a price to pay. No doubt the jogger who had found the body would have approached closer, and the Rose Garden was a popular place, making forensic collection difficult. The rain didn't help, either.

However the man had died; it looked as if his death had been violent. The amount of blood hinted as though he'd been stabbed repeatedly and viciously, but only a pathologist could confirm the cause of death. Death was never easy to deal with, even for officers or detectives, and murder was even harder, a savage reminder of how callous humanity was, especially to itself.

He thought about the culprit, wondering who they were and why they'd killed the man. Was it a random attack or premeditated? Was it a mugging gone wrong? How long had the body been there? George took another look around. The victim looked as if he were an electrician or a plumber. So why was he out in the Rose Garden? What was he doing?

No matter how hard George thought, he couldn't answer his own questions; he needed forensics and pathology to unlock more pieces of the puzzle before he could solve it.

He strode back to Isabella and Sally.

"CSI will be here soon, George."

"Thank you." George glanced at the sky, hoping the drizzle wouldn't get any worse. The last thing he needed was the rain washing vital evidence away. Then he turned to the young lady standing with PC Fletcher.

"Miss Kaur," George said firmly. "Because of what you found, we'll need to take a full statement from you. So please describe what happened, and include as much detail as possible."

Miss Kaur nodded, and her piercing brown eyes darted

towards the Rose Garden, where the body lay out of sight. When she spoke, there was a tremble in her voice, and George could see that she was still trembling despite the blanket. "I was jogging through the woods just like I do every morning. Before moving on, I always stop in the Rose Garden for a rest and a drink. The mist was very thick this morning, but I saw two silhouettes: one black and one blue. As I—I got closer, I—I saw the one in black get up and run away. So I—I called out—" The woman's voice had dropped to a whisper and then wobbled. "But when he didn't reply, I knew something was wrong."

"Was the one in black a man or a woman? Could you describe them to me?"

"Sorry, Detective, but I can't. It was too foggy. They were dressed in all black, with their hood up."

"Right, OK," George said. "Thank you. Anything else?"

"When the man in the blue top didn't reply, I went over to him to see if he was OK, and..." Miss Kaur swallowed and drank from her bottle. She turned a face twisted by dread towards DI Beaumont. "It was then that I noticed all the blood. He wasn't moving, so I checked his pulse—just his left hand. Is that why you need my prints?" She looked at George, worried.

George nodded but said nothing.

"He was cold but not freezing cold. He wasn't breathing. I dialled nine-nine-nine straight away. I felt useless that I couldn't do anything." Tears glistened at the corner of Miss Kaur's dark eyes. "I didn't do anything wrong, did I? By touching him?" She looked desperately between the officer and two detectives.

PC Sally Fletcher smiled sympathetically and placed a hand on Miss Kaur's shoulder. "It's alright, Ruby. There was nothing you could have done, so don't blame yourself. And this has been a traumatic morning for you—do you have anyone I can call to come and be with you?"

"No. I need to go home, shower, and go to work."

"Where do you work?" Isabella asked.

"I'm a receptionist at the surgery on Middleton Park Avenue."

"Opposite the primary school?"

Miss Kaur nodded jerkily and then started to cry. "I've—I've never seen anything like it before. I fucking hate this place! Always have!"

The two detectives shared glances, and George said, "Why do you hate this place?"

Ruby's answering smile was sad. "When I was younger, someone killed my best friend's kitten right in this very fucking place."

Sally squeezed and said, "Ruby—"

"It's fine; it was a long time ago. Its headless body was nailed to that exact same tree through the tail. I sometimes still have nightmares about it."

"Thanks, Ruby," George smiled. "PC Fletcher will take you home, and if you think of anything regarding the black silhouette, give me a call." He handed her his card. "Give PC Fletcher your number, too, as you'll need to come in and give an official statement."

Ruby nodded and said, "Th—Thank you." PC Sally Fletcher then marched Miss Kaur away from that horrific scene.

George stayed with a silent DS Wood, watching them go as he could do very little until CSI arrived. Their main priority was finding out who he was. Hopefully, he'd have a phone or wallet on him, especially if he was heading to work.

CHAPTER TWENTY-THREE

"How bad is it, George?" Wood asked quietly.

He thought about it. "Pretty bad," George replied. "A big guy. He looks like a plumber or electrician, maybe a tiler or a builder—somebody who works with his hands. I'm sure I saw a defensive wound to a hand. A big guy like that wouldn't have been easy to take down."

Chapter Twenty-four

Chaos soon descended upon Middleton Park Woods as CSI, the general public, and reporters all arrived at once. DSU Smith had sent an army of police constables after George had asked for the cordon to be extended, but the officers had a difficult job. There were many different ways into the woods, so George created a double cordon, with the outer cordon measuring about one hundred metres in diameter.

Lindsey Yardley stood at the inner cordon, her CSI team behind her, while the young redhead signed them in.

Moments later, they were all dressed in white paper coveralls, shoe covers, masks and gloves and had a tent erected around the body shortly after. George was always impressed with how quickly they worked.

"Morning, George," Lindsey eventually said. "What do you know so far?"

"Morning, Lindsey. Not much, just that the male, who looks to be in his thirties, died between last night and this morning. I haven't been near, but from what I saw, he may have multiple stab wounds."

Lindsey narrowed her eyes. "Interesting. Suit up, and we can go through it together." She brushed past him without a further word.

* * *

"Frank Hinchcliffe. Thirty-three." George stared at the photograph a SOCO had taken of the driving licence—the original having been bagged up for evidence. He had been right—Lindsey had found a wallet filled to the brim with notes and a driving licence inside a pocket of the victim's work trousers.

"Thought he was older, to be honest," Lindsey said, her hands folded across her chest. It was getting colder by the minute.

"Me too," George said. He'd spent some time watching Lindsey whilst she looked for clues. "Find anything?"

DS Wood caught his eye as she strolled back. He'd sent her to help the PC at the inner cordon because some walkers and curious onlookers had managed to infiltrate the outer cordon.

George drained the rest of the lukewarm drink from the thermos, still appreciative of the slight warmth it added to his bones against the persistent cold that seeped within him. The rain had begun to fall, and so George knew it was a race against the clock for the CSI team to capture all the evidence they needed from the scene and for Lindsey to conduct her initial examination of the victim.

Lindsey said, "Not much more than you already know, George. There are multiple stab wounds and a lot of blood. Once I get him back, I'll conduct a proper investigation, as usual, but whoever killed this man... well, it was a prolonged and violent attack."

George glanced at the sky once more. "Leave the body for now and search the area. The scene's degrading quickly because of this fucking rain."

"Already on it," she said and smiled. George had seen the CSIs combing through the undergrowth and surrounding area. "I do have a theory on how he died."

"Go on," George said.

"There's blood on the tree trunk, so my theory is he was pushed against the tree and stabbed." George nodded, already having the same thoughts. Lindsey continued, "The blade was long enough and used with such force that it penetrated pretty deeply into the victim's considerable stomach. There's blood spatter on the bark, arterial spray, I'd say, but it could be from the arc of the knife moving through the air between thrusts. I'll put it in the report."

"Anything else?"

"He tried to put up a fight, but it didn't do him any good," Lindsey said. "He has a nasty defensive wound on his right hand as if the culprit deliberately thrust through his palm. On his left forearm are clean, sharp slices. Left ring finger is missing, too. We haven't found a murder weapon or the finger in the immediate area, and I've had my team search the surrounding area, too, just in case. It would have been a rather long, wide knife, possibly a kitchen knife, to create these wounds. Your culprit likely took it away to be hidden or dumped." Lindsey shrugged. That was up to George to handle, and he considered stopping all refuse collection again for a few days. Middleton wouldn't appreciate it, but they would if it got a killer off the streets.

"His phone's been bagged up for you, George," she said. "And I don't think it was a mugging because his wallet was flush with cash."

George thought that was good. Phones were like goldmines during investigations such as these. Was this murder linked to the other or separate? He asked Lindsey for her opinion.

"It seems like a different MO to me, George, and the murder weapon is different. Miss Cummings was out walking her dog, right?"

George nodded.

"Then I'd suggest they're unrelated, but that's not my job." She smiled at George. "I did notice that his polo shirt suggests he owns a plumbing and heating company."

George nodded. He had DS Luke Mason looking into the company already, and the licence had an address, so he knew they would have to head there next.

"We found prints where Miss Kaur said she touched the body and matching footprints. From what DS Wood told me, it matches what Miss Kaur told you. There are other footprints in the area, but as it's a popular area, they're scuffed and overlaid."

"Any decent forensics?" George asked, his tone hopeful.

"I found a brown hair complete with a follicle, so I'll fast-track that. Hopefully, the culprit is on the system, and this case is open and shut."

"Why open and shut?"

"Because I've just moved to Middleton, and I hate to think a violent murderer is running free out there, never mind two of them."

George nodded. He felt a strong sense of déjà vu. "Time of death?"

Lindsey Yardley grimaced. "From the body's temperature and condition, I think your jogger, Miss Kaur, just missed the murder. So anywhere between..." She pursed her lips, eyes towards the sky as she deliberated. "5 and 7 am."

"Thanks, Lindsey." George scratched his head. What a

nightmare. The weather would have put a lot of dog walkers off and probably some joggers, too. He texted DS Josh Fry back at the station to put up a social media appeal appealing for witnesses. "I can't believe the mess. Who would do something like this?"

Lindsey looked between George and Wood as a smile broke out on her face. Then she uttered her favourite catchphrase. "That's your job, isn't it, detectives?"

"Cheers, Lindsey. Send us that report ASAP, yeah?"

She said nothing as George and Wood headed back towards the red-headed PC to wait for the transport to the morgue to arrive for the body.

"Right, DS Wood," George said, "we have a name, so call the team and get them to start the preliminary background checks, identify next of kin, and the like."

"I already did it, George. DC Scott is currently pulling up his files. I also asked Josh to find him on social media so we can try to find out more about his life."

"Good job," he said with a wink.

* * *

It took only five minutes in George's Mercedes to get to Frank Hinchcliffe's house because it was on Sissons Road in Middleton, less than two miles from the park. For George, this was the worst part of his job, as, after all, there was no easy way to say, "Good morning, your husband's dead. Can we ask you some questions because, statistically, you're the person who probably murdered him?"

Beside George, DS Isabella Wood liaised with the other detectives back at Elland Road, giving orders and exchanging information. The constables guarding the cordons in the woods had taken statements from everyone who had passed through, which Isabella committed to memory.

George took a right and headed down Sissons Road. He knew the area well because his great-aunt Susan lived on Sissons Road when he was a child, so he spent many weekends there with her grandchildren. He indicated left and pulled outside a russet-coloured semi-detached house with a white door.

The attached houses were surrounded by a hedge fence, and the Hinchcliffe house had a giant conifer in the front garden.

As George and Wood approached the house, he saw movement from within and didn't even manage to knock before a slim woman in her late twenties, who was most likely Kelly Hinchcliffe.

"Mrs Hinchcliffe? I'm Detective Inspector Beaumont, and this is Detective Sergeant Wood. We're sorry for coming unannounced, but may we please come in?" As George spoke, he held out his warrant card, and Isabella did the same. The woman, frowning, looked at her, then back at George.

"You wanna come in? Is something wrong?" George said nothing but smiled, and so she led them inside. Kelly Hinchcliffe led them into a modest living room with cream leather sofas that she invited them to sit on. George detected a hint of perfume mixed with washing powder and something else—the familiar smell of soiled nappies.

George's heart sank. They didn't know much about Frank yet, but looking around the living room, it seemed like he had a baby.

"Can I get you a cuppa?" Kelly asked.

"Ah, no, thank you," George said. "Please, take a seat, Mrs Hinchcliffe."

Kelly's face crumpled into worry as she sat on one of the sofas opposite where George and Wood were perched.

"I'm very sorry to tell you this, but this morning, the body of your husband Frank was found."

Stunned silence greeted the detectives.

"You what?" Kelly Hinchcliffe said, furrowing her eyes.

George nodded and waited. He was waiting for his words to sink in—there was no use repeating them.

Kelly Hinchcliffe seemed to age in front of them.

"No. It can't be Frank. He—He went to work this morning. He left the house early. Are you sure it's him?" Kelly said, her voice caught in her throat. "What happened?" Then, as she wilted, she burst into tears.

"Can you tell us what Frank was wearing this morning, Kelly?" Wood asked.

"The usual. His blue work polo shirt with the company logo on it, black and grey work trousers and black boots." A sudden thought must have crossed her mind as her eyes brightened. "Was the dead—Was the body wearing any of those clothes?"

"I'm afraid so, Mrs Hinchcliffe," George said.

"Frank had identification on him, too, but we would appreciate it if you could be present for a formal identification to confirm," Isabella said quietly. "He'll be at the Leeds General Infirmary."

"What happened?" Kelly repeated.

George shared a glance with DS Wood. "Our investigations are still in the early stages, but he was killed this morning in the Rose Garden in Middleton Woods."

Frank's wife made a wordless moan of anguish at George's response, staring desperately at him as though he could take the words back and leave. George knew there was no way Kelly could absorb such enormous news in mere seconds, but George also knew what happened next could impact the investigation.

From the photos sprinkled around the room of Frank, Kelly, and their baby—their only child from the look of it—Kelly's grief would be tremendous.

"How?" Kelly dared to ask.

"The post-mortem hasn't been carried out yet, but preliminary results from the scene suggest a stabbing."

Kelly moaned again. "A stabbing?" George nodded. "Why?" Tears carved through the foundation down Kelly's cheeks.

"We're not sure yet, but we're doing everything we can to understand what happened and to bring the person responsible to justice. So with that in mind, even at this early stage, any information would be beneficial, especially if you know anyone with a motive."

"I—I—I don't know what you mean."

"Did Frank have any enemies," Wood added, "or anyone who might have held a grudge?"

Kelly, wide-eyed, shook her head and stared at the floor. "No. Everybody loved Frank. He was a proper community champion. He owned his own plumbing and heating company and had plenty of mates." Kelly winced. "He loved living in Middleton and loved the people who live here. He was always out, tending to people's pipes and stuff, sometimes even for free. I know a few elderly folk around who appreciated what Frank did for them." She smiled sadly.

"Did he work alone?" She nodded. "Do you know whether he had any problems with any customers?"

Kelly shook her head. "He was a professional and never had any complaints. He was so open and honest with me. If he were having issues, I would know about it."

"What about his friends? Do you know about any arguments with friends?" Wood quietly interjected.

"No. Why are you asking me this? Do you have a suspect?" Kelly asked.

"From what you described, he was in the park early and wearing his work uniform. We don't know why he was there. Do you?"

She shook her head, and more tears fell.

"At this stage, I would suggest he was meeting someone, which takes me to my next question," George said. "How was yours and Frank's relationship?"

"Perfectly fine. We have a baby, Garry; he's six months old. Been married for two years."

"Any cheating?" George thought about the missing ring finger and missing wedding ring.

"Cheating? Excuse me." Kelly stood, her face like thunder. "My husband has just died, and you're asking about cheating."

"I apologise, Mrs Hinchcliffe, but your husband was meeting somebody in the park, so I have to ask these difficult questions."

"Please, Mrs Hinchcliffe, we mean no disrespect," Wood added.

Kelly shook her head. "He was always on his phone, but he had a bit of a gambling problem. He thought I didn't know he was betting again, but I did. It was obvious by his mood swings. When he won, he was happy, but when he lost..."

George said nothing and texted Luke back at the station to start gathering information regarding the Hinchcliffes' financial accounts. Then, he sent a separate text to DC Scott, asking him to collate information about local loan sharks. It didn't seem like that kind of attack, especially as Frank's ring finger was missing, but they needed to investigate all angles.

"Do you know Chanelle Cummings?"

Mrs Hinchcliffe shook her head. "No, should I?" When George said nothing, she added, "Is that the bird he was shagging?"

"Thank you, Mrs Hinchcliffe. Now, if you could tell me where you were this morning between 5 and 7 am, that would be extremely helpful."

"I was here, tending to Garry. Frieda Blake, next door, popped in for a cuppa about half six."

He would get Wood to confirm the alibi, even if it didn't entirely exonerate her. Kelly could easily have gone to the park, murdered Frank, and returned. George stood. "Thank you. I'm sorry we have brought you such awful news today. We'll do everything we can to find you answers and bring Frank justice."

Kelly stood, a shaking mess.

"I'll arrange an FLO," DS Wood said to George before respectfully saying goodbye and stepping outside.

George continued, "An FLO is a family liaison officer. They'll be your main point of contact, so if you think of anything else that might aid our investigation, you can pass that on to us via them. That also works the other way, so we'll also keep you informed of any developments in the same way. Whoever your FLO is will be here to offer you any support you need." He looked at Kelly to check for comprehension, but she nodded dully, her eyes glazed over.

"If you need anything else, for now, call me." George handed her a card from his pocket. Kelly took the card from George's outstretched hand. Then she turned and gently picked up a photo of the three of them, clutched it to her chest, and began sobbing quietly.

George showed himself out. If Kelly's involved, then she's a bloody good actress, George thought.

Outside, he found DS Wood leaning against his Mercedes. "It's getting worse around here," she said.

George knew what she meant. Middleton and murder seemed synonymous these days.

"The FLO team have put Cathy on this one," Wood said.

"Great," George clicked his fob to open the doors. Cathy Hoskins was one of the best FLOs the force had. He'd worked with her before, most recently during The Cross Flatts Snatcher case. She was an expert at putting victims' families at ease and supporting them at difficult times. Kelly Hinchcliffe would need it.

Chapter Twenty-five

George returned to the station to find it in pensive silence. DC Scott sat hunched at his desk, dark shadows under the young man's eyes and two empty coffee cups next to him on the desk.

"Alright, Jay?" DI Beaumont said.

"Aye, boss," Jay said wearily. Then, at George's prompt, he launched into an update.

As expected, DC Scott had come up blank on CCTV in the area. Like with Chanelle's murder, he was creating a list of people they saw entering the park an hour before and after the murder. DS Fry was investigating Frank Hinchcliffe's mobile phone.

Then, George checked in on DS Wood, who was just on her way back from taking a statement from Ruby Kaur, the jogger, to detail her story further and confirm the timings. According to Isabella, the young woman was beside herself, which was understandable, given what she'd found. And there was a weird connection, too. Ruby Kaur was also one of Chanelle Cummings' best friends.

George had, for a brief moment, thought about that connection. Had Frank killed Chanelle? And was Ruby out for revenge?

No, it didn't seem possible. For one, Ruby didn't come across as a calculated killer, and according to Lindsey Yardley, there was a lack of evidence left behind. The killer would have been covered in blood, and it would have been impossible to hide in such a short time without CSI finding some evidence.

That and Ruby was petite, and Yardley had detailed that the arc of the knife wounds had come from higher up, as though the perpetrator stood taller than Frank. So Ruby Kaur had simply been in the right place at the wrong time, an unlucky first witness on the scene, not the perpetrator. But George had been wrong before. So he'd get Wood to keep an eye on her.

"Any info from the phone yet?" George asked.

"Josh is working on it as we speak. But he did find something weird," DS Wood said.

"What?"

"He had a YorkshireFlirt.com app on his phone. Could there be a connection? Maybe Matthew Longbottom killed Frank Hinchcliffe?"

"What does the app show?"

"Nothing yet, George. The app has been logged out for some reason."

"Speak to the Super and get another warrant. The one we have for 'Longbottom' is only for his account and not Frank's. Once you have it signed, please send it to Josh. Hopefully, they'll send us the information we need ASAP."

"Yeah." Wood smiled. "He's downloading the rest of it as we speak."

George felt repelled by the amount of data they could seize on a phone and found it incredible that within minutes, they could download the content of an entire smartphone. He also found it scary how easily they could explore the owner's private data, deleted or not. They could also download location tracking, messages, and photos. And because they had the handset, they didn't need a warrant. It felt invasive to see such intimate details of a person's life. But it wasn't just that. It was the fact that data taken without understanding could be misinterpreted and misunderstood.

* * *

Fuck!

It was definitely me.

My hands shook as I looked at the image on Facebook again. I'd called in sick and had been scrolling through my feed, a mind-numbing habit when I'd come by a sponsored post. It was a blurry photo of me next to a crystal clear one of Phoebe Widdop and an urgent appeal to locate me.

Fucking hell. I knew I didn't have long, but I assumed I had longer.

I clicked on the post, read it, and then scrolled through the hundreds of comments, noting that hundreds of people had shared it and tagged their mates despite being only a couple of hours old.

The comments were disgusting and were all aimed at me.

Arseholes!

Anxious energy channelled through me, making me restless and filling me with fear and excitement as I trod that fine line between the panic and the thrill of being caught. The only distinguishing features I could see from the image were my brown hair and shaved chin. Yet, anybody with half a brain cell would know it was me in that picture.

Fuck fuck fuck!

I had to change my appearance immediately.

Calm down, calm down. They couldn't possibly know who I was from just a blurry image. And I'd already deleted my profile and removed the SIM. It wasn't my picture, anyway; it was just a random guy who looked like me from Google Images.

I'd been tempted to dye my hair platinum blond a year ago, like a rapper from my childhood. I'd bought the dye but left it in my bathroom cupboard after shitting myself. I could dye my hair now, then grow a beard. I'd look completely different.

It would work.

I legged it upstairs—each step pounding under the hammering of my footsteps—into the bathroom. Finally, panic overcame me, and I leaned on the sink, breathing deeply, taking in the look of worry on my face.

I tried to force my jaw to unclench, my furrowed brow to relax, and my lips to soften, but I was scared.

I'd never been so scared in my life.

But I could overcome this. I knew I could. The hair on my face had grown since Tuesday. Shaving daily has always been a pain for me.

Yes, keep the beard and dye the hair.

Bingo.

I bent and rummaged through the cupboard under the sink until my hands landed on what I sought—the box of dye.

But first, I pulled out my electric beard shaver, forcing my hands not to shake, and cut my hair short. The buzz against my skin was a welcome numbing against the frenetic anxiety. I didn't dare do a buzz cut, but I cut it long enough for the dye to take effect, then rubbed the awful-smelling lotion into my hair.

For the next twenty minutes, I sat fingering Chanelle's bracelet and Frank's wedding ring, my body shaking, my head itching and burning, telling myself it would be worth it.

After showering, I stood in front of the mirror. The difference was stark. I felt calmer, unwavering.

* * *

Ruby Kaur left her house thinking she recognised the blurry image of the man who had attacked Phoebe Widdop. Was it the guy she saw? In the Rose Garden?

She was tired and disoriented from the lack of sleep. The dark-haired shadow haunted her every waking moment yet also invaded her dreams. Ruby worried that the man watched her every step and that she was next to be murdered.

As Ruby swung open the gate, she noticed an empty cardboard box. Littering was one of her bugbears, so she grabbed it to place in the green recycling bin and paused, noticing that her name was scrawled across the top in thick, black ink.

Ruby placed the box on the bin lid and gently lifted one of the flaps to investigate. She saw lower stems. The package wasn't empty after all. Ruby smiled, thinking back to the beautiful blooms Poppy had left for her not that long ago.

Or at least she hoped they were from Poppy. She'd had a crush on Poppy since year 7, not that anybody knew. Ruby was bisexual and proud of it in her own way. But to stay close to Poppy, Ruby never told her.

Ruby eagerly pulled open the other flaps and froze. Bewildered, Ruby stared at the contents.

Someone had decapitated the entire contents.

Chapter Twenty-six

Across the table from Ruby at Costa, Shae's jaw hung open as she stared at a picture of the flowerless bouquet on Ruby's phone. Earlier, Ruby had taken a photo and promptly disposed of the stems—box and all—in the black bin. Then, as the lid slammed shut, Ruby felt eyes on her but looked around and saw nothing.

"Shit," Shae finally said. "That's fucking mental."

"Right? Headless flowers? What the hell? I'm proper freaked out."

"Were they definitely for you, Rubes?"

"Yep," Ruby said, shaking her head firmly. "They were in a box labelled Ruby, so they were definitely for me."

"That's so fucked up," Shae said, her thin hands shuddering. "Who do you think sent them?"

"No idea, but—"

"But what, lovely?" Shae said, her red curls bouncing.

"I think I'm paranoid."

"Paranoid? Go on."

"The murderer. The guy who I saw." Ruby toyed with her fork, pushing the cake around the plate. "I think he's watching me. I think it's him who sent me the flowers."

"You don't sound convinced, lovely," Shae said.

"No?"

Shae smiled and shook her head. "No."

"I just can't get him out of my mind. He's on every corner, watching me. And in my dreams, he's behind me."

Shae said, "You don't know that for sure—"

"I don't think I'll ever sleep again," Ruby interrupted. "No matter what I do, he's there."

"You want my advice, lovely?" Ruby nodded. "You need some therapy." Shae saw the look of apprehension on her friend's face. "It'll do you good. You saw something terrible happen. But the police will catch him soon. Trust me."

"Thanks, babe." Ruby straightened as a thought suddenly came to her. "The man. The one I saw kill that plumber. He kind of looks like the guy all over Facebook."

"The one who attacked Phoebe?" Shae and Phoebe had gone to school together.

"Yep. Something about the blur. He ran off when he saw me, and I couldn't take in the details because of the blur. It's the same with that picture."

"Call the police, then," Shae said. "Tell them. They could look into connections between Phoebe and the plumber."

"True. But then, what about the headless flowers?"

Shae's eyes widened. "I don't know, lovely. Have you pissed anybody off lately?" Shae asked, taking the phone and looking at the picture again. "It's quite nasty, is this."

"Only the murderer," Ruby said.

Silence. Neither woman said anything.

Then, a sudden ping shattered the silence.

The colour drained from Shae's face. "What is it?" Ruby asked.

"Holy fuck!" Shae said, turning the phone to face Ruby and

pointing to the text that had just come through:

My favourite chrysanthemums are lavender, yellow and white; await my next text, which will give you a fright.

"That's what the headless flowers were. I could tell by the stems that they were chrysanthemums," Ruby said, her voice high.

Then another ping went off, like a gunshot.

It's evident to you that violets are blue and roses are red, but what's not apparent to you is that you will soon be dead!

"Jesus Christ," Ruby gasped, her hands shaking.

"You have to take this to the police, lovely. You have to go there. Now!"

"Or I could call them and see who is sending stupid jokes?" Ruby said.

"Go on then."

Ruby pressed the telephone button at the top of the screen, but it wouldn't connect. "Phone's turned off."

"Just some dickhead texting random numbers for a laugh, then?" Shae asked.

Ruby looked up, surprised. "You said I should take it to the police a minute ago, and now you think it's a joke. Which is it?"

"I'd speak to them. See if they can trace the number. Might be one of those idiots you went to school with," Shae said with a shrug.

Ruby gave Shae a dubious look.

"I really don't think it's the murderer," Shae insisted. "I mean, how would he even get your number?"

That's a good question, Ruby thought.

And so Ruby went straight to the police. Nothing else mattered. She'd been a witness to a murder and had now received a decapitated bouquet and threatening text messages.

She only hoped the police would take her seriously.

* * *

I had felt captivated as I used the scissors that morning, snipping the head from each chrysanthemum before carefully setting each stem in the box. My hands had been shaking, and my body vibrated with a dangerous mixture of panic and the thrill of being caught as I placed the box in front of her house. I then walked away to hide, hopeful I had communicated my message loud and clear.

I just hoped it wouldn't be long before she left. I knew she was meeting a friend at Costa because I'd heard them making plans last night.

Ruby was beautiful and very different from my usual type, but then so was Chanelle. Neither were pale like Poppy, and both had the dark hair and darker skin of their Indian and African ancestors. Ruby's skin was the colour of wheat, whilst Chanelle's was black satin.

And Ruby had always been friendly to me at school. I suppose she was similar to both Harper and Phoebe in that Ruby was girlfriend material, a woman worthy of being taken to show off to my dickhead dad.

Whilst Poppy was in a league of her own. If Poppy were mine, I'd hide her from prying eyes, not wanting others to take in her beauty, so scared I was that somebody else would take her away.

And after what happened with Kai, nobody would ever take Poppy away from me! Never again!

From the bushes where I kneeled, I saw a woman walking

with her stroller, which made me smile. My body went warm and fuzzy as I imagined Poppy's slight form swelling, her glowing with child. Our child.

I thought about how Poppy would look when our beautiful child finally made its way into the world and how she would look up at me from the hospital bed with a bursting smile and say, 'I love you so much. Thank you for allowing me to carry your child.'

I was kissing the fuzzy head of our perfect baby, already planning its future, when I saw a woman watching me from her window. I'd felt her eyes on me instantly, a strange feeling that I assumed my own prey must have felt as I stalked them from the shadows.

"What the fuck are you doing out there in my bush, lad?" the woman said, her tone oozing annoyance.

When I ignored her and continued my daydream, she shouted down, "You shouldn't be here! Fuck off before I call the coppers!"

"Fine," I said, standing up. It wasn't loud enough for the woman to hear, and I had my hood up so she couldn't see my newly acquired platinum locks. My identity was safe.

"Fuck off now. I'm warning you, get the fuck off my land!"

Something inside me clenched, and for a split second, I envisioned breaking into her house as I had broken into the others, grabbing that stupid bitch by her hair and smashing her face into the window. That would really give her something to complain about.

But instead, I swallowed hard and forced my hands to unclench. Then, I held up my hands to show her my palms before walking away.

* * *

I got home and thought about my ex-girlfriend, Lois. The week after Poppy Lavell had re-entered my life, I visited Lois. Lois Chan was a primary school teacher who worked at the Church of England school in Middleton.

I knocked on her door, and when she opened the door, with a surprised look on her face, I said, "Lois, please tell me what I did wrong because I don't want to make the same mistake again."

"Again?" she repeated, her eyes narrowing. "Are you seeing someone?"

I wasn't too fond of it when her eyes narrowed. "Why? Are you jealous?" I snapped.

"No, I'm bloody not—"

"You are, aren't you? I can see it in your eyes. The way you narrowed them. That or you're thinking, how the fuck have I managed to find somebody else? Right? Always so judgemental, my love." I took a step closer

She tightened her mouth into an almost invisible line. "Don't you dare take another step!"

"You're wrong, you know. You and your friends. You're all wrong—"

"You need to leave. Now!"

"Lois," I started, softening my voice.

"I'm going back inside now, and when I flick on the kettle and come back to check, you won't be here. Right?" She stared at me so intensely that I backed off. "Do you understand?"

Do you understand? Like I was some sort of fucking idiot, incapable of comprehending basic English. I was right about her. She'd never be happy, and I deserved so much better than her.

"Yes, Miss Chan. I understand," I sneered at her.

"Good," she said, nodding. She turned on her heel, marched inside, and slammed the door shut without looking back even once. I watched her go, taking in that fine form I'd once desired. Lois was still pretty, with her exotic looks and black hair. But compared to Poppy, it was hard to imagine that I had once thought Lois was something special.

After walking away, I paused and looked back at her house for a moment, my hands shaking. I guess I still hated her, even after a year. She'd changed the locks about a week after dumping me via text, not that the new locks had stopped me. I knew I could easily break the glass panel beside the door, snake my arm through the hole I'd created, and let myself inside her house.

Once inside, I could have smashed the many vases that lined every window and every cabinet top, an affectation that drove me mad. I could have ripped the covers from her favourite crime novels that resided on her flimsy IKEA bookcase or deleted the crime documentaries from her Sky box. Though, in truth, I'd begun to like crime documentaries myself. I'd recently watched one set in LA that involved a Chinese-Canadian tourist. I also could have smashed up the Disney ornaments that littered every surface, many of which I'd bought for her during our two weeks together.

But what I really wanted to do was wait until dark and hide in the shadows until she returned home and—

But I didn't do any of that because I'd moved on.

Poppy Lavell was everything I'd ever wanted. And more.

Chapter Twenty-seven

"You just can't help yourself, can you, Son?" Bill said to me. "Always making a mess. Look at the state of the fucking tablecloth!"

"Sorry, Dad, I'll take it home and clean it for you." He was such a prick. I'd spilt gravy by accident. But accidents didn't matter to him. They didn't exist. Everything happened for a reason. And usually, the reason was that I was a clumsy bastard.

Because I was a bastard, a child born out of wedlock, and my dad never gave up an opportunity to remind me of that.

"Let us pray," my dad said. It was the same routine during our weekly meal. I didn't believe in God, but he did. The fucking idiot! God will not save you from what I have planned for you, Dad.

I cut into a juicy sausage and brought it up to my mouth, the juice dripping onto the tablecloth. Shit!

But before my dad started about the tablecloth again, he sniffed and asked in his most complaining way: "What the hell is that dreadful smell?"

"What smell? The sausages?" I sniffed at the air.

"Silly bastard. Can't you smell it?"

"I can just smell our tea, Dad."

"My food wouldn't smell bad like that. Something stinks." The prick raised an accusing eye. "I think the stink is coming from you. Haven't you showered today?"

"Of course I have!"

"But you stink of cat shit. Been hiding in bushes again, boy?"

I ate another sausage, revelling in delight as more juice dripped from the sausage and onto the tablecloth. I saw my dad's fingers clench around his knife. Go on, you prick, I dare you.

Yet the strike came from his other hand as he swung the fork through the air, stabbing the sausage.

"I'm waiting to hear you say sorry, Son."

"Sorry," I said. We both then ate, a heavy silence filling the air.

"I want to hear you apologise," Dad said.

"I apologise then," I said.

"I don't call that an apology," said my dad.

"Well, I said sorry, and I said I apologise," I pointed out. "What else do you want me to say?"

"You could say what you're sorry for," Dad suggested, a smile stretching from ear to ear.

He was taunting me, daring me to challenge him over a tablecloth I'd already promised to clean and had apologised twice for. "All right. I apologise for dripping juice and gravy on the tablecloth. I promised to clean it for you," I said, hoping it would now mean peace, knowing for a fact that it wouldn't. By adding the 'I promised to clean for you' to the end of my sentence, I'd invalidated the entire apology.

"That didn't seem like much of an apology to me, Son. In fact, I'd say it wasn't an apology at all. You always have to ruin a good night, don't you?" He stabbed his final sausage. "I don't know why you bother coming any more. You never look happy to see me."

"Do you blame me? You constantly remind me of being a bastard, and you're a prick!" I wanted to say, but I held my tongue. So, instead, I let the silence take hold; it was only broken by the clinking of metal on ceramic.

"You're the most ungrateful son a father could ask for," Bill eventually said.

I could hardly believe what I was hearing. "How am I?"

"I brought you up alone after that mother of yours fucked off!

"She didn't fuck off, Dad!" I said. "She died."

"And I've never had a thank you for bringing you up on my own—not one," Bill said, ignoring me. I don't think you realise how much of a sacrifice I made for your benefit, Son. I had so many plans I had to cancel to look after you. We've never been abroad because of your ridiculous fear of planes."

I shook my head and was about to defend myself when Bill spoke.

"So, Son, I'll say nothing more about your rudeness tonight as long as what I hear from you in return is a proper expression of thanks to me for all I have done for you."

Again, I tried to speak, but Bill held up his hand.

"Do you even care about me, Son? Do you love me? I'm your father. I've sacrificed my life for you. Is it too much to ask for you to be grateful for once?"

Desperately, I said, "What—" but was once again interrupted.

"I sometimes think," Bill said vigorously, "that you were born without a scrap of gratitude, boy. You're so much like your mother that it hurts. She was ungrateful, too. It's why she fucked off!"

"But I am grateful, Dad," I lied. In truth, I wasn't grateful to him at all. I gave and gave and gave but received nothing but abuse in return.

"Sometimes, Son, I don't think you'd even care if I were to drop dead at your feet."

"I would care," I whispered. I'd care because it would stop my ambition of killing you myself.

He said nothing, and so I added, "Fine, Dad. To prove to you that I care, I want you to come to mine for a meal. I'll cook. Tomorrow night. Please?"

My dad nodded, and I smiled.

* * *

A uniform dropped Ruby Kaur off at home that night after she had provided a statement to Detective Sergeant Wood at Elland Road Station.

The beautiful brunette detective had taken Ruby seriously and had put her mind at ease. But, despite that, she locked her doors, turned on all the lights once she was inside, and barricaded herself in her bedroom.

DS Wood had promised to find her stalker. But Ruby wasn't sure the gorgeous detective could keep her promise. From the look on the young Detective Constable's face who'd accompanied the sergeant, they wouldn't get much from only a mobile phone and a box of dead flowers.

A rustle and the sound of a bin lid snapping shut made Ruby jump.

Calm down, Ruby, calm down. It's only the police collecting the box for evidence.

But then there was a knock at the door. Firm and hard.

What did she do? Did she ignore it? I was only the police, right? Right?

But what if it was the murderer?

Or her new stalker?

What if the murderer was her new stalker?

Then her phone rang, and she screamed.

* * *

The grainy black and white CCTV printout greeted me as I entered Sainsbury's Local—just before my shift to buy a bottle of Lucozade—pinned to the automatic door. It was inevitable, really. I knew that. Even so, I stroked my scratchy chin self-consciously as I looked at the image taken outside Slice of Italy with Phoebe Widdop.

Despite the drastic changes I'd made to my appearance, the image pinned to the doors still set me on edge as, after all, I was still the man in the photo. If they managed to get a higher-resolution picture, I'd be fucked anyway, as I couldn't change the shape of my nose, chin, profile, or build. Not quickly, anyway.

"Alright, Bill, mate?" Afzal said. He pointed to the poster. "An officer brought it in and asked if they could stick it up. I won't lie to you, mate; I thought it was you at first. That brown mop of yours is proper recognisable!" He laughed, pointing to the man's head in the picture.

"Why are they looking for him?" I asked.

"Took a girl out on a date and then tried to kill her. Mad, innit! Local girl, too."

"That defo ain't me, mate," I said with a shrug, running my

hand through my platinum locks.

"Aye, I can see that. When did ya dye ya hair?"

"Monday night after work," I lied. It was a stupid lie, one I regretted immediately because I'd attended work on Wednesday, and Afzal had been on shift with me. "I think it was then. It could have been Wednesday night, actually. I'm losing track of days, mate."

Afzal nodded, but his narrowed eyes slid back to the picture.

"I wouldn't be out dating a lass anyway. I'm gay." Again, as soon as the lie left my mouth, I regretted it. Frank had been in here spouting about the fact he'd seen me with Phoebe, and whilst Afzal said he hadn't heard that part of the conversation, how could I be sure?

Did I need to kill Afzal, too? A dead man can share no secrets.

"You're gay?" I nodded. "Are you? Shit. I had no idea, mate! I thought I saw you cracking on with a bird in 'ere last week or the week before. Bloody hell."

What a gullible idiot. "I never said because it's not anyone's business, is it? But yeah, I fancy men." I winked at him, and he moved back with an awkward look. I knew Afzal came from an ultra-conservative family where homosexuality was frowned upon, so I hoped he'd move on from the subject.

Afzal laughed. "Aye, Bill, nobody's business but yours. Anyway, mate, you start in a bit, don't you?" I nodded. "Best leave you to get ready."

I started to walk into the back when Afzal said, "Oh, by the way, the boss is after you."

Shit! I gritted my teeth. I wasn't in the mood to deal with her, to be honest, but it was inevitable. As I headed for the staffroom, the stockroom door clattered open.

"Ah, good evening, young man," Jill said grimly, her severe

ginger bob unmoving as she closed the distance. And it was only 10 am. Sarcastic bitch!

"Morning, Jill."

"I'm delighted you've decided to grace us with your presence."

"Sorry, I was ill."

"It's not the first time this month either, is it?" Jill snapped. "I shouldn't have to cover at the last minute because some idiot doesn't want to work his shift." She handed me two letters.

"What are these?"

"Your second and final warnings. I'm not having you come into work when and as you want!"

"I was ill! You can't do this."

"I can, Mr Longbottom and I will, especially when you don't follow procedure. You returned to work in between your sicknesses, hence the warnings. You also didn't call in to let us know."

"I texted. And I emailed. That's enough, right?"

Jill narrowed her eyes at him. "Wrong." She looked at her watch. "You are due to start your shift in one minute. I suggest you get ready and get cracking. There are plenty of people in Middleton who would love your job, Mr Longbottom. If you want to keep it, pull your finger out!"

I was about to argue my case with her, but Jill strolled back into the stock room. So, I cursed under my breath and headed into the staffroom to put my things in my locker. One of these days, I was going to tell her to shove the fucking job up her arse.

Or maybe I could kill her? Both her and Afzal.

Now there's a good idea.

"Are you just gonna stand there all day, mate?" Afzal said,

pointing at a queue of customers that had formed.

"You what, mate?"

"You're staring into space, Bill." I looked around to find he was right. Three customers were tutting at me.

The second customer in line was pale and blonde like Poppy, and as I served her lottery tickets and scratch cards, I wondered what it'd be like to plunge my knife inside her neck.

Chapter Twenty-eight

DC Jason Scott crashed into the silent Incident Room in search of his colleagues. "You scared the shit out of me, Jay," DC Blackburn said.

"Tashan got something from the social media appeal." DI Beaumont and DS Wood entered, and the young DC turned and greeted his superior officers, "Boss, Sarge," before continuing. "A woman's rung in. Harper Verril. She had a one-night stand with a man matching the CCTV image. Phoebe's attacker. She slept with him eight days ago, the day after Chanelle Cummings was murdered."

George, Wood, and Blackburn turned to Scott as one; their attention focused on him. "Go on, Jay," George said.

Jay grinned. "They met on YorkshireFlirt.com, and guess what his name was?"

"Just get on with it, Jay," DS Wood scolded.

"Matthew Longbottom."

"Same guy," Tashan said.

Jay mimicked him. "Same guy."

They clapped hands. "Yes, mate, nice one," Tashan added.

"But, I've checked on the PNC," Scott explained, "and I can't find anyone matching the name Matthew Longbottom."

The DI nodded. "Did they sleep together at his house or

hers?" George asked.

Jay grinned once more. "Harper attended Longbottom's home address in Middleton, but as she's from Otley, she doesn't know the area. She thinks she knows which bus she got into Leeds on the way home. The number 13. Longbottom also met her on the street and brought her back to his. It was dark, so she's really unsure."

George and DS Wood shared a look. The number 13 went down Middleton Park Avenue before crossing Middleton Park Road and down Town Street into Leeds. It was a large area to search, but the net was closing every day.

"Anything else?" George asked.

"Two other things, boss," Jay said. George raised his brow. "Scars."

"Scars?"

"Yes, Roman numerals, she said. Hundreds of them."

"Like Phoebe Widdop?" George asked.

"Like Phoebe Widdop. She also provided 'Longbottom's' profile picture, boss. Like with Phoebe, it's been deleted, but Harper screenshot it. Also, like Phoebe, Harper said the picture isn't an exact match to 'Longbottom' and was probably edited to make him more handsome. However, it's a strong match for the man on CCTV. Here." Jay handed him a colour printout of a blown-up photograph of a man in his mid-twenties with brown hair and blue eyes.

"This is great, Jay. Good job." He could see the pride swell in the young lad. Good. It would make him work even harder. "Right, team, we're looking for someone who looks like this guy," George said, handing the image to DS Wood to pin to the board. "We don't know his name, but from what Jay has just told us, the profile picture matches the man she met. So, we need to focus on him."

Wood said, "The lab has profiled DNA from the brown hair found at the Rose Garden. No match on the database."

"Damn."

"Ruby Kaur saw a man with brown hair fleeing the crime scene," Wood added. "She was in here last night, putting in a statement. She thinks she's being stalked. Ruby found flowers with their heads cut off and received threatening text messages. I sent a uniform and a SOCO to collect the flowers, but somebody had taken them."

"Probably to hide the evidence, Sarge," Jay said. He turned to George. "Right, boss?"

"Right." George turned to Isabella. "What else did Ruby say?"

"She gave me the number, which I gave to Josh, and it turns out it's a burner. Only sent those two messages before it disconnected from the network."

"Right. Could be one of our killers, could be an aggrieved ex." George scratched his spiky chin. "DS Wood, take Jay and find Ruby Kaur. Take the picture of 'Longbottom' with you. See if she recognises him. Also, go over everything with her to ensure we have everything." He turned to Tashan. "Josh will be in soon. When he is, work with him on another appeal. Get that image out there ASAP. Alright?"

His team nodded at him. "I'll update DSU Smith and ask for another warrant. We need data on who 'Longbottom' spoke to using the profile he used to speak to Harper Verril. It looks like we can crack everything once we get all the info from this bloody app!"

* * *

DS Wood and DC Scott returned after a couple of hours and didn't come back with much. Ruby had never heard of the name 'Matthew Longbottom' and couldn't confirm with certainty the man in the profile picture was Frank Hinchcliffe's murderer.

* * *

"Sir," DS Joshua Fry said to George. I have an update. YorkshireFlirt.com has accepted the warrant, and I've managed to obtain some information, though the detailed messaging history, login data, and whatnot won't be available until tomorrow morning. However, basic profile data shows that the woman Frank agreed to meet was called Poppy Lavell. I also have the mobile number she used to sign up."

"The same Poppy Lavell we interviewed before? Chanelle Cummings' friend?"

"The very same, sir."

"OK, great work, Josh," George said and checked his watch. It was 5.30 pm. "Message me the details, and I'll go and see her."

* * *

I eyed the Yorkshire Water van at the end of Back Mount Pleasant, which was sitting and doing nothing. It was my dad's van. What was he doing? Spying on me? Making sure I was going to follow through on my promise? I slipped past the vehicle, down the ginnel, and into my house with my shopping bag.

I'd had a shit day at work because of Jill, and only the thought of seeing my dad had kept me going through the grind.

But before seeing Dad tonight, I had other plans—inevitable plans—something I'd been planning for a while.

* * *

When Poppy arrived home from work, her phone pinged just as she was stripping for the shower. She felt as if she'd had no peace recently. It has to be Kai, she thought as she went back into her room, a towel around her.

Hi, Gorgeous. New Number. Fancy meeting me in the park? We can go for a walk and have a coffee in the Visitor Centre? Kai. X

The park was just down the road. Poppy checked the time and texted back: *That's fine, but I have a lot of work to do, so I can only stay with you for an hour or so.*

He replied: *Brilliant babes, see you soon. XX*

She lifted an arm and sniffed her pit. She was fine but would definitely need a shower when she got home.

I love you, baby girl. XXX

Poppy smiled at the last message. Maybe he had changed. And after everything that had happened with Chanelle and Ruby finding that body, she thought being alone was overrated.

One more chance. That's all he'd get.

* * *

Poppy Lavell hadn't answered her door, even after George had hammered as hard as he could. Had she done a runner?

Maybe.

That usually meant guilt. But then Poppy was blonde, and they'd found a brown hair at the scene.

He dialled the number they had on file for her, but it rang out and went to voicemail. George left a message asking her to contact him ASAP and provided his number. He was just about to leave when a thought struck him. He checked his text messages, and the number Josh had received from the dating app didn't match the number George had just called.

What the hell?

So George called that number, too, assuming she may have changed it in the last week or so. But that didn't connect at all.

He pondered what that meant. Could Poppy have killed Chanelle and Frank? Had Frank been seeing Chanelle behind Poppy's back? Who knew? But they'd have the messages in the morning, and hopefully, that would solve everything.

George called DS Wood and ran it by her.

"I'm not sure, George. Poppy seemed to really love Chanelle, and you usually get a feeling. I didn't think she was involved then, and I'm confused about how she's involved with Frank." Wood paused. "I also don't think there's a link between Frank and Phoebe. I really don't think it was him who tried to kill her. But I do think it's possible the same man attacked all three. The brown hair keeps coming up."

"Yeah, I get that, Wood, but many people have brown hair. We're getting nowhere."

"I sent Sergeant Greenwood out in Phoebe's area with the profile picture of 'Longbottom' on it. People are coming home from work now, so hopefully, if anybody knows anything, Greenwood will find out."

"Good job, Wood. I'll stay here for an hour or so and keep trying Poppy's mobile. If I can't reach her, I have an idea about how we can, but I'm not sure I really want to follow through with it."

* * *

George hummed and hawed for a moment before picking up his mobile and calling the parasite named Paige McGuiness. She answered after two rings. "Paige, it's DI Beaumont."

"It's nice to hear from you, George. What can I do for you?"

"Let's spare the pleasantries," George said. "I need your help, and you want a story."

"I'm intrigued. Go on."

"You're printing the paper tonight. Releasing it tomorrow?"

"That's right, but I can post it on social media and our website straight away."

"I have an image I need circulating. Poppy Lavell, aged twenty-five, from Middleton. We want to speak with her in connection with the murder of Frank Hinchcliffe."

There was a fumbling sound, no doubt putting George on speaker. "Can you email it over to me now?"

"Done," George said.

"And I get an exclusive?"

"Once we find Poppy and clear everything up, I'll provide you with information for your story, alright?"

George didn't want to provide information to hurt Frank's family, but it seemed Poppy and Frank exchanged messages the night before he was murdered. That, and along with the fact that Frank's ring finger and wedding ring were still missing, suggested a jilted lover of some kind. Or an act of revenge.

Frank had brown hair, and whilst they could get no DNA from the hair left behind on Chanelle's body, they did have the partial print of Chanelle's killer.

The lab was trying to match it to Frank. Or that was what

George was hoping. If Frank killed Chanelle and Poppy killed him in revenge, those murders would be nicely tied off. Then, all they had to do was find Phoebe's attacker.

And if that happened to be Frank, then so be it, but George wasn't convinced. The profile picture didn't look anything like Frank, and both Harper and Phoebe had said 'Longbottom' looked very similar to his profile picture.

He also wasn't so sure Poppy was Frank's killer. From what George remembered of Poppy, she was petite, and the post-mortem suggested a taller attacker. That, and the attacker had brown hair and not blonde. Ruby was convinced the culprit was a male, too. But then, she was far away and could have been mistaken.

"So you're promising an exclusive, George."

"Yes."

"I really appreciate this."

George hung up, wondering whether he had made a mistake, and questioned how much the journalist's appreciation was worth.

A moment later, DS Wood knocked on his office door and entered. She shut the door behind her, and George grinned.

Chapter Twenty-nine

I regularly fantasised about the death of my dad. Sometimes, I imagined a terrible accident—like a car crash, him choking on his tea, or being told by his work that he'd fallen and drowned inside the water tower. Other times I imagined doing the deed myself, stabbing the twat, or lacing his tea with rat poison and watching as Bill choked to death.

In my youth, I scoured subreddits, searching for advice. Within minutes, advice trickled in, telling me that having occasional inappropriate thoughts was normal and didn't necessarily mean I would become a serial killer one day.

How wrong those idiots were.

Some dickhead piped up that I clearly had unresolved feelings of resentment toward my dad and advised me to schedule weekly sessions with a licensed therapist.

I remember how hard I'd laughed. I didn't need a professional to tell me I resented my dad. I knew I resented him deep within my bones.

After all, he was the reason why my mum killed herself.

Her dying wish was for my dad and me to have at least one weekly family dinner. However, surviving these dinners without stabbing him was an arduous task, especially when, inevitably, my dad tried to focus on the shortcomings of my personal life.

The dinners were so clichéd that I could predict the menu, conversation, and how much my dad would drink down to the smallest margin of error, despite being at my house instead of his.

Tonight was rare steak, followed by him asking whether I was seeing anybody and would end up with him drinking too much whisky.

"Actually," I said, slicing my steak and thinking of Poppy, "I'm sort of seeing someone."

Silence descended. I put the steak in my mouth and chewed.

"That's great," Dad finally said, his tone a little too earnest.

I knew I shouldn't have told him because he would find a way to ruin things, so I stayed silent.

"Come on, Marshmallow," Dad taunted, using the infantile nickname I had repeatedly requested he stop using. "Who's the lucky girl then?"

Underneath the table, I balled up my fists and squeezed, my nails digging into my palms. The pain steadied me and made me less inclined to grab Dad by his neck and squeeze.

Dad smiled at me sympathetically, and I hated him for it. I dug my nails deeper into my palms to hold back my dark, rage-filled thoughts.

"I'm just having fun," Dad said. "You can take a bit little fun, can't you, Marshmallow?"

I couldn't answer; otherwise, a bloodcurdling scream would come out. Instead, my nails bit through my flesh, causing crescent wounds, and I smiled tightly at my dad as blood trickled down my wrists.

I decided right there and then that I was going to kill him next. I'd poison his dessert.

* * *

It had been a busy nine days for George and his team without a day off, and today was no exception. It was supposed to have been his first weekend off in God-knows-how-long, but it wasn't to be. Maybe if they caught somebody today, he could go and see baby Jack Beaumont tomorrow as he'd promised.

And so, because of that promise, George was outside Poppy Lavell's place, knocking hard, with DS Isabella Wood at his side.

She'd spent the night, and they'd watched the first two episodes of a crime documentary on Netflix.

There was nobody home.

He peered through the letterbox, seeing open doors, stairs covered in a lush brown carpet, and a flurry of unopened mail. Then, again, George banged on the door, his police knock echoing through the house's rooms.

"Place looks deserted to me, Wood. Guess she isn't home," George said, stepping back to look through the letterbox again. "Poppy Lavell. Open up!"

"You think she's done a runner?" Wood asked.

"Looks like it." He nibbled his lip, considering their next move before realising they didn't really have one. Not without a warrant, anyway. As much as he desperately wanted to batter down the door and charge in, they had no probable cause and zero evidence. The data from the dating company hadn't come in yet, and until they had that, no magistrate would sign a warrant. "Fucking hell! I feel like even if she isn't involved in the murder, she's an important piece."

"I know, George. But you need to be patient. I'll take the houses to the right, and you take them to the left. We can ask the neighbours if they've seen her."

"Yeah, good idea, Wood."

The urgency of finding Poppy Lavell drove George. She was involved in some way. He was sure of that. But the desperation had made him sloppy recently. He didn't deserve to be a DI with the terrible decisions he'd made. Isabella would have been a better choice. Maybe he should step down? But where would that leave him? And his team? He felt like an imposter. A man held up by his team. He didn't deserve their respect.

With his head down, George started at the bottom of east Moor Flatts Avenue, where it met North Lingwell Road. As a child, he'd eaten fish and chips from the chippy on that road and even had his hair cut by the barber above the chippy. The chippy had changed hands repeatedly over the years, once owned by a couple from Kent that he regularly spoke with as a teen before being eventually closed down. The barber was now a sweet shop.

George sighed and approached the first house. It was Saturday morning, so he assumed most people would have been in, but hardly any of his searches had yielded a resident, much less anyone who could help.

He turned away from yet another unanswered door, a Yorkshire Water van chugging away, purging one of the drains. He'd seen a lot of them recently but was unsure why.

An older man finally answered a few houses up, squinting up at George through milky eyes.

Blind or visually impaired. It's not ideal, but it's not the older man's fault.

"Who, Poppy? I mean, I can't see much, love," the older man said, "especially with the state of the NHS right now. But Poppy does drop in now and then. Lovely girl."

"Yes, Poppy Lavell. When was the last time you saw her, the last time you spoke with her?"

"It's cataracts I'm struggling with. Been waiting months to get these seen to."

"Yes, well—"

But the man wasn't done. "I struggle enough wi' rheumatoid arthritis acting up wi' the cold. Always worse in October."

"Er, yes, sir. I hope the NHS sorts that out for you. I need to ask: Have you heard anything unusual in the area? Or anything involving Poppy?"

"No, I haven't," he said, turning his head and tapping his hearing aid. "I take this off at night. Some of the young people have loud music on at night! It means I get a decent sleep."

"Do you know if anybody else on this road knows Poppy, sir?"

"Sorry, love. Nothing. Look, it's getting cold. Can I go back in now?"

George nodded, and then the older man slammed the door in his face.

George dutifully went from house-to-house until he bumped into DS Wood, and they shared the results of their enquiries.

Isabella explained how she spoke with Poppy's direct neighbour, who said she hadn't seen Poppy in a couple of days, which was unusual.

Chapter Thirty

"You've reached Poppy Lavell's voicemail. Please leave your message after the tone."

Beep.

"Hey, my love, it's me. I haven't heard from you since yesterday. I hope you're OK. You haven't answered my texts, so I'm going into Wakefield alone. Yes, alone! Because of you, even when there's a murderer out there. Jokes. Well, it's partly a joke. Anyway, ring me when you get this, yeah? And I'll pop by your house on the way home. Ring me, babe. Love ya."

That Saturday morning, Ruby scanned the street and, for a moment, wondered where her car was before remembering she'd had to park it down the road because a car was in her spot last night.

Thankfully, it was gone, and she hoped it would be gone when she got back. But, before heading down the street towards her car, she checked the street for people hiding in the shadows, for people with their hoods up.

The morning was cool, and a refreshing breeze blew through Ruby's dark hair. To her left, a black cat prowled along a garden wall. It was Halloween next week. With a murderer running about, she'd lock her doors, turn out the lights, and ignore all knocking.

As Ruby approached her car, her heart dropped.

Fuck.

Her tyres had been slashed, the rubber completely shredded, and the alloy rims of her car resting heavily against the road.

"What the fuck?" she shouted, horrified. She turned around full circle, searching the houses for CCTV, but saw nothing.

As she walked the entire perimeter of her car, she saw that all four tyres had been destroyed.

Who would do something like that?

Then she thought back to the threatening messages and the decapitated flowers.

Perhaps this was the same person?

Should I call the police?

No. It could have been the scallywags that vandalised Middleton daily.

But when Ruby checked the other cars nearby, they were all fine, with only her tyres shredded. So she stood there, wondering what to do when her phone went off.

She quickly tapped at it, hoping the message was from Poppy. But it was from Shae. They'd agreed to meet at the Costa in Wakefield again. And, like last time, she'd be forced to get the bloody bus.

But then she thought about the murderer stalking the streets and decided an Uber was probably safer. Shae could drop her off at Poppy's on the way home, and she could see why her best friend was ignoring her.

So she dumped her bag on the bonnet of her car, freeing her hands to use the app for an Uber. Whoever had slashed her tyres was selfish, an idiot who just wanted to ruin people's lives. It didn't rain but poured—one of her late father's favourite sayings.

She barely had any signal outside, and the app wouldn't work right. Then she realised she had the Wi-Fi still on, and it was connecting this far away from the house. No wonder the signal sucked.

Ruby turned off the Wi-Fi and eventually entered her destination into the app to request a ride.

As the app told Ruby it was searching for a driver, a man's voice said, "Good morning!"

Shocked, Ruby turned to find a man standing there, wearing Nike trainers, black jeans, and a black hoodie. He'd dyed his hair platinum blond and wasn't unattractive. Like a Targaryen from her favourite show. Not her type, though. Not really. He wasn't a woman.

"Morning," Ruby replied, trying to quell the nerves from the shock. She smiled politely but began tapping away on her phone.

"I'm Matty." He went to shake Ruby's hand, but as she flinched back, he held up his palms and stepped back. "Sorry." He smiled and then asked, "Everything OK?"

"Yes." Matty raised a brown brow. "Well, no. I'm having some issues. An idiot has decided to slash my tyres, and I'm trying to get an Uber," Ruby explained, pointing at the car.

Matty's face fell. "Oh, shit." He looked down at Ruby's tyres, his eyes widening. "That's awful."

"Yep," Ruby grumbled.

He knelt to get a closer look. "Christ. It looks like somebody really did a number on these."

"Yep. Just last weekend, a vandalising shite rubbed dogshit all over my car. I had to wash it off. I threw my clothes in the bin after because they were beyond saving. And now this!"

Matty smiled as if he knew something about that and said,

"Oh dear, really? That's just terrible."

"Yep." She looked back at her phone, bored of the stranger already, but honestly, unnerved by his lingering gaze.

"Can I help at all?" Matty asked.

"Not unless you can get four tyres for me and then fit them for me."

Ruby smiled whilst Matty shook his head. "I could fit them, but I can't get the tyres for you. Sorry."

"There you go then. My driver is seven minutes away. Thanks for coming over."

"No problem. Hey, listen. Are you sure your tyres got slashed?" Matty asked, rising from his crouch.

"Well, yeah! They didn't exactly do that to themselves, did they?" Ruby snapped.

Matty looked at her, suddenly shocked, slighted by Ruby's tone. He raised a brown brow. He looked familiar, but she wasn't sure why. It was the way his brow arched when he was annoyed. She'd seen him recently. She was sure.

"Do I know you, Matty?"

He shook his head and went to walk away.

"Look, I'm sorry," Ruby said. "This has really stressed me out." She pointed at her car.

Matty smiled. "No problem. And no, this is the first time we've met. Trust me, I'd know."

He winked, and Ruby smiled just enough not to offend him but hopefully not enough to think she was trying it on with him.

"I only asked about the slashing of your tyres because there's some broken glass down by the kerb," Matty said, gesturing to the broken glass glinting in the morning light.

Ruby bent down to inspect the road, finding that Matty

was right. Broken glass—smashed green beer bottles—was scattered around her tyres.

Had I driven over the glass last night and not noticed?

She wasn't sure, but the paranoia was getting to her. Somebody was following her; she knew that for sure.

"It's unfair, Ruby. The council should have cleared this up," Matty said sympathetically as he went to leave, looking genuinely concerned and sorry for her. The look on his face made her feelings soften towards him. She also didn't pick up on never telling him her name. "I'll see you later," he said with a smile.

You won't, she thought. Despite how friendly Matt had been to her, she didn't want to see him again.

When Matty turned to the right to head back from where he came from, Ruby was sure she'd seen him before somewhere, but she couldn't put her finger on it. "Are you sure we don't know each other?"

"I'm sure."

She wanted to pick apart their histories and see whether their paths had crossed at some point. He sounded local, so maybe she'd seen him out and about. But no matter what she did, she couldn't figure out where she knew him from.

Then her thoughts were interrupted by the sound of a car honking behind her, her Uber driver, which she confirmed via the app.

"Sorry, Matty, my lift's here. It was nice of you to stop and offer your help," Ruby said.

Matty smiled as she got into the car. "No problem at all, Ruby. I do hope your day gets better."

* * *

After watching the taxi containing Ruby pull out of the street, I broke in. It wasn't the first time. I'd spent the last few days watching her. The stupid idiot left a key in the back garden and didn't even have an alarm. And in Miggy of all places. It was like she wanted her house to be broken into.

I searched for a while, sat on her sofa, and looked through her recordings on her Sky box. Checked the fridge. Stole some underwear. The usual, really.

I found treasure at the bottom of her underwear drawer, covered by silky knickers and thongs.

Her diary.

Dear diary, I'm having trouble sleeping. Every time I put my head on my pillow, I hear phantom footsteps and faint scratches outside my window. I thought it was just the wind, but just in case, I hung thicker curtains to shield myself from the stalker I assumed was out there and to block out the terrifying noises of the night. Unfortunately, I think the thicker curtains have stopped me from sleeping, though, because if someone is out there, then I wouldn't know about it—so I began leaving the curtains slightly cracked.

I can still hear the footsteps and scratches.

Losing Chanelle already put me on edge, and then I started having nightmares about the body I found. His name was Frank Hinchcliffe, and he had a wife and young child. Every night, I dream the same dream of running through the woods, coming across the body in the Rose Garden, and seeing that dark hooded reaper with a sharp knife in his hand.

And sometimes, when I've finished dreaming about seeing Frank's body, I dream about being asleep in my bed and awoken by a guy outside my window with a knife.

It's convinced me the murderer is the one who stood outside my window, scratching like a vampire wanting to come in, his eyes obscured by his hood and his gloved hand wrapped around a kitchen knife.

One night this week, I thought I heard a voice, so I bolted upright in bed, looking wildly around for the source that had awakened me, only to find the room empty.

I've become so paranoid that I downloaded an app to record my sleep and any irregular noises. The idea was that people used it to figure out what was disturbing their sleep.

In my case, I was the only thing disrupting my sleep.

Yes, me.

There were no phantom footsteps and faint scratches coming from outside.

There was no voice other than my own.

And when I woke up, terrified and petrified with fear, I checked the app on my phone and listened to the most recent recording to reassure myself that nobody was watching me sleep.

But Ruby was wrong.

Very wrong.

Because those 'phantom footsteps' were mine. It was me scratching the windows. I was the dark hooded reaper, watching her, waiting, stalking, my gloved hand wrapped around a kitchen knife.

Chapter Thirty-one

Ruby Kaur left the bedroom and felt a shiver run down her spine as if someone were watching her from behind. She tightened the belt of her pink dressing gown and checked over her shoulder to find nothing but shadows.

She walked down the stairs; her nerves were shot despite knowing she'd locked the doors when she returned from visiting Poppy's house, where Shae had dropped her off after their coffee.

Poppy wasn't there and still wasn't answering her phone. It was unusual, but Poppy had acted this way before. Whilst Ruby worshipped the ground she walked on, Poppy sometimes could be a bit of a drama queen. And recently, with that Billy guy catfishing her, she'd been acting differently.

She opened the fridge and took out a chocolate fudge cake she'd been eating for the last few days; the movement of her arm stretching to the back of the fridge meant her dressing gown fell open again, uncovering her toned stomach and small breasts.

Usually, Ruby would immediately cover herself up. However, she'd locked the doors and closed all the curtains, and despite still not feeling safe, Ruby knew she couldn't live with the paranoia forever.

She shivered as she pulled a chef's knife from the block and then cut a small slice of the fudge cake, not bothering to warm it up in the microwave, and popped it straight into her mouth.

Dropping the knife on the counter with a clang, Ruby left the rest of the cake out and went to the kettle, fancying a cuppa. She only drank Yorkshire Tea and liked it strong, with two sweeteners. In her opinion, it was the only way to drink it. She hated the way Poppy put milk in first and the way Chanelle liked her tea bag dunked in and out, so she was drinking tea-flavoured milk.

Ruby missed her friends dearly, and despite having Shae, she felt so alone.

The kettle clicked; she poured the hot water over the tea bag to let it stew and headed into the living room to phone her cousin, Priti. But as she picked up her mobile from the coffee table, Ruby was sure she'd heard a noise. Like a person trying to creep on the stairs.

It sent her pulse sky-high, and she considered ringing triple nine rather than her cousin.

She listened for a moment, for the tell-tale creak of a stalker, but heard nothing. So she dialled her cousin.

"Hi, Priti, it's only me," she said. "How are you?"

"Hello, cousin, I'm good, thanks, and you?"

Before Ruby could answer, she heard something rustling and looked towards the dark hallway leading to the front door, where she usually hung her coat and left her shoes.

"Ruby?"

"Sorry, Priti, I thought I heard a noise. Just the wind, I guess."

"Are you coming tomorrow?" Priti asked.

"I don't know," Ruby said as she headed back upstairs and

into the bathroom. She'd forgotten to take her medication today and found the blister pack of fluoxetine on the basin, the green-and-white capsules dull in the fading light.

Ruby looked at the sad, scared reflection in the mirror. The bathroom door was open behind her so she could see the stairs. As Ruby strained her eyes, it looked as if somebody were standing there, and her heart raced once more despite knowing it was nothing but a trick of the light. It could also be her coat that she threw on the newel post at the bottom.

"Aww, why not? I haven't seen you in ages."

Ruby smiled. It was nice to be missed. To be loved. "I'm not in the right frame of mind, to be honest, Preet." She turned to head towards her bedroom, the phone wedged against her cheek and shoulder.

It was the only window in the house she hadn't covered with a curtain, and she immediately felt self-conscious about her dressing gown being open.

"You sure I can't change your mind, Rubes?" Priti asked.

"No," Ruby said weakly as she forced herself to look away from the window, catching sight of herself in the mirror. This time, there was only the bed behind her. She took in her form, which she wished Poppy appreciated, with her small round breasts and toned stomach. She wondered for a moment what it would have been like to have had a cock. Would Poppy have appreciated her then?

Probably not.

Her crush on Poppy had always remained a secret, as had her bisexuality. The issue was at sixteen, she'd got pregnant. It had been her first and only time with a man. And as luck would have it, the condom had split.

The long pink scar above her dark pubic hair and across her

pubic line betrayed her. Ruby had told everybody that she'd lost the baby, but after the caesarean section, she'd given up her daughter for adoption. She didn't want a child back then and didn't ever see that changing. Ten years later, Ruby didn't regret her decision. She just wished she could tell someone, but the fear and the disappointment Ruby knew she'd face were too much.

The constant anxiety was the reason she was taking fluoxetine.

"Look, I gotta go, Preet. I love you. Speak soon."

"Love you, cuz!"

As she put her mobile down, she saw the trees shaking in the wind outside and considered closing the curtains.

But she decides to be brave instead, turns off the light, and takes off her dressing gown, hanging it on the door.

She then crossed the room to open the chest of drawers before becoming confused. The fluoxetine helped with her OCD, but she always ordered her knickers by colour.

Somebody had mixed them up. And that somebody wasn't her.

Suddenly, she felt like she was being watched again. She glanced out the window, squinting at the shadows in the garden and the leaves rustling in the wind.

Then, there was a thud from the landing behind her, and she jumped. It was the letterbox—probably another bloody takeaway menu. The heating was on in the house, but still, she shivered. As if somebody had walked across her grave.

She trained her ear, listening for signs of an intruder, but heard nothing.

So she chanced a step forward. Nothing.

She walked down the stairs. Nothing.

Then, a sound from the kitchen drew her to the counter, and when she walked over, the knife she used to slice the fudge cake was gone.

Did she put it in the sink? Was her medicine making her confused? Did she take it upstairs?

She must have.

So, Ruby crept back up the stairs and headed to the bathroom.

She turned to head towards the sink when, in the mirror, she saw a dark hooded form sprint towards her, knife in its hand, an evil grin on its face.

It was the person from her nightmares. This isn't real, she told herself. It's just the medication.

So she stood still, eyes closed, not believing what was happening.

But the sound of the person panting was too real, and as she opened her eyes, she saw Matty, the man who tried to help her this morning, with her chef's knife raised high.

It penetrated straight through her collarbone, high up to her left.

Ruby's legs collapsed under her just as Matty pulled out the knife, and she fell, her knees hitting the wooden floor.

"Why?" Ruby whispered as Matty dragged her to the foot of the staircase.

Matty pulled down his hood and smiled. "Because you saw me, Ruby. You saw me kill Frank. You were just a loose end I had to tie up."

She could feel the hot blood pulsing down her breast and onto her stomach, a deep burning pain spreading across her chest.

Any lower, and he'd have got her heart.

"But I didn't even really see you, Matty."

"I couldn't take that chance, Rubes."

The pain forced her to her knees, and she felt movement above her, unable to move, unable to understand Matty's motivation.

"I still don't know who you are. Leave me alone," she breathed. "Let me call an ambulance. I'll say—I'll say I can't remember what happened," she whispered.

Then she felt a blow to her head and a terrible pain in the back of her neck. She fell forward, lying flat. Then he turned her over onto her back.

He wanted to watch as the light in her eyes died.

And then he thrust once again, piercing her right lung. Ruby began coughing up frothy blood and stared at the ceiling, not meeting her murderer's eyes.

Then she felt the knife blade being thrust in and pulled out of her chest repeatedly until her heart began to stop, and everything went quiet.

* * *

DI Beaumont and DS Wood stood still until their eyes adjusted to the darkness. The smell of copper permeated the air. It was hot. And from the other smell in the air, the body was already beginning to rot.

Sticky blood had cascaded down the stairs, pooling at the bottom.

George's mask moved rapidly from his breathing as beads of sweat broke out on his forehead.

It was far too hot in here.

The pair followed Lindsey Yardley up the stairs, a safe

passage created by her team of SOCOs. Whoever had killed Ruby had left footprints on the stairs in blood. He wondered whether the prints would match the ones found in Chanelle's back garden.

She must have read his mind as Lindsey said, "We've taken pictures and will try to match the footprints to your other crime scenes. They're large, so I'd say a male did this."

George didn't want to take a long time in the house because he knew that a crime scene changed over time and was gradually destroyed as people walked in and out in shoe covers, destroying the microscopic evidence that was usually left behind.

That's why they used a common approach path, but it was difficult when evidence was contained to a narrow staircase. Luckily, the SOCOs had already taken everything they needed from the stairs. George's only job was to approach the body and the actual murder scene with caution. That, and to ask the right questions. Who. What. And why.

"I need you to be quick, DI Beaumont," Yardley said. "To get an accurate time of death, I haven't changed the temperature in here, but leaving her body here any longer means it will deteriorate further and risk compromising the evidence. OK?"

"OK," George said. "So what have we got?"

"Not much else, to tell you the truth, DI Beaumont."

Shit!

Lindsey's paper suit rustled as she pointed towards the bedroom, where two SOCOs were photographing and bagging up evidence.

"We think she was stabbed there first, where she fell down, before being dragged closer to the stairs. Marks in the blood trail suggest she was kicking at the time, so she was conscious."

"Go on."

"Then she was stabbed again, there." Lindsey pointed to where the naked body lay. "From the blood pattern, she was flat on the ground before being flipped over. Then it looks like she was stabbed again, repeatedly."

"Anything else you can tell me?" George asked.

"Not until we get her back and Dr Ross has a look. No murder weapon, so the culprit took it with him. But it looks as if a knife is missing from the block downstairs."

George nodded, and Lindsey directed him towards a window. "If I had to guess, I'd say your killer went out of the back door, then that way, over the fence into the grounds of the next-door neighbour. I have two CSIs out there, looking." Then, as if by magic, bright lights illuminated the garden.

"That's a guess, though, DI Beaumont," Lindsey stressed. "There are depressions in the grass leading to the fence, but they could be unconnected." She shrugged. "Still, he had to go somewhere, so I'd say that's your best bet."

"Wouldn't the culprit have been bloody, though?"

"True, but if he'd been careful with his clothing choice, then he might not have been covered as much as you think."

"And do you think he was?" George asked. "Careful?"

"Dr Ross would know more than me," Lindsey said.

"How many times was she stabbed?" DS Wood said. She looked down at the naked woman who was smeared in blood.

"I don't know, as I haven't moved the body," Lindsey said, raising a brow. "Dr Ross will be able to tell you."

"What I can tell you is that there are no visible marks or injuries to the insides of the thighs."

The two detectives nodded. At least she wasn't raped.

"And there were no defensive wounds. But, from the spray, the attack came from the front."

"So why didn't she defend herself?" George asked.

"Well, that's your job, DI Beaumont."

"Fair enough. Anything else?" George asked as Hayden Wyatt, the blond American, bent down by Ruby Kaur. George watched as the man expertly scraped under her fingernails, adding the contents to ten tubes—one for each nail—and labelling them.

"Nope."

Chapter Thirty-two

George pointed at the victim's photograph, which DS Wood had pinned to the board behind him, took a deep breath, and composed his thoughts. "The victim is twenty-six-year-old Ruby Kaur."

"The name sounds familiar, boss," DC Scott said.

"It'll be familiar to you all," George explained, "because she was the witness who saw Frank Hinchcliffe's murderer at the scene. She was also the best friend of Chanelle Cummings and Poppy Lavell."

Ruby Kaur's picture showed a woman who looked full of life. She looked happy and content, a stark contrast to the state of the body George had just seen. And that made him angry, and his fists balled tight.

"Ruby was at home in Middleton when she was attacked. No signs of sexual assault. Yolanda's on CCTV as we speak, looking at cameras in the area. Tashan is with her, searching for private cameras. Sergeant Greenwood is with them, too, and he will liaise with you, Luke. OK?"

"The usual, boss? Reassurance patrols and uniform conducting house-to-house enquiries?"

"That's right. DS Wood has received information from the public that she's following up on regarding the CCTV from

Rothwell. I'm going to see Dr Ross." He turned to DC Jay Scott. "That leaves you to carry out more background checks on Ruby Kaur."

"Who found her body, boss?" Jay asked.

"Priti Kaur. Her cousin. Apparently, they chatted last night, so the death must have occurred after. Wood took a statement."

"Yeah, Priti said Ruby was worried about being stalked, which aligns with her statement I took on Thursday."

Wood felt guilty for that. She'd personally taken Ruby's statement, but there wasn't much they could have done with the information. The phone had been a burner, and the SIM was a Tesco Mobile pay-as-you-go. Could she have done more?

"Josh is working on the message data from Yorkshire-Flirt.com. They didn't send it yesterday, and he had to chase it up. We needed to see if Ruby was on the same dating app, so DSU Smith woke the magistrate and got them to sign a warrant."

Then, as if by magic, Josh popped his head into the Incident Room. "Sir, there's no Ruby Kaur registered to that mobile on YorkshireFlirt.com. The messages between Frank and Poppy were flirty, and they agreed to meet up at the Rose Garden in Middleton Park. But the number, as you said, sir, doesn't match the one we had on file for Poppy Lavell. The provider of that number is Tesco Mobile. It's pay-as-you-go, and I'm on hold with them now."

Tesco Mobile again. Was there a pattern? "Cheers, Josh; keep me informed."

Then, as if reading his mind, DS Wood said, "Josh, the number harassing Ruby Kaur before her death was also a Tesco pay-as-you-go. Could they be connected?"

"I'll check, Wood," he said, leaving the Incident Room.

"Right, Jay. I need you to delve deeper into Ruby Kaur's life. Priti's statement is on HOLMES, so make sure you keep up. I want to know who her friends and colleagues are. Everything you can think of. There was no break-in, which may suggest Ruby let them in."

"Oh, actually, George, Priti told me that Ruby left a spare key in the garden under a gnome. Unfortunately, it's missing," DS Wood explained.

"Shit. Right. Let's hope Yolanda and Tashan find something on CCTV."

He looked around at his team. "Do we all know what we're doing?"

They all shouted, "Yes, sir!" in unison before leaving and cracking on.

* * *

After killing Ruby last night, I couldn't possibly go to work today. Fuck them. They didn't deserve the presence of a God! So I emailed in sick and did precisely what that bitch Jill advised me not to do.

Then I decided to see how my dad's corpse was doing downstairs in the cellar. It had been a right job hauling Bill down the steep, narrow stairs, especially with the cramped confines of the back-to-back terrace.

I'd placed Bill's dead body in the nook behind the underside of the stairs so only his legs poked out, wrapped in a dark sheet so that the cellar would look empty at a glance down the stairs. The idiot police weren't on to me, anyway. I'd made sure of that with the various burner phones and identities.

As I opened the cellar door, I could already smell Bill and wrinkled my nose in disgust. Of course, with the time of year—autumn—and the cold nature of the cellar- I'd hoped he'd remain cold and not decay. Like a morgue, I supposed. But then, they have fridges, don't they? Actual fridges. But in my case, the cellar clearly wasn't cold enough to prevent the cloying, pungent smell of death and decay that grew heavier with each step I descended.

I knew then, though I'd always suspected, I'd have to find a way to get rid of him, but there was no way for me to get a body out without being caught. I chastised myself for being so careless as I tramped back up the stairs. I should have killed him at his own house as I'd tried with Phoebe. But it was too late now. I'd have to find a solution where I wouldn't get caught.

I held my breath for a while and fingered my trophies: Ruby's bracelet, Frank's ring, and Chanelle's bracelet. I'd tossed Frank's stinking finger down the drain already.

I shut the cellar door firmly behind me and locked it before I moved through the kitchen to the living room. I swallowed great gulps of the much fresher air but could not get the smell of death out of my nose. I grabbed a beer from the fridge and went to crash on the sofa, running my free hand through the darkened stubble on my jaw.

The more beer I drank, the more my anxiety abated. My dad's body could wait for a few more days. The problem was that the more I drank, the more the hunger warred within, And I desired to seek the thrill of murder again. I'd already been warming up a girl on the YorkshireFlirt.com app who looked much like Harper, Poppy, and Phoebe, but she was taking far too long to say yes. She had work tomorrow, apparently.

* * *

An hour later, Sophia finally agreed to meet me later that evening in Morley.

I wasn't sure whether I'd take her home or go to hers, but if she left me no choice, she'd be welcome here. But the smell that assaulted me whenever I entered the kitchen was making me paranoid.

I looked at my phone, and it was too late to nip out to the shops now. I'd researched it online, and I needed strong acid to dissolve my dad's body. I wasn't relishing that part of affairs. The fun was in the killing, not the aftermath, but if I wanted to avoid the clutches of the law and keep killing, then I would have to do the dirty work, too.

I showered, changed into my best clothes, and headed towards the bus stop to get the number 46 to Morley. Unfortunately, my dad's Yorkshire Water van was still on Back Mount Pleasant, and with the late Sunday hour, I found the stillness of the street eerie. I'd need to dump the van somewhere. And soon. His keys jingled in my pocket.

The eeriness was the paranoia taking hold. The picture on the door at work. That Afzal had made a comment likening my appearance to the man.

Suspicion crept around the edges of my self-control, and I didn't like it. I wondered if this was how my prey felt. Did they feel the exact sensation I was feeling now, the one that forced you to look over your shoulder and out of sight, convinced someone was watching?

Had I been too cocky?

CHAPTER THIRTY-TWO

Were the coppers watching me?

I told my weak thoughts to fuck off!

The urge was more potent than the fear. I loved the power and how it made me feel as I watched their life fade away. And I already wondered how I'd kill Sophia.

* * *

I got off the bus to yawning shadows stretching between the tall buildings of Morley as I walked up High Street towards Queen Street. The darkness and the shadows calmed my nerves, shrouding me from onlookers and hiding my dark thoughts from any scrutiny.

Sophia Hardaker waited for me in the bar at the JD Wether-spoon on Queen Street, which was surprisingly rowdy for a Sunday night, though with the cheap alcohol and food, not unexpected. But, unlike the cosy Italian in Rothwell, we'd be lost in the crowds and not be seen on CCTV.

Sophia stood, beautiful in a brown jacket and black pencil skirt, the shiny black stilettos elongating her shapely legs so that when I greeted her, she turned, only slightly looking up. Sophia was taller than any of the other women, even taller than Chanelle. She was several years younger than me, just twenty-one, and I could see the nerves and inexperience from her body language and the way her voice shook.

How I already wanted her to succumb to me.

"Nice to meet you, Sophia."

"Hello, Matthew." She smiled, and we embraced. I kissed her on each cheek, and she blushed.

"What would you like to drink?" I asked, my tone casual as I jerked my thumb towards the bar. Sophia removed her jacket and folded it over her arm. Her tits were small, but I'd heard that anything more than a handful was a waste. "Oh, a glass of white would be great, thanks."

"Shall we sit here?" I asked, not waiting for an answer and guiding her, my hand glancing against her lower back to a table for two in a corner out of the way. Then I headed to the bar, my head down until the bartender served me.

"Thank you for agreeing to this at such short notice," I said, smiling warmly at her. "I have to go down to London for three weeks tomorrow," I lied.

She downed her glass, and I offered another. I bought a bottle this time. Alcohol was one of the steps I used to disarm them so that I could strike when they least expected it.

Chapter Thirty-three

"My name's Afzal."

"Hi, Afzal; I'm Detective Sergeant Wood. I believe you have some information for us?" Isabella answered, her pen poised, ready to record anything. The man had left his name and number with the helpline set up to help find Phoebe Widdop's attacker.

"Yeah," said the man, his tone troubled. "Look, it might be nothin', but it's about the man in the photo from that CCTV. Phoebe's attacker. Well, I thought it was him straight away, but then he changed his hair, and now I'm not sure—"

"Afzal," DS Wood said, cutting him off. "Let me decide what's relevant, please. In my experience, what somebody believes is small or insignificant can usually help break cases. Who is he, and what do you mean by him changing his hair?"

She could hear Afzal breathing deeply on the phone, composing himself. "OK, the man in the CCTV, the one with the brown hair."

"Yes?" the DS said encouragingly.

"I think I work with him."

Wood's breath caught in her throat, and she poised her pen over the pad. "Go on, Afzal, tell me everything," she said, her heart hammering and her nerves tingling at the thought of getting the breakthrough they needed.

"Please, detective, promise me I won't get in trouble if I'm wrong."

"Of course not, Afzal," she said to ease his distress. "We can check all the details here without needing to speak to your colleague, and if we can rule them out on that basis, they'll never know that you've spoken to us. OK?"

"Oh. That's so good," Afzal said, still sounding hesitant. "He's called Billy. I don't actually know his surname. We work at the Sainsbury's Local in Middleton."

"The one at the top of the avenue?"

"Aye, that's the one," Afzal said, more animated now.

She'd been hoping Matthew or Longbottom would at least turn up, but she was disappointed. Still, she asked, "Can you give me more details?"

"Not really; I don't know much about him."

"I understand. So, how did you connect your colleague with the man in the photo?"

"Well, they look exactly the same—or, did look the same. Same sort of shape and build."

"Did?"

"Aye, he dyed it platinum blond and started growing a beard. He's always had brown hair and was clean-shaven as long as I've known him."

Isabella's gut screamed this could be their guy, and she struggled to keep her voice calm. "Is there anything else?"

"No. I don't really know Billy," Afzal said, sounding troubled. "We're not friends, you see; we just work together. But at work, he's mostly quiet and keeps himself to himself."

"You've been brilliant, Afzal. Thanks for the information; it's appreciated. Can you please tell me the name of your line manager at Sainsbury's?" She needed to check out Billy's background information and make a few enquiries before she could find him.

"I'm on my day off today, but Jill's in. We don't keep Sunday hours." He provided her full name and work contact number.

"Thank you so much, Afzal; I appreciate your time today."

Wood was about to hang up when Afzal said, "Wait. There's more—that man. Frank, the one who was murdered earlier this week. Billy argued with him. He was mad. Really mad. I'd noticed them arguing before, to be honest. I don't like to speak ill of the dead, but that Frank fella wasn't very polite, and Billy hated impolite people. It might be connected. It might not be. But whilst I'm on the phone with you..."

Could the murders be connected? Wood was unsure, but she could take the matter to the DI. First, she thanked Afzal and dialled the manager's number. "Hi, is that Jill?"

"Yes."

"Hi, sorry to call you at work. I'm Detective Sergeant Wood. I have a question about one of your employees, Billy. Does he work at the Sainsbury's Local with you in Middleton?"

"I know, Billy, yes." The woman's tone sounded disapproving. "Though he won't be working under me for much longer, not with his current conduct."

"I see. As a witness in an ongoing investigation, I'm after Billy's full name, address, and contact details."

"I can check that information for you." There was a slight pause and the sound of keys clacking. "Hmm. So strange."

"What is?"

"We call him Billy Longbottom."

At the word 'Longbottom', Wood's heart thumped in her chest because of the name 'Matthew Longbottom', the name used on YorkshireFlirt.com.

"His name badge states he's named Billy. But I never realised that his legal name on the payroll is William. William Matthew Longbottom, actually." She read out a mobile number. "His address is... 29.5 A Mount Pleasant, Middleton."

Wood was grinning. "Is he working today?" She tried to keep her voice calm.

"He emailed in sick again."

"OK. You mentioned Billy's current conduct. Can you tell me what you mean by that?"

Jill snorted with disgust. "He's been off work a lot, skipping shifts without giving us notice. Then, emailing in sick at the time he should be on the till."

"Is that usual behaviour for him?"

"No," she admitted after a pregnant pause, "but the last two or three weeks have been shocking. Billy's on his final warning."

"I understand. Thanks for your help, Jill. Bye," Wood said and hung up before calling DI Beaumont out of his office.

Her hands were shaking. Mount Pleasant, where 'Longbottom' lived, and Back Mount Pleasant, where Phoebe lived, were conjoined.

* * *

You got used to the corpses. But never the smell.

No matter how prepared you thought you were, the first one was rough. That first body on that first slab always hit you hard. Of course, it hit you harder when you were the SIO, as Erika Allen's murder had hit him.

And dual offenders were rare, so the apprehension made it

worse when that second body appeared on the slab. Somehow, your mind built it up, and you braced yourself for the dread before arriving at the morgue. But then, when you saw it, it was nowhere near as bad as your imagination had tried to prepare you for.

And then serial killers were even rarer. A different breed entirely. And George seemed to attract them. So your body tried even harder to protect you from the terror; in George's case, he'd even had to go on medication to feel better.

But as the years passed and the cases mounted up, it became easier, just part of the job. George wasn't even sure how many bodies he'd seen now, just empty shells on cold slabs. And regarding their names, he could remember even less, even though he'd promised to remember them all.

But then, part of his therapy was to move on. She'd told him it wasn't his job to remember them, and it wasn't his job to avenge them, but that was always his intention, as it was to get the families justice. It was better if the remembering and the mourning were up to someone else.

Ruby Kaur lay on her back, naked and fully exposed, her torso a pincushion of stab wounds. Her wheat-coloured skin had paled, meaning each dark hole stood out. Whoever killed her had made a mess.

"Shall I run you through what I think happened, son?" Dr Ross asked. "And if you have any questions, just ask."

The older man walked around the table until he was beside Ruby's head. "Your guy stabbed her straight through her collarbone, high up to her left. That would have caused her to fall, and I'd say she fell on them hard from the bruising to her knees."

George nodded, following.

"Then, from the blood marks on the floor, it looks like she went from being on her knees to flat out on the floor. That position change resulted from an impact on the back of her head. A hard one, too, I reckon. It looks like your man smashed her head from behind as she was on her knees.

"Hilt of the knife?"

Dr Ross looked impressed. "Very good, George. Yes, judging by the shape of it."

George smiled.

"Then he turned her over onto her back," the pathologist added.

"Any signs of a sexual assault?"

Dr Ross raised an eyebrow. "None at all."

The pathologist continued down the body to where most of the attack occurred. "And then, we have this. Eight stab wounds at various depths, but mostly confined to the chest area."

"Any thoughts on the weapon?" George asked.

"The entry wounds are smooth, and the deepest measure thirty-eight millimetres across. The murder weapon had a sharp tip and was non-serrated."

"A chef's knife, then?"

"Aye, a chef's knife," Dr Ross confirmed.

That didn't help much. Chef's knives were easily available. Most shops readily sold them, and most homes carried them. Lindsey said there was one missing from the block in the kitchen, and George wondered how the uniformed officers were getting on with their search of the skips and bins. A murder weapon was beneficial because they could tie it to the murder and the killer. But he doubted they'd find anything. It was never that easy.

"And he put some force into it."

"Definitely 'he'?" George asked. Statistically, they were almost certainly looking for a man. He'd keep an open mind, of course, especially after the Blonde Delilah case, but right now, he was just happy to narrow the search a little.

Dr Ross said, "I tend to avoid definites, son, so there's less chance of me looking like an idiot later if I turn out to be wrong. Whoever killed her was strong, though. Extremely strong."

"Any other wounds?" George asked.

"No, she didn't put up a fight," the pathologist explained. "But there is this." Dr Ross pointed at the apparent caesarean section scar.

George raised his brows. They'd seen no evidence of a child. None at all.

"Anything else you can tell me about our male suspect, Dr Ross?"

"Judging by the angle of the wounds, I'd say he was taller than the victim and left-handed."

"Anything else?"

"No, son. This was a calculated, frenzied attack. And most likely, the guy kept stabbing three or four times after this poor lass was already dead."

* * *

On the way back to the station, George called DC Scott to get Ruby's NHS records.

Maybe it was a disgruntled ex who had killed her?

But it was DS Wood who answered. "George, we've got him. Get to 29.5 A Mount Pleasant in Middleton."

Chapter Thirty-four

Finally! They had him. They had Matthew, Billy, or William Longbottom, whatever the hell his name was, at last! George just hoped he was home. But just in case he wasn't, he'd put out a BOLO, a 'Be On the Look Out for', a warning flag used when a suspect is circulated on the Police National Computer or PNC.

DC Tashan Blackburn was still at the office, frantically trying to find any mobile numbers associated with the man so they could attempt to find and track him.

DS Wood had rung Afzal, but he didn't have Billy's number. So DS Wood, DC Scott, and George raced to Longbottom's address to see if they could find him there.

As George raced towards Middleton from the morgue, a ringing tone silenced the radio coming from the Bluetooth. He checked the clock on the dash. Shit. He was supposed to have picked Jack up by now.

He answered.

"Where are you, George? Jack's waiting for you. Again!" Her words were like bullets, and they struck his vitals.

"I don't think I can have him tonight."

"What the hell do you mean?" George could hear her teeth grinding behind every word she spat out. "We said seven. It's already past seven. I'm going to be late."

"I'm sorry," he said. "But I've got to work."

"When will you be here?"

"I won't be able to get there tonight, Mia." He slowed for yet another set of red lights ahead.

"Explain yourself, George. This isn't funny. It's twice now that you've let Jack down in a short space of time. Twice."

It wasn't too far to Middleton, but he admonished himself silently as he hit yet another set of red lights.

"George!" Mia snapped.

"I can't take Jack tonight, sorry."

"But I have a date—"

"Mia," George barked. "For fuck's sake! The whole world doesn't revolve around you and your dates? Alright? I'm sure you've heard about the three murders in Middleton recently and the attempted murder, too. So, whilst he's free, there's a chance somebody else is in danger. You, of all people, should know how that feels!" George regretted the statement immediately, but it got her to shut up. "We might be looking at a serial killer, two killers, or even three. I just don't fucking know, alright? So stop being selfish for one minute and get off my back. I'm not doing this to piss you off, nor am I doing this to get in the way of your date!"

"Fine, George. Bloody hell!"

George hung up before he could say anything else he would regret later and clenched his shaking hands on the steering wheel, breathing deeply, trying to still his hammering heart. Then, at last, the lights changed to green, and he floored it.

* * *

DC Scott pulled up behind George's Mercedes with DS Wood in the passenger seat at the end of Mount Pleasant. A marked car arrived and blocked the bottom. George hoped that the vehicle contained Sergeant Greenwood and the 'big red key'.

"Warrants are signed," Wood said. "I can't believe he lives in the same set of back-to-backs as Phoebe Widdop. DS Mason had uniform knocking on doors for days around here."

George shrugged. "Can't be helped." He nodded to the door. "We'll go straight in and knock down the door if we have to."

"We've got the paperwork," PS Greenwood said, panting from the run up the hill.

"Good. Gloves and shoe covers on, please." He heard them say, "Sir," in unison, and then the rustle of paper and the snap of latex gloves.

Then George hammered his fist against the door, counted to ten, and then hammered again. Finally, impatient, he said, "Longbottom's had enough time." He turned to Greenwood. "Break the door down, Sergeant."

George and Wood stood back as Greenwood and another uniform hurled the 'big red key' at the door. Then, with another hit, the door gave way, the sound of shattering wood like a gunshot.

"Police!" Greenwood kicked the door in and continued shouting as he and the other officer entered the hallway.

Then George stepped over the threshold, and all he smelt was death.

The stench of death choked him, overpowering the cloying scent of the plug-in air fresheners.

"William? William Longbottom, are you in here?" George shouted. DC Scott thundered up the stairs with PS Greenwood. DS Wood and the uniform glanced into the living room but shouted back; it was clear. George entered the tiny kitchen at the back, and whilst it was empty, the stench was more pungent.

"It's all clear up here, boss," DC Scott called from upstairs. "The loft hatch has been painted shut, and the paint looks old. Sergeant Greenwood's trying to get in."

George checked the cupboards but found nothing. Then he saw the door in the corner that he suspected led down into a cellar. There was an aura about the door. With its shabby, faded, and partly peeling white paint, it was menacing. The scuffed, round, brass door handle looked like a clown's nose and reminded him of the master of horror. Stephen King.

It was just a door, yet George already knew what he would find behind it. The source of the smell.

He wasn't even sure he wanted to open the door, to flick on the light switch, because deep within, he knew that some skeletal fingers would grasp his wrist... and then pull him down into the darkness that smelled of muck and mouldy vegetables. Instead, George stepped forward, steeling himself, and wrenched it open.

With a strength he didn't know he had, George tried to switch on the light, but there was no switch there. Fuck! It was down at the bottom of the stairs.

With the door open, the smell from the cellar strengthened, wafting out unchecked.

"Wood, Jay, I need you in here."

The tone in his voice had them running towards him, and it wasn't until they were at his back that he placed his foot onto the first stone step that led down into the cellar. Then, with the light of his phone torch to guide him, he took the second step and then the third.

His two detectives lit up their own phones, illuminating an old shelving unit with a metal toolbox so full it was jammed between the shelves to wedge the lid down. Everything else looked dust, yet the toolbox didn't, as if it had been recently disturbed. "Jay, check that toolbox for me, will you?"

He heard the word "Boss," and heard metal scraping against wood.

George moved round the bottom of the stairs, and there, on the filthy flagstones, as George raised his light, was a black-shrouded bundle lay half in the shadows.

And on the floor, emerging from the sheet, was a single pale hand.

* * *

"Who is it?" asked Wood, covering her mouth with an arm. The stench was awful.

"I don't know," George said. "I'll take a look. Wood, get CSI here and secure the house as a scene."

"OK." DS Wood thundered up the stairs.

Before his nerve deserted him, George stepped over to the body. This really was the worst part of the job. He saw that the hand was already beginning to bloat, and George only peeled back the black sheet at the top end, stretching out a gloved hand and standing as far away as he could so as not to have to lean in too close.

A man's face greeted him. A man he didn't recognise. His face was swelling like the rest of his body, and the man's bulging eyes were clouded and devoid of life. His skin had started to loosen, and George could only imagine he'd been dead for days. Lindsey and Dr Ross would confirm, of course.

And hopefully, he'd have some ID on him.

"Boss. There are three bloodied knives in here. And some jewellery. Plus three mobile phones." Jay's voice broke through his train of thought.

He turned. "Three knives and three phones?"

"That's right, boss." Jay carefully pointed into the toolbox. He'd carefully removed a few items from the top but had clearly dug no further after seeing the evidence inside. "One's a Stanley." George thought about Chanelle Cummings. Were the murders linked after all? "I don't want to touch them without forensics seeing them in situ first."

"Good job, Jay." Then he pointed upstairs. "Come on. Lindsey will have my head if we disturb anything." George tramped upstairs almost in a daze, stopping dead by the front door.

"You alright, boss?"

"No," George admitted, running a hand through his blond hair. "Where the hell is Longbottom?"

"Come on, boss, let's leave. I can't do with the stink. And I know how you feel," Jay said. "We couldn't have done anything differently."

"I'm not sure about that, Jay. I feel like we could have done more." But Jay was at least right about the stench. It wasn't helping.

The two male detectives walked outside to the quiet street where PS Greenwood was standing with DS Wood, who was busy on her mobile. George sucked in the fresh air, clearing the taste of death, and looked back at the terraced housing. Who else had Longbottom killed? And who was the man in the cellar?

Then George's phone rang.

"Sir," Tashan said. "YorkshireFlirt.com has got back to me. From the exchange of messages I've read, Matthew Longbottom is currently on a date in Morley with a Sophia Hardaker. I don't know where because it looks like they made final plans via text. Longbottom is using a Tesco Mobile pay-as-you-go SIM, but it's currently turned off. DSU Smith has managed to get a warrant signed, and we've sent it off to them. I'm on hold via the office phone. Once I know more, I'll get back to you."

"What about Sophia?"

"She's not answering."

"Shit!"

"I've used her number to triangulate her location. It's in Morley right now, sir, somewhere on Queen Street, but the triangulation isn't exact."

"Thanks, Tashan," George said, not hanging up and getting Wood's attention. "He's in Morley, Wood. We have to go now." He turned to his Detective Constable. "Jay, stay here. Do not leave the scene, and be on the lookout for Longbottom. If he returns, then apprehend him immediately." The two detectives then legged it up the street to his Mercedes.

"Tashan, keep a trace open on Sophia's phone. Wood and I are heading to Morley now. Do whatever you can to get hold of Sophia Hardaker. If she's meeting Longbottom right now, then she's in danger. While you're tracking her, find out her address, next of kin, her boss, or whatever you can find. We need to get in contact with her."

"Of course, sir. I'll see what I can find out through social media, too."

George opened the door, and DS Wood joined him in the passenger seat. He fired up the engine, the throaty roar of the

Mercedes as eager as he was to hunt Longbottom.

265

Chapter Thirty-five

Sophia laughed. "I'm really enjoying myself, Matty. I hope you are, too."

"I am. If you don't mind me saying, you have a beautiful smile." I grinned, my eyes warm. I leaned in and brushed a stray hair from her face, sliding my fingers down to her chin. The ladies always loved the story of how I fell into Middleton Pond. "But please, you can't tell anybody. I was proper embarrassed."

"I promise," she said, leaning into me. She wasn't hungry, so we ordered more drinks at the JD Wetherspoon instead, although she was out-drinking me. Like I'd planned.

Sophia's phone vibrated on the table again, and she scowled. I thought she'd never looked so beautiful. I looked down and saw it was an unknown number. "Again? Why don't they get the message and piss off!" she exclaimed. "Sorry, Matty. You know what? I'm just going to switch the stupid thing off. Then we can't be bugged by anyone."

"Good idea," I grinned. "I already switched mine off. I don't want anything to distract me from you and your beauty."

She coloured at the compliment. She looked at the time on her phone before turning it off. "I'd better head home soon," Sophia said with a sigh. "Work in the morning."

"Yeah, same for me. London." I winced, then smiled, hoping she didn't notice. "I'd much rather spend the time with you. Of course, we could always head back to yours for a coffee?" I placed my hand on her bare thigh.

Sophia bit her lip; then they parted around her tongue. She was so fucking sexy. "I'm not sure, Matty. I live with my mum, and she wouldn't like it if I took you home."

I put on my saddest expression and nodded my head. "I understand." Whilst my place reeked of my dead dad, and it was a fucking ball-ache getting rid of dead bodies, I hungered for Sophia. I yearned for the folds between her legs. And her death. "I really like you, Sophia. Surely you can forgive me for not wanting to say goodbye yet?" I grinned and held my hands up. Then I winked.

The wink worked. I saw Sophia looking at me, a sparkle in her eye. She was still shy, but the flattery was working.

"I guess I'm saying you could come back to mine?" I suggested, shrugging. "We can chill."

"Just chill?" she glanced up at me, and I could see the worry in her eyes.

"Yeah, and have a coffee, and then I'll book you an Uber. I'll even pay for it, too. No pressure from me. None at all." Not yet, anyway. I wanted to strangle her this time like I'd tried to strangle Phoebe.

"An Uber?" I nodded. "And you'll pay?" Shit. Had I fucked up by saying that?

"Yeah, if you liked?" I smiled again. "No pressure, like I said. Say no, and we can go out when I return from London, alright?" She nodded and took a large gulp of her wine. "I have a place in Miggy. We can put Netflix on, and—" She raised her brow at me. "—we can have a drink and just chill." I grinned and raised my brows. "Or we can just sit in the kitchen and drink coffee. I have a machine. It grinds the beans and everything. It's amazing."

She drained her glass, and I filled it up with the rest of the bottle. The small amount of alcohol I'd consumed had given me a buzz of confidence.

"OK, you've twisted my arm," she said with a grin. "Let's go back to yours and do that."

"Great. Drink up, then, and I'll book an Uber." I pretended to turn on my mobile. "There's no signal in here. Mind if I pop outside?" She nodded, and I gently kissed her lips, gripping her tightly around the waist. "I'll be back in a minute."

As I headed outside, my stomach churned with excitement. A million butterflies fluttered. Sure, I'd had to play a slow game with Sophia, but I understood she was young, shy, inexperienced, and scared. But the alcohol had already begun to coax her from her shell. And the fresh air would hit her like a sledgehammer.

I turned on my phone and called a taxi. They didn't have this number, so I didn't need to turn it back off. I'd sent shots to the table on my way out, and she'd have drunk both of them with any luck to quell her nerves.

I was very much looking forward to taking control of her before I watched her die.

* * *

As he searched for Sophia Hardaker, DC Tashan Blackburn had hundreds of windows open in his laptop's browser—every social media website and various police databases.

Her Instagram was private. Shit.

Her Facebook was also private but had her employer's details on. Unfortunately, it was a Sunday evening, so they were closed when he called.

She held a provisional driver's licence—bingo. Blackburn texted DI Beaumont her address, and then he checked on the cell triangulation again.

Gone.

Shit.

Tashan blinked a few times and then refreshed the feed. Nothing. Longbottom's had turned back on, though. Why?

The final pings from both phones came from Queen Street. Where would they be on a Sunday night in Morley?

Then it clicked.

Spoons.

Nowhere else was open. So he dialled his DI, who would decide whether to head towards the JD Wetherspoon or Hardaker's house.

But that still left the issue of Longbottom. Would he be heading home, to Sophia's, or neither?

* * *

Sophia and I slid into the back of a taxi. "Mount Pleasant in Middleton, mate," I said to the driver up front, draping my arm around Sophia.

"Is she OK, pal?" the taxi driver asked, his stare lingering between the two of us.

Sophia flushed and nodded. "A little tipsy," she said with a laugh.

The driver nodded slowly. "Just making sure, pal. I have a daughter her age, and I worry, you know?" He released the handbrake and set off.

I grinned. With a monster like me around, all Dads should be worried.

The taxi driver's eyes lingered on me in the rear-view mirror for a few seconds before they moved back to the road, continuing down High Street towards Middleton.

* * *

"Sir, I have an update for you," DC Tashan Blackburn said as soon as DI Beaumont picked up from the Bluetooth in his car. He and DS Wood were racing towards Sophia Hardaker's house in Churwell.

"Go for it."

"They're going back to Longbottom's, sir."

"What?" George questioned, pulling over immediately. "How do you know that?"

"He's turned the burner back on. I'm tracking it as we speak. It looks like they're driving towards Middleton."

"Great work!" George said and immediately floored it around the Elland Road roundabout on the A6110 and floored it towards Middleton.

"Thanks, sir. Is Jay still at the scene?"

"He is. Call him. Let him know. And send everyone! We need to catch this fucker!"

* * *

The taxi driver didn't like the young man's vibe. So he texted the office with the word, 'RED'. It meant the office would call the police and get them to attend the address where he dropped them off. He hoped anybody in his position would do the same, especially if daughters were involved.

He knew something had been off about the lad the moment they'd set foot in the taxi. He was quiet and had a weird look about him. Plus, he was aware of the recent bout of murder in Middleton and that a young woman named Phoebe Widdop had been recently attacked.

So he'd decided to stick under the speed limit tonight and not race home for this lad. And whilst he'd taken the longest route, down Bridge Street, and then across Tingley Common, onto Bradford Road, he was less than ten minutes from Mount Pleasant now.

He glanced in the rear-view mirror again, noticing the lad in the backseat was focused on groping the young lady. Anger coursed through his veins. His own daughter was a similar age, and he dared any man to do what that lad was doing to his own lass. But, twenty-one or not, she was his baby and probably would be forever. It was his job to protect her. As such, he felt like he had to protect the young blonde lass in the back of his car.

A marked police car drove past him in the opposite direction, and his heart hammered with fear. He considered flashing his lights right there and then and slamming on his brakes. But then what if he were wrong? What if the acts behind him were consensual? The guy could be innocent. He was blond, and the guy from the CCTV images he'd seen plastered around Middleton had brown hair.

Yet there was something strange about the lad. Something menacing. And whether he was wrong or not, if he was somehow right and stopped the lad from killing the pretty lass, then his actions were justified.

* * *

George drove like a man possessed, with DS Wood clinging on for dear life beside him in the passenger seat. He flung the car up the slip road on the Ring Road near the White Rose Centre roundabout, heading towards Dewsbury Road north, and flooring it up Middleton Ring Road, no idea how far behind the taxi he might be. Tashan had called, and the taxi was definitely dropping Longbottom off at his home address on Mount Pleasant, but if they didn't intercept him, then they could lose him.

* * *

The driver accepted the fare from the young lad, his heart hammering. He'd asked to be dropped off on Town Street, his excuse that the short walk would sober his lass up. The driver had tried to dissuade him, especially considering there was no sign of any police, but the young lad had laughed and asked him to keep the ten-pence change.

How generous.

"Well, at least let me open the door for you and your lass." He slid out of the car and opened it for her, looking up Lingwell Avenue for signs of activity. "Are you alright, love?" He frowned as he helped her out because she was bleary-eyed and certainly not as sober as the lad had made her out to be.

"She's fine, mate. Leave her to me," the young lad snapped, glaring at the driver as he pulled Sophia away, supporting her around the waist with a strong arm. "I'll give her some coffee back at mine. Alright?"

The driver watched them stagger away. His gut instinct told

him to try and stop them, to help her. What if he was wrong? The lad could assault him. But what if he was right?

They passed under the first streetlight towards the junction of Mount Pleasant.

But that gut instinct was strong. Stronger than ever. The driver dithered, agonising.

Then he made a decision.

"Damn it!"

If his daughter were at risk or in a similar situation, he'd want someone to help her. So, the driver locked his car and legged it after them.

Chapter Thirty-six

Lindsey Yardley and her SOC team were behind DC Scott inside the lit-up house, a white forensics tent shielding the small front garden and a cordon of police tape stretching across the gate. He'd been guarding the scene just like the boss had asked, but after the call from Tashan, he needed to abandon that duty.

DC Scott sprinted up Mount Pleasant, away from the floodlit scene, his phone still in his hand as DC Blackburn hung up on him. Two figures were at the end of the road—on Lingwell Avenue, who drew closer—a staggering woman and a man holding her up. Despite the newly dyed platinum blond hair, Jay instantly recognised Longbottom from the YorkshireFlirt.com app profile picture.

"Police! William Longbottom, you're under arrest!" DC Scott roared, his legs and arms pumping as he sprinted towards the pair.

William stopped in his tracks at the shout and raised his free hand to shade his eyes, no doubt so he could see where the harsh illumination of the forensics light behind Scott emanated from. William dropped Sophia after realising that the light coming from his own house meant he'd been busted, and he legged it in the opposite direction. Sophia crashed to the ground with a cry.

"Stop!" DC Scott yelled as he sprinted up the street.

A man came out of his house and looked down at Sophia.

"Watch the woman!" DC Scott ordered as he passed the man, who immediately sprinted towards the fallen young woman. "Cheers, mate."

William had disappeared around the corner at the end of the road, and DC Scott slowed for a moment, looking left and right up and down Lingwell Avenue until he spied the figure ahead, legging it towards the main road.

Headlights raked the darkened street as a silver Mercedes A-class turned into it, lighting up William Longbottom like a beacon.

In the middle of the road, William slowed and jerked back as the Mercedes screeched to a halt horizontally across the street, cutting him off. William changed direction, darting back towards DC Scott, who collided with him. With an almighty crack, they both went down.

Longbottom wrestled with Jay, trying to push him away to escape, but DC Scott hung on doggedly.

The two young men fought, with Longbottom breathing heavily. Jay was fitter and stronger. He gripped tightly until Longbottom screamed, "I can't fucking breathe!"

With no witnesses around and afraid of hurting the criminal, Jay loosened his grip, and Longbottom used it to his advantage, viciously headbutting him, the back of William's skull meeting the bridge of Jay's nose.

Pain blinded DC Scott, and he could taste blood. He fell, and Longbottom slipped from his grasp. But with adrenaline coursing through his veins, Scott lunged, ankle tapping William, who went down and crashed down, hitting his head on the kerb.

As Scott got up to launch himself onto Longbottom's back, a taller blond man rushed from the Mercedes and pushed Longbottom onto the rough surface with a knee on his back, his two hands restraining Longbottom's arms.

"Police brutality! Get the fuck off me!" Longbottom screeched, the sound drilling into DC Scott's already-pounding skull.

DS Wood joined them then and said, "Do the honours, DC Scott." She handed Jay her cuffs, who then wrenched Longbottom's arms behind him and cuffed him. The man continued to scream profanities.

Panting heavily and with blood still dripping from his nose, DC Scott groaned and went down on one knee.

"Nice one, Jay!" DS Wood smiled.

"DC Scott, good job," George said.

"That lass. She's on his street," DC Scott forced out, his lungs aching from the sprint. "She was staggering about and might be hurt. But, fucking hell, he got me good," Jay groaned.

"Hurry up and charge the bastard, DC Scott," George Beaumont said as two marked cars entered Lingwell Avenue. George sprinted towards Mount Pleasant.

DS Wood helped Scott stand, but Jay bent down, hands on his thighs. She said, "You listening to the boss, or what?"

DC Scott glared at Longbottom. Then, with Wood's help, they hauled William up to his feet, an arm apiece. His skull was bleeding from where he'd hit the kerb.

Then William coughed up a bloodied globule of spit and launched it towards DC Scott, who managed to dodge it. "You dirty fucking prick!" Scott screamed.

"Come on, Jay. Charge him!" Wood said.

"William Longbottom, you're under arrest for murder,

resisting lawful arrest, assaulting a police officer, and preventing the lawful burial of a body."

He read the police caution as Longbottom spewed profanities at the detectives.

"Get him back to the station, will you, lads?" DC Scott said to the two PCs approaching from one of the marked cars, which lit the street with blue flashes. "Think he needs a night in the cell to take the edge off that attitude."

The PCs nodded and took Longbottom away, forcing William's head down and into the back of their car. His tirade of profanities was silenced as the door slammed behind him.

"Bloody hell. What a dickhead," DC Scott said. "Crazy bastard!"

Wood smacked him on the shoulder. "Well done, DC Scott."

DC Scott and DS Wood followed the DI back to Mount Pleasant, where a sobbing young woman sat drinking water from the bottle, and an older man hovered about. He looked up as they approached.

Jay spoke first. "Thanks, mate, for looking after her."

"My pleasure."

The men shook hands, and George smiled. "Brief me, then take a statement from him, DC Scott."

"Sir, Longbottom's in custody and heading to the station and the cells."

"Great job, DC Scott." George gave him a thin smile.

A rush of pride filled Jason Scott. It was true that he'd been a bit of a prick to the DI last year as a green DC, and then the tables had turned, and the brilliant DI had been hard on him during these past few months. But Jay hoped he'd finally proved himself to the brilliant DI and showed what he was capable of. "Cheers, sir."

"You're welcome, kid. You deserve it." George sucked in a large breath. "Right, this is Sophia Hardaker. Thank God we made it in time. An ambulance is en route. DS Wood, can you take over here and get in touch with her next of kin? Like her mum or dad or something, and see if they can come and comfort her." He turned to the drunk young woman. "I'm afraid we'll need a statement, though, Miss Hardaker, before we can let you go."

As George headed into the house to see how CSI was getting on, the three detectives shared tired grins. They'd found William Longbottom before he'd struck again, and Sophia Hardaker was safe. They'd caught the murderer of at least one man and stopped him from murdering a young woman.

* * *

It had been a long night already, and they worked late into the morning. Lindsey Yardley and her team of SOCOs eventually finished up at Longbottom's house. The body had been removed to the hospital morgue to await a post-mortem and formal identification by Dr Ross. Lindsey had found a wallet on the corpse, identifying him as Bill Longbottom, and after some checks from DC Tashan Blackburn back at Elland Road, they knew he was William's father.

What had possessed William to kill his father?

An upset Sophia Hardaker had given a brief statement at the scene and had been taken home by her equally traumatised mother, with the promise that Sophia would attend the station on Monday morning to give a full witness interview. When DC Scott shared the horrifying news that she'd been in the company of a man most likely planning to kill her, she broke down even further.

Likewise, Declan Ridley, the taxi driver, had given DC Scott a complete account of what had happened. The person they really needed to talk to, however, was William Longbottom. They needed to figure out why he'd killed his dad and get Phoebe Widdop to formally identify William as her attacker. George didn't know what drove a person so far as to commit murder, but then he admonished himself. For he, too, was a murderer.

George's eyes burned, and he yawned as he drove back to the station. It was already one in the morning, and there'd be a long night ahead interviewing Longbottom. It was the same for Forensics who gathered evidence to make their case watertight. That way, it didn't matter whether the psycho admitted to anything.

George's biggest fear was that they wouldn't find enough evidence to put him away for good so that he couldn't harm anyone else.

But then he remembered the knives, the jewellery, and the mobile phones.

Back at the office, DS Wood, DC Scott, and DC Blackburn were busy filling in the paperwork and assembling the evidence. All the while, William Matthew Longbottom, totally oblivious to the hum of pent-up anxiety within the office, sat in a cell as they prepared the interview.

* * *

"Got a minute, sir?" DC Holly Hambleton asked, nodding to her screen. With Yolanda off sick with COVID, one of the DCIs had lent her to them.

"Aye, what's up?"

She said, "DS Fry managed to link the numbers together. The pay-as-you-go SIMs?" George nodded, and Josh came over.

"Hiya, sir." George nodded back a greeting. "With DC Blackburn's help, I managed to link the SIMs. They were purchased together in sequence from Tesco, in Batley, alongside burner phones."

"What do you mean by 'in sequence'?"

"Well, just that, sir. He bought six SIMs together. In one transaction. And whilst they paid with cash, Tesco tracks where and when SIMs are purchased."

"So you have an exact time?" George grinned.

Holly cut in. "Yep. And Batley has just sent the CCTV to us. Josh and I have looked at it."

"Go on, the suspense is killing me," George said.

"William Matthew Longbottom," Josh said, pointing at the monitor. "They're sending us all text messages and call data for the six SIMs."

Then DC Jay Scott shouted from across the room. "Boss, Dr Yardley called. She's found six phones in Longbottom's bedroom with missing SIMs."

"Looks like you've got him, sir."

"Yeah, maybe."

Chapter Thirty-seven

After a few hours of kip and armed with evidence, George strode down to the custody suites, bracing against the vile stench of sweat, vomit, piss, and shit, ignoring the moaning, screaming, and shouting coming from the detainees. It wasn't a pleasant place to be holed up, to say the least, and he didn't envy William Matthew Longbottom. He waited as the desk staff unlocked Longbottom's cell.

William regarded him impassively; the lad was tired, no doubt after no sleep in the hard, barren cell.

"Would you like a drink?" George asked.

William looked up in surprise, frowned, and then nodded hesitantly. "Please."

"What would you like?"

"Coffee, milk and two sugars. Thank you."

"Can you make that for me, constable?" he turned to the uniform beside him.

"Of course, sir. Can I get you anything?"

"No, thanks." He looked at the solicitor. "Anything for you?" The solicitor shook his head.

He waited until the young constable left before turning back to Longbottom. "Mr Longbottom, I know I don't need to tell you, but you're in a lot of trouble." He stared levelly at the man.

Longbottom shook his head but kept his head down.

DS Luke Mason entered, and DI Beaumont reeled off the usual spiel after pressing the recorder's button.

"What happened to your hand, son?" Luke asked. Bloodied bandages were wrapped around the thumb and forefinger of Longbottom's left hand.

"I cut it at work. Box cutter. My fault." William then paused. "Why am I here, detectives?"

"You killed your dad, William." It wasn't a question, and George filled his voice with earnest shock.

Longbottom finally looked up from the table he'd been staring at since George entered. "No comment."

"And it looks like you've killed other people, too. How many, William?"

"No comment."

George turned to the solicitor. "Is this all I'm getting?"

"Yes, until you disclose evidence," the duty solicitor, Ethan Miller, said. DS Wood had warned George about him. They had history. Of the romantic type.

The constable entered with William's drink.

"Thank you," William murmured. He shifted in his seat as the DS stared through him.

"So, Mr Longbottom," George said. "The post-mortem has been carried out on your dad. You killed him with rat poison. Is that correct?"

"No comment."

"Don't be shy, William," DS Mason said. "You did a number on your daddy. The rat poison caused internal bleeding, organ failure, and paralysis before putting him in a coma. After all that torture, only then did he die. So why did you do it?"

"No comment."

There was no trace of rat poison in the house, but uniform was checking bins and skips. They'd cancelled collections again. But without any evidence, William was innocent of killing his dad until proven guilty.

"Your prints are all over the body and the black sheet he was covered in," George said.

"No comment."

"OK, we'll return to your dad later, William."

"Tell me about Chanelle Cummings," DS Mason said.

"Who?" William said.

"The woman you murdered. You slit her throat with a Stanley knife. That's right, isn't it, boss?" Mason said.

"That's right, DS Mason." He slid another document across the table. "CSI found a partial blood fingerprint on Chanelle's arm. We took your DNA and prints when we booked you in. Guess who that print belongs to?"

"No comment."

"It belongs to you, son," Mason said. He slid another document across. "This is document two. It's an image of a black fibre and a report. It matches the fibres from a hoodie found in your house. How do you explain that?"

"No comment."

"Is it because the explanation is you killed Chanelle Cummings?" DS Mason chuckled, then slid another document across. "As we said, your DNA is currently being profiled, and we already have your prints. But we have Chanelle's DNA profile. Guess what?"

William coughed and looked nervously between George and Mason. "What?" William crossed his arms.

George took over. "CSI found your prints on the Stanley

knife. And on that Stanley knife, they found Chanelle Cumming's blood."

"Am I right in thinking that this ties William to the murder weapon and the murder weapon to Chanelle, boss?"

"That you are, DS Mason." George turned to look at William, whose eyes quickly returned to the table. From the brief look they shared, George knew Longbottom was scared. "Do you recognise this?" George slid across a photo.

"No comment."

"Tell me what it's a picture of."

"A toolbox."

"Ah, good. Is that toolbox yours?"

"No comment."

"Well, in that toolbox, we also found these." Again, DS Mason slid across three more documents. "Your prints are all over the bracelets. Document four also states that there's DNA that belongs to Chanelle Cummings. We showed it to her parents, who identified it as belonging to her." William shrugged. "But that's not all, son. The Cummings family identified the bracelet in Document Five as belonging to Ruby Kaur and the bracelet in Document Six as belonging to Poppy Lavell."

"Now, as you probably already know, Ruby Kaur was recently murdered in her home. She was wearing her bracelet the day she died. We know that because of a witness who saw her not long before you murdered her. We're in the process of profiling Ruby's DNA, and when we link that bracelet to her as we've done to you, you're fucked, mate."

"Why's he fucked, boss?"

"Well, because we found a chef's knife in his cellar. Inside that toolbox." He pointed at the photo. "The box and the knife were covered in his prints. That same box held the bracelets, as I said, and the Stanley and a kitchen knife we will get to in a bit. A wedding ring, too." George grinned. "Now the pathologist told me there were traces of something in Ruby Kaur's wounds. And we found that same trace on the chef's knife. Do you know what it was, William?"

"No comment."

"It was chocolate fudge cake. As per Ruby Kaur's stomach contents—from the post-mortem—she had eaten a slice just before her death. So we assume she cut the cake and then left the knife and cake out just in case she wanted another slice."

Mason grinned. "I do the same, boss. I leave the knife resting on the sink when I can't decide whether or not I want another sandwich."

"Your fingerprints are all over that knife, William. How do you explain that?"

"No comment."

"Why do you have Poppy Lavell's bracelet?"

"No comment."

"Did you steal it?"

Nothing.

"William?"

The young man grinned.

Mason slid across yet another document. "Document ten is a cast of a footprint." He slid another across. "Document eleven is an image of a trainer found at your house. An expert tells us they match. So you were in Ruby's garden the night of her murder. Why was that?"

"No comment."

"They also match casts taken from Chanelle Cummings' property. Did you stalk her before killing her?"

"No comment."

George shook his head. "OK, so let's move on to Frank Hinchcliffe. Do you know Frank?"

"No comment."

"We found Frank's wedding ring in your toolbox. We know it's his because his wife identified it. It also has his DNA on it."

"And your fingerprints, son."

George nodded. "And your prints. Probably your DNA, too. We'll check." He grinned. "We also found Frank's DNA on the kitchen knife. His blood."

"And your fingerprints, son."

George nodded. "And your prints. What we don't have is the finger. Where is it?"

William took a deep breath before he replied, and George thought they were getting somewhere. But all Longbottom said was, "No comment."

"Are you going to give us anything, William?"

"No comment."

George and Mason shared a look, bemused. The pair stood up. "Well, considering you've given no explanation as to why you killed these people and the threshold test has been passed, it is my lawful right to charge you for the murders of Chanelle Cummings, Frank Hinchcliffe, Ruby Kaur, and Bill Longbottom. Do you understand?"

William Longbottom nodded unhappily. "For the record," George said, "Mr Longbottom nodded his head."

"And," Mason added, "once we profile your DNA, we'll be able to charge you for the attempted murder of Phoebe Widdop. Do you have anything to tell us, son?"

Longbottom shook his head. "No."

"Interview terminated," George said. The two detectives

left the room. Two uniformed officers entered, handcuffs out, waiting. Longbottom would spend his time in a cell at the station before being taken to the Leeds Magistrates' Court.

* * *

Later that afternoon, George dragged William Matthew Longbottom and his solicitor back into an interview room.

This time, he brought DS Wood with him, hoping her presence would put the solicitor off. After saying the usual spiel and pressing the record button, George said, "We know all about the catfishing, William."

"That's why you bought the phones and SIMs from Tesco, isn't it? To set up multiple fake profiles on YorkshireFlirt.com and lure these people to their deaths?" DS Wood said and pushed documents thirty to thirty-nine across the table, which showed William on CCTV purchasing the SIMs and burners from Tesco in Batley.

"Just because you have this picture of me buying them doesn't mean I used them," William smirked. "What if I told you I lost them?"

"Documents forty and forty-one are images of a box found in your bedroom at Mount Pleasant and the contents of said box, respectively."

William turned to his solicitor. "I've never seen that box and the contents before in my life."

"Of course you have," George added. "It's got your fingerprints all over it, as do the contents. Document forty-two is a report from a forensics specialist which confirms this."

"So what contents did we find?" Wood asked.

"Who knows? Probably contents planted there."

George shook his head before he laughed. "Burner phones. We've matched the phones to the SIMs used to contact Harper Verril, Phoebe Widdop, Frank Hinchcliffe, Ruby Kaur, and Sophia Hardaker. The text message and call data from the phones and SIMs can be found in documents twenty to twenty-nine, by the way." George left the smirk there. "What I don't understand is why Frank Hinchcliffe? And why pretend to be Poppy Lavell?"

"No comment."

George turned to Wood. "'No comment'? Now, where have I heard that before?"

A knock at the door interrupted the silence. George terminated the interview and found DC Scott waiting for him outside.

"You need to see this, boss. A misper's been reported in the Middleton area," Jay said.

"And?"

"DSU Smith's assigned it to us, boss. Poppy Lavell. She didn't turn up to work this morning, and I know you've been struggling to find her."

George frowned. With capturing William Longbottom, he'd forgotten all about trying to find her.

DS Wood exited the interview room, a curious look on her face. "What's wrong?"

"Poppy Lavell's work has reported her as missing," Jay supplied.

"And I tried finding her but got nowhere," George added. Then he remembered something. "I asked Josh to try to trace her phone. Because of the other number used to catfish Frank Hinchcliffe, we can trace the mobile."

DC Scott nodded, then looked at the door to the interview

room. "Who do we know who catfishes people, boss?" Jay asked.

"And who do we know who has Frank's wedding ring?" Wood added.

George scratched his beard. "You think he had something to do with Lavell's disappearance?"

"He did have her bracelet," Wood added.

"But not her mobile phone." George shrugged. "I thought he'd just stolen it. Especially after the stalking. You know, the messages and stuff."

"Guess we should just go ask him ourselves."

Chapter Thirty-eight

George sat in silence, reading over his notes.

DS Wood had turned on the recorder and had already reeled off the usual spiel. It had been going for nearly five minutes so far but had recorded nothing but the sound of pages turning, the occasional slurping noise coming from the DI's lips as he drank his coffee and an angry, "Can we just get on with it then?" from Longbottom's solicitor.

The solicitor's anger had resulted in a long, harsh scowl from George and a promise that they'd get on with it when he was good and ready.

"Where is Poppy Lavell, William?" George eventually demanded.

"I'd prefer you to address my client as 'Mr Longbottom,'" the solicitor on the other side of the desk sneered.

George turned to William Longbottom. "I'm sure you would, William, and I'd prefer to be at home rather than here with you. But, unfortunately, it looks like we're both going to be disappointed." He continued before Longbottom's solicitor once again had a chance to object. "Where is Poppy Lavell, William?"

Longbottom shrugged.

"For the recording, William Longbottom shrugged," DS

Wood said clearly.

George smirked. "It's not a difficult question, William. Where is Poppy Lavell?"

Longbottom glanced at his solicitor, who nodded. "Why would I know where that bitch is?" William let the words hang in the air, but both detectives knew better than to interrupt.

But Longbottom added nothing else.

"Where is she, William?" George repeated. "You have her bracelet. And from one of your burner phones, we know you pretended to be Kai and lured her into the woods. So where is she?"

"No comment." William snorted as he laughed.

"Tell us where she is, William," George said, who was boiling with rage inside. "CSI is combing the route you advised Poppy Lavell to take as we speak."

George watched the murderer, and something dangerous flashed in the blue of his eyes as if he were daydreaming something.

* * *

The previous Friday night, Poppy Lavell walked down the narrow path between the Witch's House and Middleton St Mary's Church, which took her down into Middleton Park. As she headed towards the Visitor Centre, she looked down into the dark blue water, and Poppy saw only the constant motion of weed in the wind, with any fish present hiding in the shadows.

Her message tone interrupted her, and she pulled out her phone. It was from Kai. Hi, Gorgeous. Sorry if you're at the Visitor Centre already. Fancy meeting me at the bike park instead? Their food's better. Kai. X

Poppy stood stock still. There were two quick ways to the bike park, and she relished neither. The murder of her friend, Chanelle Cummings, and the murder of a stranger, Frank Hinchcliffe, were the reasons why.

That and Billy's behaviour had unnerved her. She'd walked the entire way to the park, looking over her shoulder.

The only safe route would be a third and twice-as-long option. She'd have to head back up to the main road and walk to the bike park up Town Street.

It would be dark soon, but there would be enough light for her to walk up to the park gates and then head through the woods, past the Rose Garden, and into the bike park. It would only take ten or fifteen minutes. And so that's the way she went.

About halfway down, with the golf course to her right, a movement caught her eye. Out from the trees, it appeared, walking steadily on the path, oblivious as yet to the woman who stood there. A fox, bright red, with a white belly. Then it stopped, nose quivering, smelling the foreign presence. Poppy watched, scarcely daring to breathe, as the fox turned its head and stared at her. For a moment, they watched one another, the wild creature in its own habitat and the intruder. Poppy saw its ears flick as it watched her. Then, lowering its head, the fox crossed the path and into the woods to her left.

So Poppy continued, marvelling at the first fox she'd ever seen. They weren't uncommon in the woods, but she'd never seen one. Suddenly, a bird's cry made the hair on the back of Poppy's neck rise.

She turned towards the sound and blinked, but the woods were empty now save for the dancing trees.

For a moment, she shivered,

Was that the shadow of a person standing watching her?

Poppy froze.

Then the shadow moved, and she saw it for what it really was: a sapling moved by the wind. Every little thing was making her jumpy, recently, especially after the two murders that had happened in the woods. She thrust her hands into her coat pockets and cursed Kai for the change in plans. They could have been at the Visitor Centre now, drinking hot chocolate. But no, he had to—

Poppy's ringtone shattered the silence of the woods.

It was another text from Kai.

Hi, Gorgeous. I'm driving up Town Street. I can pick you up by the water tower if you like. Kai. X

She shook her head, cursing. Kai was always on his phone while driving. One of these days, he was going to crash. Hopefully, the selfish prick wouldn't kill someone.

But the timing of the text had been good. To Poppy's left was a path out of the woods that led to Town Street, where she'd only have to walk another hundred metres until she got to the water tower.

Fine. See you in five. No kiss.

Turning, Poppy made her way up the track of beaten earth that led towards the burgundy gate she knew was at the top of the hill.

* * *

After pretending to be Kai and texting her that Friday night, I followed her from her house. I was the shadow in the trees.

I was the one leading her to her doom.

It was genius, really. I'd stolen Kai's phone, so I knew how he spoke to her. I knew what words to use. It was so easy. All I had to do was wait patiently in the gym for him to put it down.

So easy.

Even getting her to follow my instructions was easy. I'd planned her route carefully so that she wouldn't be seen on CCTV once she entered the park. There was the risk that she would leave the park by the park gates and head to the bike park up Town Street. But it was getting dark, which would have taken her twice as long.

Not that it mattered because I had a contingency plan. If she walked up Town Street, then I'd tell her to meet me at the top of the bike park where the jump line started and intercept her in the woods. From Kai's phone, I knew she'd watched him there before, showing off in front of her.

But getting Poppy to walk through the woods had been easy. She had done exactly what I expected her to.

And once I told her I'd give her a lift, I knew she'd walk up the path to her left. Then, all I had to do was follow behind her.

* * *

I sprinted towards Poppy from behind, forcing my right hand over her mouth and my left arm around her neck. I'd always longed to embrace Poppy Lavell and shivered with ecstasy as she tried to scream. I forced my hand over her mouth as she struggled against me, gripping my arms with her hands, her sharp nails digging into the black hoodie I was wearing. But I was so much stronger than her, and within seconds, I'd lifted her from the ground and pulled her into the undergrowth, dragging her west towards a flat spot.

Breathing hard, I eventually laid her gently on the wet

ground and took in the beautiful features of Poppy's face. Her eyes were shut, but I knew they were a marvellous shade of emerald. The light was fading by the minute, but I watched as her flawless, pale skin glistened in the rain and her damp blonde hair slayed out behind her, contrasting against the pillow of dark leaves.

* * *

Poppy Lavell awoke, and the memory of the attack flashed through her mind as she looked around. Where was she? Everywhere she looked was the same. Darkness. Tall trees and dense foliage.

"Hello, Gorgeous," a voice said. Poppy couldn't pinpoint where the voice came from and blinked against the darkness, her eyes darting around. Poppy couldn't see a face to match the voice but knew who it was, anyway.

Billy.

Billy stepped closer, and Poppy's heart hammered. Terror rose from her stomach and threatened to choke her. She opened her mouth to scream but couldn't as Billy had used tape to seal her mouth. Poppy began heaving against the tape as bile rose into her throat. Poppy tried to move but couldn't. Her hands had been taped together at her chest by the wrists. The tape wouldn't budge.

Billy came closer, and Poppy kicked out with her legs. All that exertion resulted in was a firm laugh from the crazy man.

Then she noticed a knife in his left hand—a Swiss Army Knife.

"You can't reject me now, Poppy Lavell," Billy said as he pulled down his joggers.

"No. Please, Billy," she tried to cry, but only a muffled noise came through the tape. "Please don't!"

"You humiliated me, you bitch! And now you're going to pay for it!" Billy spat as he rolled her over onto her knees.

He taped her ankles together and pulled down her jeans and knickers.

She tried to kick out but had no strength; instead, writhing on the damp ground.

* * *

Having Poppy to myself felt fucking glorious.

Everything I'd ever wanted.

Poppy was now mine. And mine alone!

She'd never have anybody else ever again.

I pulled out my phone from my joggers, a problematic manoeuvre with Poppy flailing about in front of me, to check the date and time, which I then carved into the back of her neck using Roman numerals.

I felt her arch and shudder and heard her screaming against the tape with every stroke of my wrist.

Blood oozed down her back.

But I wasn't finished yet.

So I let the knife in my left hand fall, again and again, raining blows down upon Poppy Lavell as the blood gushed from the wounds on her back. Her breath came in loud gasps as I pierced her lungs. Again and again, I thrust the knife into her back. She coughed, spurting frothy red foam over the grass.

The knife fell again and again until Poppy couldn't hold on to life any more. Her lungs filled with blood, and her vision blurred at the edges.

CHAPTER THIRTY-EIGHT

Soon, all would go black.

And from how Poppy's body tightened, I knew then that she was dying. She probably wished for it all to end quickly.

But after humiliating me, I'd not offered her any respite. Instead, I forced her to lay there as the sharp thrusts kept coming.

* * *

With a grin that stretched from ear to ear, William spat, "No fucking comment!"

"Fine, you can spend the rest of your time in a cell. Interview terminated," George said. The pair of detectives stood up to leave. DS Wood left first and asked an officer to take William back to his holding cell. As George was about to leave, William laughed at him.

The young man knew something. It was obvious. But what?

Chapter Thirty-nine

A tall white structure appeared out of the fog to George's left, surrounded by sharp, metal fencing that was supposed to deter people from trespassing. The water tower had been a fixture of George's life; a white monolith sat atop Town Street with its radio antennas pointed high up into the sky.

Behind the burgundy metal gate to its right was the area where Poppy Lavell's phone had last been switched off.

CSI had found nothing during their sweep of Poppy's route, which didn't surprise George, as it had rained heavily the last few days. But still, George searched every nook and cranny, desperate to find Poppy and evidence that William Matthew Longbottom had murdered her.

After an hour, George returned to his car, which he'd parked on Town Street.

There were a lot of Yorkshire Water vans milling around; George noticed and took a minute to speak to a greying man who was having a cigarette outside his house.

"Having issues with the water and the drains," he said when George asked what the issue was. "It's a funny colour and tastes rank. I wasn't putting up with it any more."

George hesitantly sniffed the air; sure enough, he could smell something waste-like, but that was hardly a nuisance, more the norm in built-up urban areas. In Middleton, there was a problem somewhere if you couldn't smell the pig shit from the farmer's fields or the human shit from the drains. George glanced down the road and saw a couple of overflowing black bins.

"Council not collecting bins at the minute, either, because of all those bloody murders!"

"Yes, but they should be up and running again soon. Thanks for your time, Mr—"

"Butterfield. John."

George made a mental note. "Thank you, Mr Butterfield."

George stepped away from the cigarette smoke wafting in his face and saw a middle-aged man wearing a bright yellow Hi-Vis jacket and a white hard hat.

George held up his warrant card and introduced himself. "I'm Detective Inspector Beaumont. Everything OK around here?"

"The people living in this area of Town Street and Middleton Park Road have been complaining about the lack of water pressure," the man said, peering at George's warrant card. "Some are even complaining that their water has a funny taste."

George nodded, remembering what the greying fellow had said, and was about to turn back to the water tower—and his car—when the Yorkshire Water worker added, "Some have even said there's black-coloured water coming from shower heads and bath taps."

The DI shuddered.

As George asked more questions, an image of the water tower flashed through his mind, though he didn't know why. No doubt the image had come through an association with the

Yorkshire Water vans milling around. But why? He thought about the black-coloured water and the funny taste.

He turned to the tall, white tower. "It can't be," he said aloud.

"What can't be?" the Yorkshire Water worked asked.

"The water tower..." George paused to take a breath. "Is the entrance to the water tower usually kept locked?"

The man tilted his head to one side, puzzled as to why the detective had turned the conversation to the water tower. "Yeah, it's kept locked so people can't get in."

"When is the tower opened?"

"Monthly, to check the water quality. Why?"

George thought about the Netflix documentary he'd watched. It couldn't be. Could it? "Can you tell me when the last check took place? And who checked it?"

"I can, but it's getting late—"

"Tell me when the last check took place and who checked it?" he repeated, unable to bottle his impatience. "Now!"

The man walked away, grumbling, and came back five minutes later.

"Bill Longbottom checks it monthly. He lives locally and has worked for us for years, apparently."

Of course, George thought. William's dad. They knew from the background checks that Bill Longbottom had worked for Yorkshire Water for forty-odd years.

"In fact, Detective, that's Bill Longbottom's van, right there." The man pointed to a van blocking the entrance to the water tower.

It all fits.

It couldn't be a coincidence that the water tower just happened to be maintained by the father of their suspect, a suspect who had not only stalked Poppy Lavell but had her friendship bracelet locked away with his other trophies.

And her phone had been turned off in this area, too.

George thought about the documentary. About a woman who went missing after going in a lift. But by forcibly disconnecting one event from another, George sought to find a logical reason and a logical understanding. Yet, no matter how hard he tried to disrupt his train of thought, the only way to make sense of it all was to link the events together again. In truth, George was already aware of the fact but didn't want to accept it. The one and only possible conclusion. The inescapable conclusion.

There was no mistaking it; Poppy Lavell was in the water tower.

And William Matthew Longbottom had put her there.

In that water-filled coffin.

He tried desperately to suppress the thought, only to have the scene unfold in his mind.

And then a tap on his shoulder made him turn. The Yorkshire Water fella stood there, patiently waiting. "Look, Detective. I've got to sort out these customers. They're complaining about the quality of their water."

Poppy had gone missing on Friday. That had been five days ago. And all George could think about was how people in Middleton had been drinking that water over the last few days. He, himself, had been drinking the water since Friday. He'd cooked pasta with it. He'd made tea and coffee with it and showered in hot water that probably teemed with putrid, rotting cells.

He'd brushed his teeth and washed his face with it.

George retched violently.

His eyes were bloodshot, and he could feel a stinging sensation that burned the back of his throat and nose.

Then he called DSU Smith and asked him to send Lindsey and her SOC team.

* * *

After CSI had taken prints and samples from the ladder leading up to the tank above the water tower, they'd asked the middle-aged Yorkshire Water fella to suit up and open the tank up.

The man's stomach was heaving, but not from nausea. Instead, it was a complex mix of tension and fear. It was a windy night, and he hung to the ladder's rungs, yet the swaying didn't seem to be the source of his anxiety. Instead, he couldn't stop thinking about what the detective had told him.

The man rested his hand on a rung and looked down at the crowd of police. He could hear the sound of water splashing inside the tank surrounding him and something thudding against the sides.

There was definitely something inside there.

The man steeled himself before climbing up to the top and then off the ladder. The hatch was to his right, and he twisted the key and pulled it up. A hideous stench arose from the tank, and the man forced his face into his armpit. Then, still determined to look in, he moved closer and shined his torch inside.

The light revealed the water at the bottom of the tank was lapping against the sole of a pale foot. The man poked his head inside the hatch to peer deeper into the tank. The foot was attached to the legs, which were attached to swollen hips. Those swollen hips were connected to a plump, pale torso bobbing against the tank's middle wall.

The man continued to sweep his torch around when another hard thump shattered his nerves. It was the head hitting the wall of the tank. And that head was attached to a pale body.

The body of a naked blonde woman, who looked up at him, her eyes unseeing, her mouth wide open as if in a scream.

Chapter Forty

George only managed a few hours of sleep before the case dragged him back to the office again. Poppy's post-mortem confirmed she had died late on Friday night by exsanguination, and dental records confirmed her identity. She was moderately decomposed and bloated, her skin green, with some marbling evident on the abdomen and skin separation evident. Dr Ross also noticed subcutaneous blood pooling in Lavell's anal area and marks between her thighs, suggesting sexual assault.

William Longbottom had given them nothing in his interviews again, but it was alright; by the end of the day, the CPS had agreed to charge him with Poppy Lavell's murder.

There were no more leads to tie up. And George told his team as much.

The blood on the knife found in the toolbox in Longbottom's cellar matched Frank Hinchcliffe's. The phones belonged to Bill Longbottom, Chanelle Cummings, and Ruby Kaur. Prints belonging to William Longbottom were found on all three friendship bracelets, as were DNA from each respective owner.

Bill Longbottom's dental records formally confirmed his identity. The keys to the water tower were once his but were stolen by his son, which was how William had gained access. George had no clue how William had managed to carry Poppy

Lavell up the ladder in the centre of the tower without being seen or how he'd managed to lift her up there with how narrow the rungs were, but then people were capable of huge feats of strength when required. And George had no doubt his adrenaline was running high.

Poppy had been stabbed a total of thirty times, and they'd found the murder weapon —a Swiss Army Knife with Longbottom's DNA lodged inside a screw in the handle—at the bottom of the water tank. William had said, "No comment," to every question again, but they'd found DNA and prints belonging to him on Poppy's corpse, too.

They'd found Poppy's mobile in her clothes that had been tossed into the water tower, and through some wizardry, the tech guys with whom Josh was on good terms managed to restore all data from the phone.

The messages Poppy and William had exchanged hadn't made for good reading but proved William had stalked Poppy Lavell for weeks, revealing the WhatsApp messages they had exchanged and the many attempts he'd made to contact her after she threatened to call the police. George felt an extreme pang of guilt at reading the messages. If only she'd contacted them. Lives could have been saved.

But the frenzy of the attack upon Poppy now made sense. It was a crime of passion, and George could now understand why—because Poppy had rejected Billy in all forms, physically, in person, and virtually, where he had catfished her in an attempt to present a more attractive character.

The burners they'd found in the house, which contained all his YorkshireFlirt.com contacts and messaging history, backed up with disclosures from YorkshireFlirt.com that morning, showed William's messages sent to Poppy, Phoebe, Harper,

Sophia, and Frank.

They also had underwear bearing their owner's DNA inside a box under William's bed.

The DNA harvested from Phoebe's fingernails and the profile from the blood on her bedsheets matched William Longbottom, too.

It was a clean sweep.

George returned from the final interview, where an emotionless Longbottom hadn't given any comment when presented with the evidence before him nor any explanation of his crimes. George had happily charged him with a list of offences that would see Longbottom serve a life sentence without parole and remanded back him into custody until he could appear in court. George wouldn't attend this time; he'd made that mistake after capturing the Blonde Delilah.

He'd done his job, and it would now be up to a judge and jury to hear any lies and excuses Longbottom used to try and get away with it.

Whilst Forensics was open to interpretation, the CPS was confident in the overwhelming case he and Lindsey Yardley had put forward, especially since Longbottom's DNA profile had come back and matched DNA found on every murder weapon and trophy he'd kept in his cellar. As such, George knew with total certainty that they'd found the culprit behind the murders of Chanelle Cummings, Frank Hinchcliffe, Ruby Kaur, Bill Longbottom, and Poppy Lavell and knew that catching him had foiled at least one more murder.

George could at least walk away knowing that Longbottom would serve life—but still carried the sour guilt of Longbottom's victims' deaths, all the same. Catching the sick Middleton Woods Stalker wasn't enough. It never was because it could never bring them back and erase what had been done.

* * *

"Ready?" George asked Isabella. He stood behind her with his hands covering her eyes.

He could feel the skin of her cheekbones raise against his palms as she smiled. "Yes."

Together, they walked through the door of George's flat, Wood's sweet fragrance enveloping George with every awkward step.

"Right, now close your eyes. And keep them closed."

"OK," she said, spreading another gigantic grin across her face. Her cheeks were rosy red.

"Isabella, there's something I've been meaning to say, and now seems like the right time."

A smile played on her lips. "OK?"

He felt his chest swell. "Take three steps forward, then open your eyes."

George was down on one knee.

He looked into her eyes, his smile broadening from ear to ear. "Isabella Wood, I love you. Will you marry me?"

Also by Lee Brook

Book 1: THE MISS MURDERER

Book 2: THE BONE SAW RIPPER

Book 3: THE BLONDE DELILAH

Book 4: THE CROSS FLATTS SNATCHER

Book 5: THE MIDDLETON WOODS STALKER

Book 6: THE CHRISTMAS HIT LIST

Book 7: THE FOOTBALLER AND THE WIFE

Book 8: THE NEW FOREST VILLAGE BOOK CLUB

Novella 1: MISSING: MICHELLE CROMACK

Book 9: THE KILLER IN THE FAMILY

Book 10: THE STOURTON STONE CIRCLE

Novella 2: A HALLOWEEN TO REMEMBER: THE LEEDS VAM-
PIRE

Novella 3: ECHOES OF THE RIPPER: THE LONG SHADOW

Book 11: THE WEST YORKSHIRE RIPPER

Book 12: THE SHADOWS OF YULETIDE

Book 13: THE SHADOWS OF THE PAST

Book 14: THE ECHOES OF SILENCE

Book 15: BENEATH THE SURFACE

More coming in 2024

www.ingramcontent.com/pod-product-compliance
Lightning Source LLC
Chambersburg PA
CBHW071130180726
48291CB00007B/2119